Out Played

SHERWOOD OUTLAWS
BOOK TWO

HAYLEY OSBORN

LEXITY INK
PUBLISHING

Copyright © 2019 by Hayley Osborn

All rights reserved. No part of this publication may be reproduced, distributed or transmitted in any form or by any means, including photocopying, recording, or other electronic or mechanical methods, without the prior written permission of the publisher, except in the case of brief quotations embodied in critical reviews and certain other noncommercial uses permitted by copyright law.

Lexity Ink Publishing
Christchurch, New Zealand

Publisher's Note: This is a work of fiction. Names, characters, places, and incidents are a product of the author's imagination. Locales and public names are sometimes used for atmospheric purposes. Any resemblance to actual people, living or dead, or to businesses, companies, events, institutions, or locales is completely coincidental.

Book Layout ©2017 BookDesignTemplates.com
Cover Design by Covers by Combs
Editing by Melissa A Craven

Outplayed/ Hayley Osborn. -- 1st ed.
ISBN 978-0-473-49487-2
Also available as an eBook

For
Jacob, Ashleigh and Zach

One

I WAS lost.

Not physically. Physically, I knew exactly where I was. I'd just taken an eight-hundred-year journey through time that had landed me, eventually, on the front doorstep of my family home. A place I never expected to see again. If I were honest, I couldn't wait to see the faces on the other side of that door.

The problem was, once I opened it, I would be a different kind of lost. Back in my own time, I no longer had a purpose. For the past month, I'd had a mission, a reason to get up every day. A legend to make. A cause to follow. Just surviving the day had never been a given. Here in the twenty-first century, none of those things applied anymore and I felt empty, as if I might just crumple up into myself like a crushed lemonade can.

The late afternoon spring sunshine hit the top story of my red brick home. I wasn't sure how I'd gotten here. To my house, that is. Tabitha had used her witchy magic to make it happen. We came through the portal at the Major Oak in Sherwood Forest, I remembered that much. The next thing I knew, I was here. On the street where I grew up. Wearing the exquisite twelfth century gown of blue and white I'd started the day in, thanks to the hospitality of the Sheriff of Nottingham, and with a navy fur-lined cloak around my shoulders.

I raised my hand and knocked on my door. It felt strange. I couldn't remember ever having done that before. But, when I left for the twelfth century, I left my house keys at home. Knocking was the only way to announce my return to my family. My heart did a funny pitter-patter in my chest. I'd missed them all so much.

I touched my hair, suddenly and stupidly nervous about my appearance. The past few hours had been trying—not just because of the trip through time—and my once stunning updo with flowers woven through the strands, now resembled more of a bird's nest than a bun.

OUTPLAYED

The wooden front door swung open and there was no more time to worry. My little brother Josh stood on the other side, with Mom hovering a step behind. "Maryanne?" Mom whispered.

Josh's eyes narrowed into a squint.

I'd spent many days wondering how they were doing, many nights dreaming of Josh missing me. Seeing them now was so much better than seeing them in my dreams. "Hey, bud. Hi, Mom."

"Maryanne?" Josh took an uncertain step forward.

"Yeah, bud. It's me." I was trying to play it cool, but my voice rose in pitch as I spoke.

"Oh my God!" He turned and yelled over his shoulder, "Dad, Maryanne's home. The real Maryanne!" Then he jumped onto me, wrapping his arms around my neck and his legs around my waist. "You're back! Dad said we'd never see you again."

Maybe they wouldn't have, had I been given the choice. Still, I wasn't lying when I said, "It's good to see you, Joshy." I squeezed my arms around him, a giggle escaping my throat. I'd spent the last month wanting to feel his little hands around me. "Did you get taller?"

He laughed. "I think so. Do you know what else?"

I shook my head. He was blind, but he'd be able to feel the movement since he was still attached to me.

"I can see some stuff again!"

"No way!" I leaned back and glanced at Mom for confirmation. She was looking at me as if I were a ghost but managed a small nod. We'd been waiting two years for this to happen. I'd begun to think it might never. "What sort of stuff?"

Josh shrugged. "Like outlines. Dark and light. That sort of thing. One day soon I might be able to see you again." He gave my neck another squeeze, pulling me close.

"I'd like that." My greatest wish was for my brother to see again. I wanted him to be able to do all the things a normal nine-year-old did with his friends, like riding a bike or playing soccer.

"Maryanne?" Dad peered around the corner, his voice incredulous and head shaking. Josh was right. Dad really hadn't expected me to return. Not that I was surprised. What surprised me was how much it hurt to hear what I already knew. What sort of father would send their daughter away forever?

His voice seemed to push Mom from her stupor. A grin spread from one ear to the other and she ran forward and wrapped a hug around both me and Josh, almost knocking me off my feet. "You're back! Thank goodness." She pulled away to stare at me. "Are you okay?" She looked different than she had a month ago. There was more grey lining her auburn hair, more wrinkles at the edges of her eyes and mouth.

"I'm fine, Mom. It's good to see you." I pulled her back into our hug, inhaling the baking cookies and Gucci perfume smell that would always remind me of her.

"And you, darling. And you." She pulled back, flapping her hands and making everyone move. "Come inside, Maryanne. Are you hungry? Tired? What can I get you?"

I followed her into the house, Josh still clinging to my hip, and shrugged. "Another hug?" The last time I'd seen Mom, I had no idea I wasn't coming back. I hadn't had the opportunity to hug her goodbye that morning, and I'd spent the last month wishing I could wrap myself around her.

Mom hugged me again and hiccupped back a sob. I put Josh down and squeezed her as tightly as he'd squeezed me.

"Give me that cloak." She held out her hand. "As stunning as it is, it's too hot to be wearing it inside."

I slipped it off and she placed it on the coat rack as if everyone stopping at her home shrugged off a fur-lined twelfth century cloak. She put her arm around my waist and led me through the kitchen and into the lounge.

Carrie was watching TV. She glanced up as I entered, then returned to stare at the screen before looking at me again. "Maryanne?" I hadn't even answered before she jumped to her feet and ran to hug me. God, how had I thought I could stay away and never see these people again?

Carrie stepped aside, her voice tentative. "I'm assuming you don't know about our house guest?" She nodded her head toward the other side of the lounge, to a person sitting in my favorite chair, munching on popcorn.

I smiled. I was fine with them having someone to stay, but for some reason Carrie spoke like she thought I wouldn't be.

I took a step toward the guest as she turned to look at me.

I could have been looking in the mirror.

The girl in my chair looked exactly like me.

Two

"You weren't supposed to come back." They were Dad's first words since I arrived other than my name, and it pissed me off. He was the one who'd sent me away, and he was upset because he hadn't expected me back.

"So, you found a replacement?" My tone was biting, and Dad stepped backward.

He stared like he'd never seen me before. Or perhaps he was trying to remember my face before he forced me to leave again. No need. He had another face exactly like mine living under the same roof as him.

"She found us, actually." Mom stepped between us as if she could sense a shouting match brewing. She gave the other Maryanne an apologetic smile over her shoulder, which only riled me up further. Mom shouldn't be apologizing to her. She should be apologizing to me. I was the one whose life was turned upside-down to repay a debt my father owed. I was the one who'd spent the last month never knowing whether I'd survive the day. I was the one who'd grown up in this house and who surely should be able to come home to it whenever I liked without someone replacing me. To top it all off, I was getting damned sick of discovering there were other people in the world who looked exactly like me.

"And you couldn't wait? Maybe see if I might find my way back?" I glared at Mom, knowing none of this was her fault. Dad was the one I should be glowering at, but he hovered behind her. Hiding, more like it.

"It wasn't like that, Maryanne. This will always be your home." She took a tentative step toward me.

Dad moved out from behind her. "Your mother...she didn't deal well with...what happened to you."

That was okay by me. At least it meant someone had missed me. Unlike him, from what I could tell. "What happened to me? You say it like I could have avoided it. Newsflash, Dad. I tried.

You ignored how I felt and what I wanted, and sent me back in time anyway." All the anger I'd held inside for the past month spewed from my mouth, and I didn't care. It didn't matter that my words caused Dad to suck in a deep breath, or Mom to wipe tears from her eyes. It didn't matter because it made me feel better. And I really needed to feel better right now. There was a huge empty hole inside me where Rob and his friends had been, because, as much as I'd once thought I wanted to return to my family, I'd made my choice to stay with Rob.

Dad gave a half-hearted nod, agreeing. "Your mom called the police, went on TV, put up flyers, did everything she could to get you back."

I stared at him, shaking my head. "You didn't tell her where I was?" That was taking the word bastard to a whole new level.

"Oh, I told her. She just didn't believe me."

I glanced at Mom. I'd always known about the time travel, and how it would be part of my future when I was older. Mom knew, too. Dad told her, the same way he'd told us kids.

Mom shook her head. "I didn't. Never had. Not really. I mean, it just never seemed possible. I went along with it because…because I love your father. But after he sent you away…" She shot him a look that would have turned a lesser man to stone. "I was certain, if I made enough noise, told enough people, someone would know where you were." She reached out to touch my shoulder, then thought better of it, dropping her hand to her side. "I was right. The police found you for us."

"I've been gone a month!" My raised voice didn't interrupt imposter-me's TV-fest. She stuffed popcorn into her mouth, so relaxed it seemed as if this had been her home for longer than a few weeks. I might have considered she was the girl whose name I'd been constantly called for the past month had she not looked quite so at home in a modern environment.

"You should have been gone longer. Didn't you find a reason to stay?" Dad. He was a man of few words, but the ones he said cut right to the bone.

"Oh, I found plenty of reasons to stay. Like a family who cared about me and who wanted me around." I paused, letting that sink in. Whatever reaction I expected from Dad, I didn't get. He just raised his chin and looked over my head. "Yet here I am, by some wicked twist of fate, back with the family who replaced me at a moment's notice. To hear you say that I should have stayed away." I deepened my voice into a bad imitation of him. "Welcome home, Maryanne. When will you be leaving?" Tears welled in my eyes as reality struck. Dad didn't want me here. And given Mom had let him bring in a new me, she probably felt the same way. I'd thought I was alone those first few days in Sherwood Forest, but that was nothing to how I felt now. "I knew you hated me, Dad, but I never thought you'd be so cruel as to wish I'd stayed away." My voice broke and the tears I'd tried to hold back, slipped down my cheeks.

Dad took a half-step forward. "Sorry, love. I didn't mean...that did sound cruel, I didn't mean it to. I just meant, well, I really thought you belonged where I sent you. I thought you might have preferred to stay there."

"I'm not Marian!" I spat the words at him. I knew what he thought. I'd worked it out myself because he hadn't bothered to share his theory with me before I left. More than sending me back in time to fix his mistake, he thought I belonged there. As Robin Hood's Marian. For a second or two when I was with Rob, I'd wondered the same. Then I was suddenly back here, and all those thoughts dried up. Unlike my feelings for him.

Dad's shoulders slumped. "You're not?"

"I'm here, aren't I? If I was her, I'd still be there. Robin Hood's Marian must have been around for longer than a month, otherwise she wouldn't be part of his legend." It came out harsher than I'd intended, yet I wasn't sorry. I was angry. So angry. I wasn't back by choice and I didn't want to be reminded of what I'd left behind.

"You could, you know, go back again, if you miss it that much." It was the first thing the other Maryanne had said, and the tone of her voice grated on my nerves. So did the fact that she felt she had any right to take part in this conversation.

I glared at her a moment, then shook my head. "Can't go back. Ever." Dad told me so the morning he sent me back in time. He couldn't return to fix the mistakes he made in the twelfth century, so he sent me.

Even so, with every part of me, I hoped Dad would disagree, tell me I was wrong. Partly so I could throw more of my fury at him, but mostly because I wanted to be wrong. Dad knew about time travel. At least, he knew more than I did. I wanted my life to have purpose—the kind I'd had living in Sherwood Forest. I wanted to be wanted, to be part of that other family I'd just started getting to know. Everything I wanted made me feel like a traitor, especially since I'd spent a good chunk of the past month wishing I were here.

Dad sagged into his favorite chair, the lines on his face suddenly much more prominent than I'd ever seen them, making him appear ten years older. He gave no disagreement. All I could do was let out a deep breath and let it all go. I was back.

I couldn't return to Rob. The only thing I could do now was get on with my life.

Mom flapped her hands, pointing us toward the kitchen. "Come, Maryanne. Let's get you changed into something more comfortable. Then we'll eat dinner. You can talk more after some food."

Dinner was roast lamb with roasted potatoes, kumara and pumpkin. It tasted divine. I couldn't recall the last time I'd eaten—breakfast at Nottingham Castle I guess, and goodness knew how many hours ago that was. I shoved down mouthful after mouthful while Josh plied me with questions.

"Did you really meet Robin Hood?" He obviously assumed that was a given, not stopping to let me answer before the next question came from his mouth. "Did he look the same as in the movies?"

I smiled. Rob looked nothing like the Robin Hood in the movies. He was better in every way. He certainly had a smile that did more to me than any movie star Robin Hood had ever done, though I guessed that wasn't what my nine-year-old brother was asking. "He wore dark green and carried a bow and quiver on his shoulders, just like the movies."

"So, can he use a bow?"

"Uh-huh." That was around a mouthful of potato.

"A sword?" Josh had stabbed a piece of meat with is fork. It was halfway to his mouth, waiting for my answer. Or for his next question.

"Mmmm."

"Did you learn to use a sword? Or your bow again?"

I glanced at Dad. We didn't talk about me and a bow. We especially didn't talk about it at the dinner table. Then again, I hadn't thought Dad would send me away either, so what the hell. "I can't use a sword. But I did save Robin Hood from the gallows with my bow."

Josh's eyebrow's rose. "Whoa! That's so cool!"

"You've really been back in time, huh?" The girl that looked just like me was sitting opposite. So far, I'd totally ignored her. "Back to 1196?"

I nodded. That was about as far into a conversation with her as I wanted to get. I had so many questions about her, but they were for my parents and they would be asked when she wasn't around.

"Did you go to Nottingham? Did you meet any nobles?" she pressed.

I'd met plenty of nobles. Most of them probably wished they hadn't met me or the people I traveled with. "Yes, to both."

OUTPLAYED

"What about Robin Hood?" Carrie put a tiny piece of potato into her mouth. I'd been watching her out the corner of my eye and was pleased to see some food making it to her mouth, even if it was nowhere near enough. "Did he treat you like a princess?"

Her voice was wistful, and I was growing tired of all the questions. I wanted to ask a few of my own, and there was never enough silence to give me the opportunity. "Don't go thinking my time in Sherwood Forest was a walk in the park. It was dangerous. Every day was a battle to survive. I never knew if I'd end it with a sword in my gut or an arrow in my back."

"Maryanne!" Mom scolded.

"Sorry," I murmured. Blood and guts weren't suitable dinner conversation according to Mom. She definitely wouldn't approve of the recounted battle stories often told around a fire in Sherwood Forest as we ate.

"Oh, we know what it was like back then. We've heard all about it." Carrie glanced at their houseguest.

I started to disagree. To tell her that all the books in the world couldn't show her how terrifying it was to have a sword held to your neck, knowing the swordsman wasn't afraid to use it. Then it hit me.

She looked exactly like me. There was an emerald ring on her left hand. And she'd been asking about nobles and Nottingham. My fork clattered to my plate and I leaned back in my seat, looking at her with new eyes. "You're Maud Fitzwalter."

Three

I PUT my head in my hands and rubbed my temples. This was screwed up. No wonder everyone confused me with Maud Fitzwalter when I was in the twelfth century. The girl across the table could have been my twin. Her hair fell in large auburn curls down to her waist where mine was straight and a little shorter, but other than that, we had the same brown eyes, same full lips. Everything about us was the same. And here she was, sitting with *my* family, at *my* dinner table, in *my* time.

"You see why we had to take her in?" Mom asked, scooping a spoonful of peas from the bowl to my plate. "Dad hoped her father would do the same for you, should you need it."

It made complete sense. He'd even told me to go to Maud's father if I was ever in trouble.

It was still screwed up.

"So, what's your plan, Maryanne? Are you really back to stay or just here for a visit?" Maud was probably worried about where she would live now I was here, because judging by how relaxed she seemed in my house, I didn't think she was planning on returning to her home anytime soon.

Suddenly, I didn't feel like talking. To her, or anyone. I just wanted to bury my head in my pillow and wake up to a normal life. One that didn't involve time travel, or legends, or anyone that looked the same as me. I put my head in my hands. "Already told you. I can't go back."

"Why not?"

My God. Could no one here read my cues? "Because that's the rules," I snapped. "It's always been the rules. Nothing's changed. We can travel twice. No more. That was the entire reason Dad sent me back to fix his mistake rather than going himself."

Dad shifted in his seat.

I ignored him. He'd also wanted me to be Rob's Marian. That was the other reason he'd sent me.

Maud shook her head. "That's not what Tabitha told me."

OUTPLAYED

A flame lit inside my gut. I didn't like Tabitha or her sister, and I was surprised Maud would listen to her given the two of them sent her through time against her will. Tabitha had a billion reasons to lie, and in both our cases they started with her sister. "It's not like I have a lot of information to go on. I went back to your time knowing nothing about anything."

She drew in a breath.

Okay, that may have been unfair. She had probably come here knowing about the same amount. Less actually, since I had taken history at school, and had my research with Dad to go on.

Maud put a hand on Dad's forearm. "That's not true, is it? In certain circumstances we can travel more than twice."

Dad lifted one shoulder. "As far as I'm aware, Maryanne's correct. Those of us who can travel, can do it only twice. Once there, and once home. If Tabitha knows a way around this, it's not common knowledge. We'd have to talk to her if we wanted to know more." Asking Tabitha wasn't an option, and Dad knew it. The only place we knew where to find her was on the other side of the world. At a full moon.

Maud's eyes went distant. "I'm sure it can be done, that there's a loophole in the rules." She shook her head. "I don't recall what it was—it's been two years, and I didn't think it applied to me. I did write it in a journal at the time because Tabitha was so insistent I remember." She gave a sheepish shrug. "But my journals are still locked in my storage locker in London."

I shook my head. Sure they were. I felt as if she'd spin anything into what Dad wanted to hear just to make sure she had a place to stay. I trusted Dad in this, because I was fairly certain he'd send me back to Rob tomorrow if there was a way. Maud's words didn't give me hope. They weren't even worth spending another second thinking about.

I pushed up from my chair. I was bone tired and done talking for the night. It was even an effort to speak nicely to Mom. "I'm sorry. Can we talk more in the morning? I'm exhausted."

"Of course, dear." Mom hugged me before sending me off to the spare room since Maud was living in mine.

All I wanted now were a few hours of nothingness. A few hours where I could forget about everyone I'd never see again. Forget about Maud. Forget about how disappointed Dad seemed to be at my return.

I showered—total bliss—and climbed between the sheets. Stretching out in bed was another exquisite moment. For a month, I'd slept on the hard ground, often with just a cloak as my blanket.

I closed my eyes.

Rob faced away from me and the hood of his cloak was up, but I knew it was him by the line of his back, the deep brown color of his cloak and the fur lining the hood. Just seeing him made me smile. He was standing at the edge of a grassy field, watching something in the nearby forest in the early morning light. He carried no bow with him, no sword. Somehow, I knew they were nearby, close enough to reach should he need them, but nowhere I could see.

There was a noise, a whooshing, a sound I should have recognized but didn't. He grunted, dropped to his knees, then toppled forward into the long grass, an arrow embedded in the center of his back.

No!

I ran. I had to help him. To stop the bleeding, to remove the arrow. Blood bubbled from the wound and Rob was still. I tried but couldn't get any closer. Horse hooves pounded into the dirt behind me. A woman screamed. Perhaps it was me. Mocking laughter assaulted my ears.

Gisborne. He did this.

Rob was dying.

My heart was breaking. I couldn't help him.

I woke in the darkness, my pajamas plastered to my body with sweat. The dream felt so real, like it had actually happened. I could still smell the lingering metallic tang of blood in the back of my nostrils. The only thing that made me certain it was my imagination playing a cruel trick, was that Gisborne had done it, and before I left the twelfth century, I'd seen him die. He couldn't still be hunting Rob.

I moved to my window seat, dragging my duvet with me, and propped my pillow behind my back. I stayed that way for the rest of the night, throwing my window open for fresh air. Every time I closed my eyes for longer than a second, I saw it all over again. Staying awake was the better option. The only option. Sometime after the sun rose the dream faded, and I climbed back between the sheets and closed my eyes.

I woke to someone knocking at my door. It seemed only minutes had passed since I lay my head against the pillow. Carrie walked in holding a tray piled with food. "Dinner?"

I rubbed my eyes and squinted at the clock. "I've slept the entire day?" If only I felt more rested for all the hours in bed.

She placed the tray on my lap. "You must be exhausted." She opened her mouth like she wanted to say something more and then changed her mind, leaving me alone with my thoughts.

The meal looked tasty—lasagna and lettuce salad—but any hunger left with the sound of my family laughing together around the dinner table downstairs. It brought back memories of my life before Sherwood Forest, when I'd taken every meal in my room and barely spoken to any of them. Nothing had changed. I was still eating in my room on my own. And they still thought that was all right. What had made me think for the past month that I needed to get back here?

I put the tray on the floor and closed my eyes.

The crowd was big, and I was in the middle of it. People jostled, talking quietly to the person next to them, pushing and shoving for a better view. I stood on tiptoes, searching to find what took their attention.

Gisborne. Standing high on a platform with Nottingham Castle looming behind him.

He was dressed well. Not in his riding gear and chainmail, but in grey pants and a blue top that matched his eyes. His wavy black hair fell around his face as he talked quietly to someone. Someone wearing a brown cloak. I couldn't see his face, but I knew it was Rob. Gisborne turned to speak to the crowd. "Sherwood Forest is safe once more. Robin Hood has seen the error of his ways. No longer will he make travel through the forest difficult. He'll instead spend his days with me, his brother."

Then Rob and Gisborne were gone, and Miller was staring at me. His eyes were filled with unshed tears, his face so bruised and swollen it was almost unrecognizable. And in the distance, Gisborne laughed.

Josh came to my room the following day. At least I think it was the following day. My sleep pattern was so out of whack it could have been two days later. I hadn't left my room since the first night. Couldn't. I was too tired. Too angry. Too scared.

"Will you read to me?" His favorite book was tucked into his right hand.

I nodded and he snuggled into bed beside me. I didn't need the book. Knew the words already. I wasn't even through half the story when he interrupted. "Are you going to leave me again, Maryanne? Do you wish you weren't home? Is that why you won't come out of your room?"

Excellent questions from the nine-year-old. Questions I couldn't answer honestly because the truth broke my heart. Yes, I wished I was somewhere else. Aside from Josh, there was nothing here for me. Hadn't been for a long time. I'd missed the familiarity while I was away, nothing else. I wasn't leaving though. That was a question I could answer truthfully. "No, Joshy, I'm not going anywhere. Why would you think that?" Apart from the fact that I'd been all kinds of anti-social since I returned.

"Dad says so."

The hackles on my neck rose. Anything to do with Dad seemed to push my buttons lately. "Dad hasn't talked to me at all since I got home. He doesn't have a clue what I want."

Josh shrugged. If he heard my anger, he ignored it. "He said if that's really what you want, he'll find a way to send you back. He said it would rip him apart to watch you leave again, but he can't stand it that you hate being here so much you won't come near any of us."

Was that how it looked? "I'm just tired, Josh. It's only been a couple of days. Give me time." I wrapped my arm around his shoulders and gave him a squeeze.

"Try a couple of weeks."

"No." I shook my head. "There's no way it's been that long."

"Take a look in the mirror. You don't eat, and you've got extra skinny." He jumped up and grabbed a hand mirror off the dresser, holding it out so I could see my reflection.

I winced. My hair was a knotted mess on top of my head, my skin pallid, and my cheeks hollow. Two weeks? How could that be?

"So, are you going to leave again, Maryanne? Because I need you to tell me if you're going this time. I need to say goodbye."

Josh was like a light on a dark night. I hugged him tight. "I'm not going anywhere, bud." And starting tomorrow, I was going to come out of my room more often.

"What are you doing out here all alone?" Rob's voice floated to me from behind. I turned to find him watching from high on the bank of the river. He looked good in his dark green pants. No cloak, no bow, just a sword strapped around his waist, and a short-sleeved tunic that showed off the muscles in his arms.

I looked past him, trying to work out where I was. My feet were soaking in the cool water, but I didn't recognize the river, had never been here before. It was another dream, born from a vivid imagination. I stood up. My dreams of Rob lately had all ended badly. Usually with him shot in the back. I wasn't sticking around to watch that happen again.

He jogged down the bank and grabbed my hand. "Where are you going?"

I shrugged. Away, I guessed. Somewhere I didn't have to see him die again.

He shook his head. "Not going to die."

I'd spoken aloud?

His thumb ran across the back of my hand and I shivered. I'd give so much to feel his touch again in real life.

I shook my head, trying to dislodge him from my dream. I knew how this would end. I didn't need to see it again.

"Maryanne? What's wrong? Aren't you pleased to see me? Because I am beyond pleased to see you."

I could sit and drink in his profile all day. "I'd rather I didn't have to see you in my dreams."

He frowned. "This isn't your dream."

I nodded. "It is." Rob was all I'd dreamed of since I came home.

"It's mine."

I laughed. Dreams never made sense. "What makes you so sure?"

"Ever since Tabitha ripped you away from us, I've been wishing to dream of you. Finally, my wish was granted."

I looked down at myself. I was wearing the beautiful blue and white gown the Sheriff gave me. Maybe this was his dream. If it was mine, I'd probably be wearing jeans and a t-shirt. Or maybe my pajamas since that's all I ever wore these days. I grinned. "Can't be. I remember you telling me how you'd like me to dress in your dreams, and it wasn't like this."

His answering smile was wicked, and my heart faltered. He remembered. He spread his hands in the direction of the water. "You want to swim? Don't let me stop you."

"After you." I was tempted, if only because I knew this was a dream.

He shook his head.

"Why not?" I laughed. He was all talk.

His eyes turned sad. "Because I don't want to turn my back on you. You might disappear again."

I sighed. Way to bring the mood down. "How is everyone?" Tuck, Miller, John. I wanted to hear about them all.

He shook his head. "Winter's hard, Maryanne. We can't help the people who need it. The Sheriff made sure of that."

"I'm sure you'll find a way." He always did.

He shook his head again. "I could do it if you were here. You always find a way past every problem that seems huge." He met my eyes with a smile. "Plus, I miss you."

"I miss you, too."

I wanted so much for that dream to be real, to have a real conversation with Rob. I also wished

I'd had more time. Time to hear how he was doing, how they were all doing. I wanted to know about the carriages they'd robbed and the people they'd helped, and how crazy they'd driven the Sheriff with all the things they'd done. The dream—the wishful thinking—had faded too fast, and instead we'd talked about things that didn't matter.

I hugged the dream tight, hoping it'd get me through the night, but I woke while it was still dark to visions of villages torn apart by soldiers, maimed and dead people, always accompanied by Gisborne's hollow laughter. I even saw John, curled around himself and screaming out in pain as blood spurted from one hand. It seemed as if I was destined never to sleep again because just closing my eyes brought tongue-less or eye-less victims.

I climbed out of bed, weary, but wary of sleep. If I couldn't get rid of the dreams, I had to get used to operating on little to no sleep. The night was warm, and I wandered outside and sat on the swing Dad built when Carrie and I were little. I still remembered how excited I'd been watching him hang it from the lowest limb of the huge oak in the backyard.

The back door opened and Maud, wearing a nightdress that covered her all the way to her elbows and knees—I guessed some habits die hard—stepped outside. She was carrying a book which she placed on her knee when she sat on the garden seat nearby. "Can't sleep?"

"Bad dreams." Terrible nightmares to be more exact.

Her nod was slow. "About?"

I sighed. Maybe talking about the dreams would make them stop. It was worth a try. "The people I knew in your time. About them dying horrible deaths. Or doing things totally out of character."

"And Tabitha didn't warn you this might happen?"

I shook my head. Tabitha hadn't spoken to me once she dragged me into the portal. Or if she had, I didn't recall. I barely remembered any of the trip back through time. "Do you think the dreams are a side effect of the time travel? Because I didn't get them when I went through the first time." Instead, I'd lost memories, only to have them all return at once. This felt different though.

She lifted one shoulder. She had no more answers than I did. "Do you wish you could go back? To marry Gisborne? Is that why you're so...sad?"

I almost choked. Marrying Gisborne wasn't on my list of things to do. "I'm not sad. Gisborne and

I...we didn't exactly see eye to eye." Not to mention, he thought I was her. "He tried to kill Rob while I was there." As well as almost succeeding before I met either of them. "Anyway, I think he's dead."

Maud sighed, her eyes going distant. If hearing of her fiancé's demise bothered her, she didn't show it. "You know, Gisborne always felt like their mother loved Rob more, and that she thought Rob's father had been a better man than his own. He felt he had something to prove, and if I know him, he wouldn't have wanted to lose everything he'd gained when his little brother returned from the dead." Meaning he didn't want to lose his land or titles. Land and titles that should belong to Rob.

I lifted my eyebrows, a sudden flash of anger heating my words. "And that's a good reason to try to kill someone? Just because he didn't get the love he felt he was entitled to? Rob didn't get it either—he was tossed out into the forest to die—and he doesn't spend his life being a bastard to everyone he comes across."

"It's not a *good* reason, no." Maud's voice was soft. "But it is *the* reason Gisborne behaves the way he does." Her lips turned up into a weak smile. "He was a good man when I knew him. He just needed some direction to stop the jealousy and self-entitlement from driving him. I thought I'd been making a difference..."

"Until he acted with the ultimate sense of entitlement." When he kissed Eliza Thatcher. "Sorry," I mumbled. "You probably didn't need to hear that." There was nothing she could say to make Gisborne seem reasonable.

She obviously got the same feeling because she dropped the subject, watching me a moment before returning to our previous conversation. "I think you are sad. If you weren't, you'd get out of bed and spend time with your family."

That was a reprimand if ever I'd heard one. She didn't get to pass judgement on me just because she was living my life. "My family don't care about me. Never have. Why would I want to spend time with them?"

"I've lived with them for a while now, I know more than you think. I know they love you, a lot." She was quiet and self-assured, but not in a way that felt like she was rubbing her knowledge in my face. I'd expected her to be a spoilt brat. Like Eliza Thatcher.

However, she was wrong. Especially where Dad was concerned. "If they did, they wouldn't have replaced me with someone else the moment I left." My angry words were at total odds with her calm demeanor.

OUTPLAYED

Maud sighed. "Look at it from your mother's eyes for a moment. Time travel is foreign to her. She knew about your dad doing it, but she never really believed it happened. Then your dad sent you away without giving either of you the chance to say goodbye. Your mother already knows she's neglected you these past two years since the accident, but she always thought she'd spend time with you soon, once Josh was better. Then you left and she had no chance."

Still didn't mean she should replace me.

"She blames herself. She thinks she should have known what your father planned that day." Maud ran her fingers through her hair, pulling gently when they stuck in her curls. "What I'm saying is that she did everything she could think of to get you back. She even spent two weeks pretending my impersonation of you had her fooled." Her smile was uncertain.

"Let me guess, you just couldn't help yourself and told her who you really were?" I was wrong to be pissed at her for impersonating me. She'd done what she needed to survive in a foreign place. I'd done the same thing in her time. It was starting to feel like everything made me upset and angry these days.

Maud shrugged. "Josh kept saying I wasn't you, that I couldn't read his book the way you did. I thought my time was up, that they'd demand answers and I'd be back on the streets. I told them who I was, and what year I'd come from, and they told me I could stay. It was like I had a second chance."

"How lovely for you all." I was in full-on bitch-mode tonight and I didn't seem to be able to stop.

Maud sighed. She gave me another of her never-ending stares, probably ready to tell me to lose the attitude. "Carrie feels indebted to you for letting her leave that morning. Josh misses you like crazy. And your Dad, everything he did was to make your life in the past easier."

Somehow, I'd come to the same conclusion when I was eight hundred years away. Now I was back here, I didn't see it that way at all. "They might say that, but they all have a funny way of showing it."

"They've been trying for two months to get you out of bed to show you exactly that."

Two months. It didn't feel like I'd been back that long. The days and nights all melted together. "You think I'm being unfair."

A gentle breeze blew a few strands of her long hair across her face and she flicked them away. "No. I think you're being a lot nicer than I would be in the same situation. I also think you're not seeing things clearly."

She might have a point. Staying in bed for weeks on end didn't exactly scream *I see why you did that.*

Maud curled her feet up beneath her. "You think you're angry at your dad for sending you away. I think you're angry at him, and at Tabitha, for taking away your choices."

"Speaking from experience?" Still with the snark. I needed to stop. Next time I spoke, I'd make a conscious effort to reign it in.

"A little. And because it doesn't take much to imagine how I'd feel if someone ripped me away from my life here and sent me home."

Was I really playing the victim? It wasn't intentional. I didn't even know where the weeks had gone. "Do you like it here?"

"I do now. It was difficult to begin with."

I could relate to that. The differences between our times were huge, yet we'd both been dropped in and forced to survive. "Where did you live? Before you came here?" She'd been here two years before she found my family.

"On the streets of London, mostly." She looked past me, off into the distance. "Sometimes I went to a shelter. Sometimes I worked in exchange for board, cleaning, looking after children, whatever it took. But I never felt like I was in the right place. Always felt like I was searching for something. Or someone." She turned to me. "That's why, when I saw your family were looking for you, I had to contact them. Anything was better than life on the streets."

I could have had the exact same struggle had I not found Rob that first day. "How was it you came to this time? I had to have a tether, to put me in the right place." I held up my wrist where the coin Dad gave me on the day I went back in time was tied with a piece of leather.

Her smile was faint. "I found this…stick, when I was a kid." Her lips quirked. "Or I might have been riffling through Father's desk and taken it from there."

I frowned. "A stick?"

"That's what I called it. It fascinated me. There was a button I could push on one end, and it felt so lovely and cool in hand. The day I took it was the first day I met Gisborne. He was the best-looking boy I'd ever seen, and he liked me so much that I thought the stick must bring good luck. I expected Father to discover it missing and ask for it back. He never did, and I carried it everywhere. For luck."

I nodded, still not following.

"I had it with me the night I went to the Big Tree. It's only since I've been in your time that I discovered I was carrying a Parker pen. Then, when I met your father, I discovered it was his, left behind by accident in the twelfth century. He knew my father."

"No wonder you never felt like you were in quite the right place. You were tethered to Dad."

She nodded.

"Why didn't you go back home? If life was so hard before you met my family." She'd stuck around a lot longer than I would have in her situation.

"Are you kidding? There are so many possibilities here. Things I couldn't do in my time because I'm a woman, and because so much hasn't been invented yet. I want to see everything, go everywhere, learn everything. I can't do any of that if I return home. You know what it's like there. Here, I have so much freedom. And there's no sexism—or not much, anyway."

I giggled. Rob hadn't been like that, but I had seen it. "True. But there are no guns in your time."

She nodded. "Yes, but swords." She made an exaggerated shivering motion. "No internet back then, either."

"You know, I really don't miss the internet. There's probably only one thing I do miss."

"Hot running water?"

I laughed. She had it in one.

"And baths," we both said together.

It felt good to laugh. It had been too long.

Maud held up the book on her lap, her eyes serious. "I had my journal sent over from my storage locker. The one I wrote Tabitha's warning in."

I gave it a side-long glance. If she'd found something good, something that meant I could go back to Rob, she would have come right out with it.

"There are things in here you'll want to know."

"But not good things? Right?".

She shrugged one shoulder. "Some are good, some aren't." Her raised eyebrows told me I should hear them all, whether I wanted to or not.

And I didn't. But her expression also said something else. It told me I'd been waiting for a choice, complaining because Dad and Tabitha took mine away when they sent me back in time, and again when Tabitha brought me home. Now I had one, and if I chose not to hear what that journal said, I would keep being a victim. Complaining about what had been done to me rather than standing up and doing something for myself.

I never behaved that way when I was with Rob. It was time I started acting like the person I was around him, whether he was nearby or not. Make a choice, then make it happen. It was what I needed to do.

I nodded. "Tell me."

OUTPLAYED

Maud looked over her shoulder at the house. The desk lamp in Dad's study was on. I hadn't noticed before. "You need to tell your father about those dreams. Then we'll talk about my journal and make a plan from there." She nodded in the direction of his study. "Come on."

Four

I HADN'T been in Dad's study for years. I used to hang out here for hours every week when I was younger. We'd sit on his brown leather couch together and talk about school, or archery, or friends, while we researched people Dad knew in the twelfth century. After Josh's accident, this room became Dad's retreat. His place to get away from everyone and everything. His place to get away from me.

It still looked the same as it always had. Warm, calm and inviting with the dark red walls. The room was meticulously tidy, except for the few papers he was currently reading on the huge wooden desk in the center of the room.

"Maud said I should tell you about my dreams." I poked my head through the door, leaving the rest of my body outside. "Maud's here, too." I added the last sentence in case he was planning to turn me away. I had a feeling he wouldn't do that in front of Maud.

Dad looked up and nodded as if it wasn't the middle of the night, and I always dropped in for chats about things like dreams. He gestured to the brown leather couch beside the window and took the chair opposite. Maud followed me into the room and sat in the other chair.

"Before we do this, I have two questions."

Dad's head tilted to one side. "Sure. Anything." His beard was grayer than I recalled. His hair, too.

"Why did you link my return to this time to Gisborne's death?" I would never be sorry he was dead—not after everything he'd done to Rob—what I hated was that Dad had said he must die before I could return home. What sort of person did that make him?

Dad shook his head. "I didn't ask for Gisborne to die. I asked for revenge, for Avery's son. Rob must have felt he had it for the magic to allow you to come home."

I nodded. At least Dad wasn't a murderer.

My other question was something I'd wanted to know since the moment Dad told me he was sending me to twelfth century England. I'd never had the chance to ask. Before I bared my soul to him, I needed him to offer the same.

"Why are you so invested in Robin Hood?"

A frown creased his forehead. "Because it involves you, of course."

I shook my head. It might involve me now, but it hadn't when he sent me back, and he hadn't known for certain it ever would. "Not now. Before."

"You know this already." Dad gave a weak smile. "I owe a debt to his father."

"Because you ran on the night he was killed?"

He nodded, his lips stretching into a thin line.

He seemed so interested in the lives of the people of that time, almost to the point of obsession. There had to be more to it. "Is that all?"

Dad got up from his chair, walked over to the window and stared out into the darkness. "I never wanted to tell you, but you deserve to hear." He was silent for a long time. Maud and I waited, hands in our laps. When he finally spoke, it was the last thing I expected him to say. "I loved him. Avery Woodhurst."

I stared at his back, unsure if he meant he loved Avery like a brother, or as something more. "Because he was such a good friend?"

"Because of that, yes. But..." He took a deep breath. "I was in love with him, too."

OUTPLAYED

My mouth fell open. I glanced at Maud to find her eyes were wide. I didn't know what to say. This wasn't the usual sort of dad and daughter conversation.

Dad turned, his eyes falling on me. "Your mother knows."

I wasn't sure I could make my voice work. "Knows what, exactly?" That they'd been lovers? That Dad didn't love her?

"How I felt about him. That I was once in love with…a man." He looked at his feet like he thought him loving a man might upset me.

It didn't. As long as it was history. As long as it wasn't hurting Mom. "Do you still love him?"

"It's been a lot of years, Maryanne. There will always be a place in my heart for him, but I am no longer in love with him. I love your mother. However, his death and the way it happened, has made me take an extra interest in the lives of the people that were there that night. And their families. I'm sorry. I should have told you sooner." His voice dropped to a whisper.

He should have. It would have made understanding everything that had come since so much easier. "What happened that night?" What I knew of Dad's last day in the past took on new meaning with his confession. I couldn't imagine leaving Rob to die while I ran to the safety of a different time.

He sighed. "Avery and I were traveling back to Woodhurst from Nottingham. We were late leaving because his horse had thrown a shoe. In hindsight, we should have left the next day rather than riding through the forest at night. We stopped in the dark at a stream deep in the forest to let the horses rest. The moonlight fell across Avery's face, and he smiled at me. I couldn't stop myself, and I told him how I felt about him." He shook his head. "I never should have done it. Avery was married and I had no business saying any of those things. It was just...impossible to keep them inside any longer."

"He didn't know?" Because that was a pretty big confession to make out of the blue.

Dad shrugged. "He probably did. We'd never talked about—or acted on—our feelings before then, though, if that's what you're asking." He turned back to the window again.

I glanced at Maud. Her mouth was a small circle. I imagined I looked just as shocked.

"Avery resisted my words. He said he was married, that he loved his wife. I refused to believe him, kept pushing him to say what I wanted to hear." He shook his head. "If I'd given up then, everything would have turned out so differently. Instead...." In the reflection of the glass, Dad closed his eyes, remembering, I guessed.

I cleared my throat, reminding him we were here. I was uncomfortable enough to have this conversation with my dad. I didn't need to watch him recall such a private moment.

Dad's eyes fluttered open and he squared his shoulders. "Avery didn't admit anything that night. And rightly so. It would have been disrespectful to his wife. Did he love me?" He lifted his shoulders. "I think so, but he never said. I suspect he didn't want anyone to find out about his feelings—it was the quickest way to the end of a hangman's noose."

I drew in a breath.

Dad took my shock at the medieval penalty for homosexuality for disgust. "I know. He was married. I should never have told him. I regret it every day."

"So, you left? Came home because you couldn't have the person you loved?" That wasn't how he'd made it sound the last time he'd told me about this night.

He turned back toward us, shaking his head. "There was no time. Jerimiah, Avery's brother, and four of his men showed up. They'd followed us through the forest with the intention of killing Avery for his land. Instead, I gave them something better. What I'd just confessed was against the law."

"But it was just you in trouble, right? Avery did nothing wrong." Perhaps running had been the smartest thing to do.

Dad shook his head. "Avery admitted nothing. But he refuted nothing, either."

My shoulders sagged. "Jeremiah took it as an admission of guilt?" I could not like that man. It was little wonder Gisborne was the way he was.

Dad gave a slow nod. "We fought hard, the two of us together. Avery was like a demon, but he had no chance. Jerimiah had a plan, and however it happened, he wanted Avery dead. Had Avery not ended that night with a sword through his belly, we'd both have been hanged. So, he fought knowing he was going to die. He fought for me, so I could come back to this time. He fought to give me a life. When he took a shot to his arm, he screamed at me to run." Dad swallowed, his memories of that night dancing in front of his eyes. "It wasn't until he was on his knees, blood dripping from his arm, shoulder and thigh, that I listened. I wasn't yet too injured to leave, but it was only a matter of time. With one final glance at him swinging his sword even though he couldn't stand, I left. If he hadn't fought for me, my life would have ended. Everything I've done since, was to repay the gift he gave me."

"Dad," I whispered, because I couldn't think of anything else to say. His story was miserable, on so many levels.

He shook his head and shook off his memories. "It's fine. I'm fine. But you asked, and you deserve to know the sort of person your father is." It was plain to see what Dad thought of himself, the guilt and shame was spread across his face.

I stood up, walked over to the window and took his hand. There were things in that story I didn't like. Things he should never have done because he had no right—like confessing his feelings to a married man. But, better than anyone, I knew how different life was in the twelfth century. It wouldn't have mattered if Avery was married or not, the two of them could never have had the relationship Dad desired because of the laws of the time. And that just made me sad. "I don't hate you, Dad. And you shouldn't hate yourself, either."

He nodded, squeezing my hand. "Thank you, Maryanne. It means a lot to hear that from you." He ran his palm down his face. "Now, do you want to tell me about these dreams?"

I returned to the couch, tucking my feet up under me and pushing off the images Dad's story had brought forth, in favor of other, more disturbing ones. "Every time I close my eyes, I see my friends...see Rob...die. The dreams feel like they're taking over my life. I'm losing track of time." I told him everything the way Maud asked, the words spilling from my mouth in a rush.

Dad sat on his chair and pulled off his glasses, resting them in his lap. "Have you been to the places you dream about?"

I shook my head. "I recognized Nottingham Castle in the background of one. The other places are entirely figments of my imagination, but the people are those I know." Mostly.

"It feels real? Like you're actually there?"

That was exactly how it felt. "So much so, I can't sleep properly."

Dad nodded, chewing on the end of his glasses. He looked at Maud, and then nodded.

Maud shuffled forward in her seat, her fingers wrapped around her journal. "Tabitha was very nervous the night she took me through the portal."

I lifted my eyebrows. "That would be because she basically kidnapped you."

"It could have been a little of that. But I got the feeling that the trip forward through time can be...messy."

"Okay." I drew the word out.

"Just hear her out." Dad reached around and placed his glasses on the desk behind him.

"She told me that whenever a person traveled forward through time, there was the possibility of them leaving unfinished business behind. She said my dreams would tell me if that was the case. She also told me not to give away my passage back in time. At least, not until I knew for certain I was finished there."

I shook my head. "Am I supposed to understand what this means?"

"It means the past wants you back, Maryanne." Dad rested his elbows on his knees as he watched for my reaction. "The dreams are a sign of your unfinished business there. What you see in your dreams are things you would have changed if you'd stayed. If you go back, you can stop them happening. You can save your friends."

It couldn't be that easy. "What's the catch?"

"There are a few."

Of course there were. "Hit me." Might as well have all the information.

Dad got to his feet, and walked over to the window again, resting heavily on the sill and staring out into the darkness for a moment before speaking. "It's most likely a one-way trip."

"Okay." So, goodbye to my family would be goodbye for good, which would totally suck. I'd been prepared to do exactly that when I'd decided to stay with Rob, though, so as hard as it would be, I knew it was possible.

"And you'll need someone to give you their passage through time." He turned looking between me and Maud.

"That's where I come in. I have one trip back to my time that I don't ever intend to use. It's yours. If you want it."

"You don't want to go home?" Not even as a backup option if everything turned to custard with life here? Because that seemed like a huge thing to give away to a near stranger.

Maud shook her head, her smile serene. "I told you already. There are so many possibilities here. Like university. Or travel. Things I'd never get the chance to do or learn about if I returned home. Father would have me married off straight away. No." She shook her head again. "I will never go back."

Dad licked his lips, like he was suddenly nervous. "Maud is family. She'll always have a home here with us. She could never replace you, but we will treat her like a daughter."

I wasn't biting, not the way he seemed to expect. Maud deserved a place to call home. I was happy to share mine and glad she had a place to live now.

Dad moved away from the window to sit on the edge of his desk facing me. He smiled, but his eyes were sad. "Maryanne, I want this to be your decision. You can choose to stay. I want you to stay, more than anything." He swallowed, looking somewhere over my head as he tried to compose himself. Then he drew a deep breath before continuing. "I hate knowing I might never see you again, never see the woman you're growing into. Maud might look like you, but she isn't you." He glanced apologetically at the girl who could be my twin, before returning his gaze to me. Blinking hard, he took another deep breath. "But if you want to go, you have my blessing. All I've ever wanted is for you to be happy." His voice wobbled.

I'd wished so many times in the past to hear him say something like this, to hear he cared. For years, I thought he hated me, and I hated myself because of that. I couldn't stop the smile that formed on my lips. Didn't even want to. "Thank you," I whispered.

Maud flicked through her journal, placing her finger in the middle of a page below her ornate writing. "Once you make your decision to stay here or go back, you'll start to feel more like yourself. The anger and sadness, and everything else you've been feeling, will disappear."

"Along with the dreams?" I hoped she'd say yes.

Maud shook her head. "There are only two ways to stop the dreams. Do something to stop what you see happening..."

I blew out a breath. "Or don't, and he dies anyway." What a cheery thought.

"Make that three." Maud gave a shrug of one shoulder, her voice somber. "The other way to stop them is by telling someone in the past that you're having dreams and what they're about."

I tilted my head, trying to work out why she said that like it was a bad thing. "I can save Rob and stop the dreams just by telling someone about them?" That seemed like the perfect solution. There would be no need to find the place I kept seeing Rob die, no need to figure out when it would happen. Yet neither Maud nor Dad seemed thrilled by this option. Their faces were gloomy, their eyes downcast.

Maud flicked forward another two pages. "According to Tabitha, if you tell anyone, you'll suffer a violent death."

"You mean I'll save Rob but die in the process?" I shook my head. A way out that wasn't a way out. I shouldn't even be surprised.

Maud nodded. "That's what Tabitha said."

Keeping secrets from Rob was what had started the events that led to me returning home. We'd argued when he realized I was pretending to be Maud Fitzwalter, and everything had spiraled from there. I didn't want to lie to him again, but if I went back, I'd have no choice in the matter. "This is a hard decision."

"Only because it's a one-way trip. If you knew you could come back and see us any time, you'd have made the decision by now." Dad pushed off the desk, sat next to me on the couch and threw his arm over my shoulders. Just like he used to when I was little. I leaned into him.

Make a choice. That's what I'd told myself to do earlier tonight. Now there was one right in front of me.

I could do it. Go back. Be part of Rob's legend.

Or I could stay here.

Either way, I'd be in charge of my life.

Make a choice, then make it happen.

I took a deep breath. I'd known what I wanted since I saw Rob's face fade into the whiteness as the portal stole me away. "I want to go back." My words were quiet but deliberate. I'd miss Josh. I'd miss my entire family. At least this time, I could say goodbye. "I want to go back," I said louder.

Magic swirled around me the moment I spoke. With Maud's offer accepted, it kicked into life, like a light in my heart, or electricity across my skin. I felt whole again in a way I hadn't since I returned. I was going back.

To the twelfth century.
To my friends.
To Rob.

"Are you totally sure you want to leave?" Mom's sandals hung from one hand as the two of us wandered along the beach, water lapping at our toes and the sun beating on our backs. She glanced quickly my way. "You know it's not too late to change your mind."

I was leaving tomorrow. Getting on a plane and flying across the world to the portal in Sherwood Forest. The last few weeks with my family had been amazing, especially my time with Mom. We'd had pedicures, and coffees, and long talks every day. It was everything I'd wanted since Josh's accident. "I'm sure." Surer than I'd ever been of anything.

"What if Rob's not the one?" She made quote marks with her fingers. "Just because your dad believes it, doesn't mean it's true."

I turned, walking backward through the shallow water, unable to stop the smile that spread on my face when I thought about Rob. "He treats me like I'm the most important person in the world. He talks to me like my opinion matters. He trusts me, and I trust him. I want to be part of his legend and I want to save his life."

She blew out a deep breath. "I know you weren't getting what you needed from us before you left, but you've helped us see what you were missing. We could give you those things, too."

I smiled, swallowing back the sudden lump in my throat. "I know you can, Mom. But…" I wasn't changing my mind and I hated disappointing her.

She gave a single nod, then plastered a smile on her face. "They're lucky to have you. Never forget that."

I nodded, tears pricking my eyes. Just because I wanted to go back didn't mean I was looking forward to leaving. "Any other wise words you want to pass on?" My voice was thick with tears. I turned away so Mom couldn't see them. She was sad enough; I didn't want to make her feel worse.

She pulled me into a hug. "I have so many things I want to tell you and no time to say the words." She drew in a deep breath, letting go of me. We started along the beach again. "Just remember how much we love you. We'll always love you that much, no matter how long it's been since we've seen you. And trust in Rob. If things get tough, remember how you felt about him here, today." She took my hand and squeezed. "You're going to be fine."

"Thanks, Mom," I whispered. "You're going to be fine, too."

My entire family, including Maud, came to see me off at the airport the next day. It would take three flights and a taxi to end up at the Major Oak. Mom and Dad offered to come to England with me. I'd refused. It would be harder to leave with them standing there watching. We could say goodbye just as well here.

I'd had no nightmares since I made my decision and I felt better than I had in weeks. The dark cloud that had hovered over me since I'd come back disappeared with the dreams, just like Maud said it would.

I hugged Carrie goodbye.

"Thank you," she whispered, squeezing me tight.

"What for?"

"For letting me go back to Mom that day in the forest." There were tears in her voice. "I wouldn't have been as good as you were in the past. I'd probably have died."

She underestimated herself. She could have done it. If she'd had to. I was just glad she didn't. "It's okay. I think it was me he needed to send anyway."

A sob escaped from where her face was buried in my neck.

I hugged her tighter. "It's okay, Carrie. I didn't want to go that day, but I do today." Apart from the goodbyes. They were never fun.

She pulled back. "Make sure those people, that family you talked about, look after you." Tears ran down her cheeks.

"They will. Make sure you look after yourself." Make sure you keep trying to eat was what I meant. Not something I could say without putting her under pressure, and I didn't want to do that. I'd talked to Mom about her though, and they had a plan going forward to help her heal.

She nodded. "I'm trying."

Josh pried us apart and climbed into my arms. "I got you something." Tears streamed down his face, too.

How had I ever wondered if these people missed me? The darkness of the dreams had a lot to answer for. "You did?"

He nodded. "I got the idea when you were buying presents for your friends in the past."

I did have presents for Miller, Tuck, John and Rob in my bag. What Josh didn't know was that I'd left him, Carrie, Mom and Dad a present each that they could open on Christmas Day. Maud had them. I'd given her enough to last the next five years. I really hoped Josh didn't forget me after that.

He pressed a package into my hands. "Don't open it yet. Save it. Until you miss us."

Tears made my eyes swim. "But I miss you already."

He smiled. "Wait until you miss us more."

Mom hugged me for so long I thought she'd never let go. When she finally did, she couldn't speak. She was crying too hard. She moved aside.

"Bye, Dad."

"Bye, Maryanne." He gave me a hug. "You make me prouder than you'll ever know. I know you don't believe that, but it's true. I love you so much."

Dad was proud of me and he loved me. It was all I needed to hear. "I love you, too, Dad."

"I'll spend my days looking for your name in history texts, Maryanne. Believe me, I'll be following your life however I can."

I nodded goodbye to Maud and bent to pick up my pack. I'd get rid of this modern one at the Major Oak. Inside was a hessian bag I'd use to carry my things when I got back to the twelfth century. Maud stepped forward with her hand outstretched. "Could you give this back to Gisborne for me if you get the chance? I don't think it's fair I keep it knowing I'll never go back to him." Between her finger and thumb was the emerald engagement ring Gisborne once gave her.

I hesitated. I'd seen Gisborne take a sword to his stomach. As far as I knew, he was dead.

She pressed the ring into my hand. "Just give it to him when you get the chance. There's no hurry."

I sighed inwardly and slipped it into my pocket. "You know he might be dead, right?"

"You saw him in your dreams." She shrugged. "I think he's still alive, but if not, sell it and use the gold however you need. I don't want to keep holding onto the past."

I didn't want to have to hunt Gisborne down. I'd rather not see him at all. But Maud was staring with hope-filled eyes and I couldn't say no. I ran three fingers down the side of my face where Eliza's scar ran. "Good job. With Eliza."

Her eyes widened. "You know about that?"

"She has a scar. Like I said, good job." Eliza Thatcher was one of my least favorite people on this earth. After what she'd done to Maud, she deserved worse than a scar on her face.

Maud took another step forward, whispering in my ear. "Listen, I didn't know whether to say this or not, and I don't know him well. I just think you should watch Tuck. I once saw him take a bribe."

I frowned, twisting to look at her, to make certain she was serious. "Are you sure?" Because that didn't sound like the Tuck I knew. He was prickly, for sure, but he was also honest to a fault.

She nodded. "He didn't know I was watching until after. He wasn't happy when he saw me."

"That's why he doesn't like you? Me." Tuck and I had never seen eye to eye. He'd once mentioned he knew Maud, but I'd never thought any more about it.

Maud nodded.

"Who from?" I had so many questions.

"Jerimiah Woodhurst." The man who'd tried to kill Dad and who Rob had called Father.

Somehow, I wasn't surprised. "What was the bribe for?"

Dad stepped between us. "Last call, Maryanne. Time to go be Robin Hood's Marian."

I glanced at Maud. She shook her head. Either she didn't know, or she didn't have time to tell me.

Five

"You lied."

Tabitha finally showed up at the Major Oak after I'd knocked on the rough bark of the ancient tree three times. She'd taken just long enough that panic increased my heart rate and I started to wonder if Dad was wrong about me being able to go back. Because I was worried, I was more than a little annoyed when she finally arrived.

She shrugged, regal as always. "Technically, I didn't. It was more of an omission." Total omission. If Maud hadn't known about the dreams or that she could give me her passage back through time, I'd never have found out.

I bristled. She knew how much I wanted to return to the twelfth century. "You could have told me there was a way to go back."

Another shrug, this one with pursed lips. "My sister doesn't want you there."

"Well, Eliza's going to be sadly disappointed."

Tabitha gave one of her long, slow blinks. "Are you ready?"

I nodded. I was more prepared than the last two times I'd done this.

She touched my shoulder and I waited to open my eyes beneath the Big Tree in the twelfth century. Instead, I found myself flanked by Tabitha, in a white room, bright with hidden lights. A black beanbag sat in one corner, a navy-blue occasional chair in another. Tabitha touched the wall with the tips of her fingers, and a drawer opened. She pulled out a thick textbook and fell into the chair, hooking her legs over one arm.

"Where are we?" Because I didn't remember a waiting room the last two times I'd done this.

"The portal." She licked her finger and flicked through the pages until she found what she was searching for.

I backed up a step, into the wall. There were no doors that I could see, no windows. And that drawer, now closed again, was completely hidden. "It wasn't like this the other times."

"It was." Her eyes remained on her page. "You slept through it." She nodded to the bean bag without looking up. "Take a seat. It takes time to travel back eight hundred years."

"Why aren't I sleeping this time?" I needed her to answer some questions before I sat quietly and waited. I needed to know she wasn't playing some elaborate hoax.

Tabitha let out a deep sigh and clapped her book shut. She spoke evenly, like it was an effort to keep her annoyance in check. "Because you're not fighting it this time. There's no chance you'll fly into a rage and hurt me or damage my portal. And staying awake is gentler on your body."

That was probably an accurate assessment of what would have happened the last two times I'd moved through time, had I been allowed to stay awake. I edged down onto the beanbag, wriggling to get comfortable. Tabitha opened her book again. The deep breath she blew out her nose gave me the distinct impression the swishing of the moving beans was annoying her. All right. I'd keep quiet.

I stared at the four white walls, the white floor, the white ceiling. The room was deathly silent. I was tempted to hum, but given her reaction to the beans, I refrained. I had no idea how long this was going to take—a long while, judging by the textbook—and I couldn't sit in silence the entire time.

To pass time, I looked Tabitha over. Her black hair was loose and fell halfway to her waist—longer than I'd imagined. Paired with her sparkly green top, tight cropped black jeans and strappy stilettos, it seemed as though I'd interrupted her evening. "You look nice. Were you on a date?"

She nodded, eyes still down.

"I'm sorry. I hope he...she...understands." It was no wonder it took three knocks to get her here.

"Given it was our first date and I walked out straight after we ordered telling him I had an emergency to attend, but without having received a phone call about said emergency, it would seem certain he thinks I'm a flake and won't be in touch again."

"Sorry," I mumbled again, watching as she read. Was this where she spent her life? In this tiny box, going on an occasional date with someone else who couldn't enter this place? I'd never considered what life was like for Tabitha. All I knew was that she hated being away from her family.

"What?" she sighed, closing the book again, this time with a louder bang.

I shrugged. "Don't you get bored, being in this place day in and day out?"

Mild amusement flooded her face. "I don't spend all my time in here. I can leave, you know.

I go to University." She held up her textbook—Gray's Anatomy for Students. "I go out with friends. Occasionally, I date."

I lifted my eyebrows. She had a life. Who'd have thought? Clearly, not me.

"Don't look so surprised." Amusement still flickered across her face.

"I guess I expected you were as desperate to see Eliza again as she is to see you." That's how it had seemed at the Big Tree.

"Sometimes the only choice is to make the best of the situation. I might not be able to leave the portal for good, or return to my own time, but I can partake in anything else I want to, from any other time I choose."

"You can go anywhere?" That sounded too awesome to be true.

She nodded.

"So, you could go back in time and meet Anne Boleyn? Or Cleopatra? Or Princess Diana?" I had a list as long as my arm of women from the past I'd like to meet. And a few men.

"I have, as it happens, met all three of them." Tabitha was so calm when she spoke. Not emotionless exactly, simply stating fact. There was no bragging. "I've also met Robin Hood." Okay, there was a hint of a smile in her voice that time.

"That is about the coolest thing I've ever heard." I had no idea her life was so glamorous.

She shrugged, her smile turning sad. "It would be, I guess, but none of those places are where I want to be."

"Because you'd rather be with Eliza?" In the twelfth century. Where I was going.

She nodded.

I suddenly felt sorry for Tabitha. She wasn't mean like her sister, and she seemed so unhappy. I knew what it was like to be far from my family and know I'd never see them again. Just like Tabitha. "Do you want me to give her something? A message? Or...a gift?" I imagined I'd see Eliza Thatcher sooner or later—especially since I had Maud's ring to give Gisborne—so giving her something from Tabitha wouldn't be too difficult.

"Thank you, but no. There's nothing else to say and I don't have anything to give her..." Her voice was wistful.

She must have something. If Josh or Carrie could ever send me a gift, I wouldn't care what it was, because it came from one of them. "What about the hairclip you were wearing the night you brought me back home? Or...or a photograph? Or a letter—"

Tabitha swung her legs onto the ground, then flicked to the back of the textbook. "I have a photo," she said quietly, staring at the picture. "Would you take it to her? A letter's just...there are too many things I can't say."

I nodded.

She stared at it a moment longer before drawing in a deep breath, her words coming fast. "I saved Gisborne's life. I know he's a horrible person and he's been awful to you, but he's my cousin and he's been good to my sister. And it was the least I could do for them."

"He's really not dead, then?"

She shook her head.

My shoulders drooped. I wasn't surprised, just disappointed. I'd tried to put all thoughts of Gisborne aside since I decided to come back. I wanted him to be dead and I thought I'd seen him die. But. He was in almost every dream I'd had. Which meant he had to be alive. And still hunting Rob. "Did you save him with magic?"

"I wish." She laughed. "No. My magic is limited to moving between times." She gave me a wry glance. "And knocking out unruly travelers to keep my portal safe. With Gisborne, I used my own knowledge." She held up her textbook. "And modern medicine." She stood and placed her hand on the wall, opening three different drawers. One held cloths and bandages, one held an array of medical instruments and the other was filled with medicines.

"You're like a full-on medical center."

She lifted one shoulder. "You'd be surprised how many people are injured and running for their lives to reach the portal. Healing is a useful skill to have. And Gisborne was lucky his injury missed any vital organs. Otherwise, I couldn't have helped him."

"My dad was injured and running when he came back through time," I said, my voice soft.

"Before my time, but yes. I believe so." She closed the drawers. "I brought you in here and made you sleep, dragged him in, did what I could, then took him back out to Eliza. I have no idea how she got him home, but she did, and he's still alive."

I shrugged, trying to sound like I didn't care. "I guessed as much. From my dreams."

Tabitha drew herself up. "I don't regret saving him, but he's a very angry man, especially with you and Rob. You should watch your back when you get back to his time."

"Noted." I nodded.

She marched over to me and grabbed my wrist, her eyes begging me to hear her. "I mean it, Maryanne. That man is filled with hatred, you must be careful around him."

I pulled myself gently from her grip. "Nothing's changed. I've always had to be careful around him." I appreciated her warning, but Gisborne's hatred was nothing new.

She shook her head. "He would never hurt Maud Fitzwalter, and that's who he thought you were when you were here last, right?"

I nodded, dread filling my gut as the reason for her worry dawned on me. "But now he knows otherwise." He might have been fighting with Rob when Tabitha arrived at the Big Tree, but he would have seen her there. Eliza had probably filled him in on the rest. Including the details about me and Maud.

Tabitha lifted one shoulder. "I think you should keep pretending to be Maud around him. I think he cares for her enough to overlook the things he thinks he knows." A frown settled on her forehead.

"You're really worried." I'd been able to handle Gisborne last time I was here, but perhaps things were different now.

"Don't give him any reason to think you're not her. If there's any way to curl your hair, do it. If not, keep it tied up and pulled off your face so he can't see the difference. Soften your voice when you speak to him. Do everything possible to make him think you're her." Her voice grew urgent and she grabbed my arm again.

I watched her a moment, my mind working. Tabitha knew Gisborne better than I did. If she was concerned, then I guessed I should be, too. "I have Maud's engagement ring with me. Do you think wearing it would convince him I'm her?"

"Yes!" Tabitha spoke before I'd even finished.

I bent and pulled it from the bag at my feet. Putting it on felt wrong—like I was cheating in a test. I'd wear it for a while, just until I figured out how much of a threat Gisborne really was, then I'd return it to him, the way Maud had asked.

Tabitha handed me some hair ties and I pulled my hair from my face. Once I was done, her shoulders fell as if she had released a deep breath.

"I think you should go and see my family." I hadn't planned to suggest it, but Tabitha seemed lonely, and I felt sorry for her.

She shook her head. "I don't need a substitute family. I've got my own. I just never get to see her."

"You misunderstand. I think they might be able to help you get out of the portal."

Tabitha's eyes widened and she sank down onto the edge of her chair. "You do?" She breathed out the words.

I had no evidence to suggest I was right; it was more of a hunch. "I'm not certain, but if you tell them the same things you've told me tonight, they might be able to find a way to get you out of here."

She looked at me through narrowed eyes like she didn't believe me.

I shrugged. "What's the worst that can happen?"

Tabitha let me out of the portal without speaking another word. When I was ten steps down the trail, she called, "Three months."

I pulled on a beanie and a pair of gloves, and wrapped my cloak around my body against the cold before turning to find her watching me with her arms crossed over her chest.

"If your father can help me, I'm going to need some time to say goodbye to my friends. Meet me back here in three months and I'll tell you if I'm free. And bring Eliza." She didn't give me time to answer, just disappeared back into her portal with a flash of light.

I started down the trail toward Edwinstowe, wondering exactly how I was going to get Eliza Thatcher to do anything. Or if I even cared.

Right now, my thoughts were on Rob, and how to find him. And maybe there was the occasional stray thought about the color of his eyes, too. I had enough food to last me a week, though I hoped to find Rob and the others sooner. The new hiking boots I'd bought before returning here were far more comfortable than the Converse shoes I'd worn last time, and if it wasn't so bitterly cold— even my twenty-first century thermals weren't helping—I'd have felt like I could walk for days.

Edwinstowe was my first stop. The same place I came to on my first ever day in the twelfth century. I came here that day because I was drawn by the noise of the massacre. Today I was here because it was the closest village to the Big Tree.

If it could still be called a village. Where homes had once stood, there were now tents, the houses having burned to the ground.

I pulled my hood up and made my way to the closest man, one of three working in the fields. "Excuse me." The man remained focused on his work. I had no time for pleasantries anyway. "Can you tell me where I might find the man known as Robin Hood?" There were places I could start looking for them, places we'd stayed last time I was here, but I was hoping to save myself the guesswork.

The man shook his head. "Never heard of 'im."

After so many months away from this time, I'd almost forgotten the way magic helped me understand their twelfth century English. What I heard and what he said were two different things. I was noticing it now, the same way I had the first time I arrived here, but it wouldn't be long until I grew used to it again and forgot it even happened.

I laughed. "Of course you have. He brings gold to the villages that need it."

He shook his head, shoveling out a pile of manure and working it into the land.

I tried again. "It's very important I find him."

"Aye. He was important to all of us, too. Until he disappeared." The words were mumbled, and I thought perhaps I'd misheard.

I pulled my hood off, so it no longer covered my ears, and snatched my twenty-first century beanie off my head, too. "Disappeared?"

The man stopped his shoveling, finally looking at me, his mouth dropping open. When I was in the twelfth century last time, the staring had annoyed me. Now I understood why everyone thought I was Maud. "You're her."

I nodded, rubbing my gloved hands together against the cold. Might as well work on my act now so I had it perfected should I run into Gisborne.

"You're his girl. Robin Hood's girl." He nodded, grinning and pointing at me. "I was there. In Nottingham, looking for work. I saw you shoot an arrow at the Sheriff of Nottingham."

"I didn't actually shoot at—"

"You ran right past me as you left. You and him. It was some mighty fine shooting." He glanced behind him and I was certain he was about to call his friends over.

I didn't have time for that. Nor did I want it. I had no doubt the Sheriff would be looking for me after my stunt at his tournament. The fewer people that knew where I was, the better. I put a hand on his arm, and he immediately stopped turning. "Do you know where Robin Hood is? It's important I find him."

The man shook his head. "Sorry, love. No one's seen or heard from him in months."

That wasn't good. "Where were they the last time you heard about them?"

The man thought for a moment. "Clipstone, I think." He nodded. "Yes. Clipstone. But that was before Christmas. They're probably dead."

My stomach rolled. It was the last thing I wanted to hear after making the one-way trip to find him. That he hadn't been seen for over a month made it even more likely, but I refused to believe it. I was going to find him. "Thank you," I said, pulling on my beanie and dropping my hood back over my head, before retreating to the relative safety of the forest.

I didn't sleep a wink that night. It was too late in the day to make it to Clipstone, so I stopped at

OUTPLAYED

Frog Rock. It was one of the most beautiful places in the forest in summer. Now, toward the end of winter, it was bleak and cold. I built a fire beside one of the large rocks, hoping the rock would give some shelter and the fire some warmth. It did, but not enough for me to sleep comfortably. Plus, I'd forgotten how noisy the forest could be at night, so I sat awake, clutching my bow until the sun began to lighten the sky.

As soon as I could see, I gulped down the freeze-dried breakfast I'd brought with me and headed to Clipstone. No one there had seen them, either. Not even John's sister. I tried to ignore the biting worry in my gut after hearing she'd had no news of her brother in weeks.

My next stop was Kings Cave. Even if they weren't there, at least I'd have somewhere sheltered to sleep tonight. The walk to the cave took most of the day. With each step, I hoped I was drawing closer to them.

Just as I started up the hill that led to the cave, with darkness beginning to fall, branches cracked to my left. I reached for an arrow from the quiver on my back. Before I could get hold of it, a strong hand backed me up against a tree, and a knife pricked the skin on my neck.

Six

A scream bubbled up inside my chest, but I knew better than to scream in Sherwood Forest. Screaming could bring something worse than whoever held the knife.

"Where do you think you're going?" A hood covered my attacker's head, hiding him from my view. His voice was unfamiliar, and he was taller than me. Scrawny, but strong.

"Looking for a friend." I spoke loudly, hoping to disguise the wobble in my voice.

"What friend?" My attacker bent, looking for my face in the shadow of the hood and the growing darkness.

As he drew close to me, I shoved my fist into his solar plexus, striking hard and fast, before he saw it coming.

My attacker grunted and took a surprised step back.

That was all the space I needed. With no knife at my neck, I ran. Back along the trail. I dodged branches, jumping over roots and stones. All with my attacker just paces behind.

My knife was in my boot. No chance to get it now, and he was too close to use my bow.

"Stop," he called, closer than I would have liked.

I ran faster, ignoring the stitch in my side.

"Lady...Maryanne? Is that you?"

Maryanne. Not Maud.

I stopped, pulling my knife from my boot and spinning around. The person behind me was no one I recognized. But he recognized me.

He pulled back his hood.

"M...Miller?" It couldn't be. The person who'd held a knife to my throat was tall, his voice gruff. Yet when he spoke my name, I heard a trace of what used to be.

He wrapped me in a hug, his arms strong around my back. "I didn't think you were ever going to overturn. Rob said you weren't. He's been so sad. We all have, even Tuck."

I smiled. Definitely Miller. I hugged him tight as he towered over me. I'd missed him so much I wasn't even going to bother correcting him. "You grew."

He pulled back. "You noticed? I keep telling Rob and John that I'm nearly as tall as them and they say I haven't grown since I was ten."

"Do they now?" I couldn't keep the smile from my face. They must be alive. Miller had used their names in present tense. I hadn't realized how much I'd dreaded their deaths until that moment. "Well, as someone who hasn't seen you in months, I can confirm, you have most definitely grown."

Miller beamed and grabbed my hand, dragging me up the hill. "Come on. The others will be so excited to see you."

The cave was near the top of the hill, with a rocky overhang to protect us from the weather, and a flat area out the front, perfect for a fire. It was beside the fire John was sitting when we pushed through the bushes and came out at Kings Cave.

He jumped to his feet and looked from Miller to me, then broke into a huge smile. "Lady Maryanne?" His brown hair stuck out in all directions, and his right hand was wrapped in layers of bandages that hid all but the tips of two fingers.

I grinned. "I would say 'the one and only', but..." Maud Fitzwalter looked too much like me to be able to say that ever again.

He laughed and lifted me off my feet in a one-armed hug, holding his injured hand to his chest.

"What'd you do?" I laughed as he put me back on the ground. "Burn yourself on the fire?"

He ran his good hand through his hair, laughing. "Need to learn to be more careful."

Tuck came out of the cave and stood in the opening, watching. I nodded to him. Our relationship had never been close, though it had started to thaw before I left. After Maud's information, I wasn't sure what to make of him.

"Good to see you, Lady Maryanne." He wandered out and perched on the log John had been sitting on and stoked up the fire.

I turned a full circle, unable to keep my question to myself. "Where's Rob?" When I'd first seen Miller, I'd been sure he was alive, but doubt niggled at me. If he was all right, he'd be here. Wouldn't he?

"He can't be far away." John sat and patted the log beside him, scooching over until Tuck had to slide across. "I assume you're staying for dinner?"

I nodded and sat next to him, pulling my beanie off and warming my gloved hands on the fire. "You're hard people to find. No one's heard from you in months." I shot him a judgmental stare. "Not even your sister."

John looked at the ground. "Been meaning to visit her. Been busy."

"Well, you should. She thinks you're dead." I sounded harsher than I intended. But Josephine had been worried and one quick visit would put her mind at rest.

"Who thinks who's dead?" Rob stepped over the crest of the hill, a rabbit in each hand. He stopped short when he saw me. His mouth fell open and he dropped the rabbits onto the dirt. "Maryanne? What the…?" He took an unsteady step forward, shrugging his bow off his shoulder and letting it fall to the ground.

I stood up, a grin pulling at my lips. "Hi, Rob." He looked good—thinner in the face than when I left—but still good. His blond hair was pulled to the back of his neck, and his green eyes were wide with surprised confusion.

He pinched himself so hard he winced.

I knew the feeling. I'd wanted to pinch myself since the moment I realized Miller had held a knife to my neck. "It's not a dream, Rob. I'm here. To stay."

"You sure? Because I've had some pretty realistic dreams since you left, and they always start with you standing in front of me telling me you're back." He shook his head like he still couldn't believe it, but his eyes never strayed from my face.

I looked down at my clothes. Pants and a tunic, and a cloak pulled tightly around my shoulders. "Does this look like dream attire to you?"

Sudden amusement flashed across his face, tension, worry and confusion gone. Rob folded his arms over his chest and considered me for a long moment. "I don't have a clue what you could mean." Which meant he totally got it.

I glanced at John. This conversation could now go in a variety of directions, all of which made me uncomfortable with everyone listening. But sometime in the last few moments, he and the others had disappeared, slipping silently off to the cave. Rob and I were alone.

Okay, then. I took a couple of steps in his direction, then stopped, still too far away to touch him. "If you don't understand, there's no possible way I could explain it," I said, innocently.

His grin grew wider. "Well, that's...disappointing."

I was so happy to be back. So pleased to be doing...this...with Rob. I hadn't realized how dead I'd felt inside these past few months at home until I saw Miller, John and Tuck. And especially Rob.

A piece of hair fell from the tie at the back of his neck to rest in front of his eye. He batted it away and took another step toward me. "How...? Why...? I mean, I saw it happen. I thought you could never come back. How are you here?"

"Long story. Maybe I should tell everyone at once. I'm sure they'll want to hear as well." Not only did I want to tell it just the one time, I wanted to hear about them. What they had been doing, how they'd fared these past months, how they'd tried to defeat Gisborne.

He glanced around as if he'd only just noticed the others were gone. "They were quick to leave." A slow and wicked smile grew on his face. "Must have expected me to ravish you up against the tree over there."

My cheeks heated. He always knew exactly what to say to elicit that sort of reaction. I was pretty sure he expected me to bite back, and I didn't intend to disappoint. Folding my arms over my chest, I lifted my chin. "Why? Do you do that sort of thing often?"

He laughed, surprise making his eyes widen, before he said, "Only with the most beautiful women."

"And these beautiful women, they're happy to be ravished by you?" A stupid question. I'd seen the way the women in carriages reacted to him. He had a way with words that made them giggle and stammer. If they were given the chance, I imagined many would take it. They weren't ever given that chance, though.

He pointed to himself using both hands, his eyes dancing as though he relished this as much as I did. "Best archer in the forest. They *are* only human."

"The best archer in the entire Sherwood Forest? That's a very bold claim." And likely correct. No sense in adding to his ego, though.

He shrugged, strutting over to stop directly in front of me. "It's hardly bold if it's true."

"You know," I said, enjoying the way he watched me. I'd missed just hearing his voice, let alone seeing his face. "I heard a story once of an archer who split an arrow in a target held to another person's chest. *That* was a pretty good shot. Some would say one of the best ever made."

His lips flickered as he tried not to smile. He inclined his head. "I agree. It was a good shot."

"I'm confused, though. I'm sure it wasn't you, the best archer in all of Sherwood Forest, who made that shot," I said, with mock seriousness.

"Sadly, that is correct." He pressed his lips together, perhaps to keep from smiling.

"I also heard that same archer then made a shot that trapped the Sheriff and Gisborne under an awning."

Rob gave a slow nod. "I believe you are once again correct."

"And that shot wasn't made by the greatest archer in all of Sherwood, either, was it?"

He stepped closer; his smile not quite so well hidden now. The strength of his stare made my heart hammer. I'd missed him so much. "Are you suggesting you might be a better archer than me, my lady?"

I was, but only in jest. Rob was a million times the archer I'd ever be. "Current examples would suggest that to be the case."

His eyes went to my lips and he took another step toward me so there was no longer any distance between us. He leaned in to speak in my ear. "If you want that title, Lady Maryanne, you'll have to fight me for it."

The tone of his voice and his breath on my ear brought all sorts of images to mind, not all to do with archery, and I was grateful he couldn't read my thoughts.

He laughed, a deep sound that traveled along my spine. It made me wonder if he did, somehow, know what I'd been thinking.

My cheeks heated and I moved away. I needed space between us to clear my head. I could never think straight with him so close. "Would that be before or after you ravish me against that tree?" I managed to keep the wobble from my voice, but not the breathlessness.

He raised his eyebrows. His grin, if possible, grew more mischievous than before. "After, of course."

How I wished I could just once say something he had no response for. Instead, it was me groping for words as he fixed me with his intense stare. Besides, no matter how good it sounded, there would be no ravishing against a tree or anywhere else when there was an audience of boys in the close vicinity. Or before we'd had the chance for a proper conversation. "As tempting as that sounds," I said, dryly, "I very much doubt you will have any idea how to get into my twenty-first century clothing." My current attire had zippers rather than buttons. And…had I really said that out loud?

He looked at his feet, then back at me with a grin. "I'm a quick learner?"

A giggle bubbled from me.

Enough.

This conversation was going places I wasn't prepared for.

He must have decided the same thing because the laughter left his face and he held out his arms. I stepped into them, resting my head on his chest. If I thought I felt like I was home when I first saw him, I was wrong. This was the place I belonged, where I felt safe.

"Missed you," he said, quietly.

"I missed you, too."

SEVEN

AFTER the cold night I'd spent in the forest last night, I was pleased our fire was so hearty I could strip off my gloves for the first time in two days. Even happier there was warm food to fill my belly.

There was a weird vibe around the fire as we ate. It felt different than when I first arrived, but I couldn't put my finger on what the problem was. The boys talked and laughed, the way they always had. But something was off. Or I was tired and seeing things where none existed.

I caught Rob watching me as I moved closer to the fire to warm my hands. I smiled, feeling like this was a dream: I'd never expected to have his eyes on me again. But he looked away and started a conversation with John.

A few minutes later, the boys stood and slid their bows over their shoulders and belted on their swords. "What's going on?" I asked.

"We're going to kill my little brother." Rob looked up from his buckle. "Come. If you want."

"You're what?" They couldn't have mentioned this sooner?

"We're going to kill Gisborne, milady," said Miller, as if I truly hadn't heard.

"Okay." I stretched the word out, looking at the moonlit sky above us. "But why right now?"

"Because he's nearly recovered, and he isn't expecting us." Rob paused for a second. "Because he's at Woodhurst."

Rob's home. Or the home that should have been his, had Gisborne not stolen it from him.

I was totally onboard with killing Gisborne. In my opinion, it couldn't happen soon enough. I just wasn't sure doing it where he lived was the best idea. "Won't he have the advantage if we go into his home?"

"I know that place as well as he does," Rob snapped.

I watched him carefully. He usually only spoke that way when something else was going on. Like when he was worried. Or scared. I tilted my head, my question—*what's going on?*—unspoken, but understood.

Rob shrugged. "Things are different now. We're like prisoners. We can't do anything in case Gisborne hears of it and takes his anger out on an innocent village. See how skinny Miller is?" He threw his hand out in Miller's direction, his voice hard with anger that almost seemed directed at me.

I turned to look Miller over by the light of the fire. He was skinny. Maybe I could have put it down to all the growing he'd been doing these past few months, were he the only one of them to have lost weight.

"Last time Miller killed a rabbit in the forest, a soldier saw him. Gisborne used it as an opportunity to burn a village down in Miller's name. Now Miller doesn't hunt. No one hunts, in case that happens again."

"You do." He'd had two rabbits with him when he arrived here earlier tonight.

"Only because he won't take his own advice," said Tuck, shifting his bow on his back until he was comfortable.

"Meaning?" I had a pretty good idea and looked between Tuck and Rob for confirmation.

There was silence for so long, I didn't think anyone was going to answer. Finally, Rob drew in a breath. "Meaning it's safest not to hunt. I only do it when we're so hungry we have no other option." He slid his quiver over his shoulder.

"Because you refuse to allow anyone else to take the risk." John held his bandaged hand against his chest, his other hand clutched his staff.

Rob swiveled to face John. "Neither you or Miller are in any state to hunt, and Tuck's time is better spent in the towns, talking to people he trusts and finding out what Gisborne's next move will be. Don't try to make it sound like I'm some kind of martyr. I'm doing what I must for us to survive. The same as you. And Tuck. And Miller." His words were sharp. I'd never heard him speak this way to John. Tuck, yes. But never John.

"I'm not making you out as a martyr," John said quietly. "I'm grateful for all the risks you take for us."

"We all are," interrupted Tuck.

"We'd follow you anywhere, including into Gisborne's home. But we just want you to know, we can help you. As far as hunting goes, I'd be happy to try it, injured or not. As for everything else, you don't need to carry it all on your own shoulders."

"Carry all what on your shoulders?" There was so much tension in the air, I wasn't sure if something had happened between the boys or if it stemmed from something else entirely.

"Rob thinks everything is his fault." John watched Rob as he spoke, and I wondered if this was the first time he'd voiced such a thought.

"Don't." Rob shook his head but said nothing more. His eyes flicked my way then away so fast it was like he'd never looked at me.

"He's wrong of course," John added.

"I'm not." Rob's jaw jutted.

"Everything, what?" I asked.

John continued to watch Rob. "The last time we stopped a carriage, not long after you left, soldiers came to the village where we handed out the gold and lined all the men up in one of the fields. They shot them in the back and told the women they'd be next if they ever took anything from Robin Hood again. Rob tried to help the women who were left behind."

"Fat lot of good I was." Rob kicked at a stone on the dirt. "They all preferred to starve to death than take anything else from me."

John's eyes shifted to me. "And starve they did," he said quietly.

I drew in a breath. How awful. From every angle.

"I don't even know why we're talking about this. I'm sure Maryanne doesn't want to hear."

Rob's voice was harsh, and he still wasn't looking my way.

Something was wrong, and I couldn't figure out what. Of course I wanted to hear about it. I'd never given them any reason to think I wouldn't be interested in what was going on in their lives. "I do. I'll always want to hear. What's changed? Since I was here before?" And why would he think I wasn't interested?

Rob turned away; his lips clamped shut.

I glanced at the others. No one met my eyes. I didn't understand what was going on. It was as if a huge wall was sitting between me and them. "Rob? Talk to me."

Rob spun to face me. "Gisborne." He spat his brother's name. "It ends tonight." Rob's jaw set in a hard line, and I doubted anyone could talk him out of what he had planned.

Not that I wanted to. But it would help to know what I was walking into before I got there. "Why now? What makes you suddenly think killing Gisborne is a good idea? Surely he'll have guards who will come after you the moment you try to touch him."

"I've always thought killing my brother was a good idea." Rob's voice was soft. "It's just that now we have the perfect opportunity. He arrived at Woodhurst Manor yesterday from Nottingham. He's there to finish recuperating."

"You mean he's been doing all these horrible things from his sickbed?"

Rob nodded, his jaw still tight. His eyes barely rested on me before he looked away again. The easy conversation we'd shared before dinner was gone, and instead it felt as if Rob was holding back. "We're going tonight whether you like it or not. There are fewer soldiers there than when he was convalescing in Nottingham, and I know that place like the back of my hand. If we ever had a chance to succeed, it's there, tonight."

If Gisborne was still recovering, this really might be a chance to be rid of him for good. And with Gisborne gone, what I'd seen in my dreams couldn't happen. "Better get going, then." I shot him a grin. "As if I'd ever let you go off and do this without me."

It was late when we reached Woodhurst Manor, easily one in the morning, maybe later.

I'd never seen Rob's home before. I'd heard a little about it from him, and a little more from Dad. A stab of anger went through me that Rob would never again live here.

The house itself was a simple rectangle shape. It was three stories high with a timber roof and beautifully kept gardens, from what I could see in the moonlight.

OUTPLAYED

We watched from the forest for a few minutes, checking for guards. Rob clenched and unclenched his hands at his sides, his jaw stiff. We were waiting for Rob's signal because it was obvious he needed a moment. I could imagine he had mixed feelings about going back into his old home. He'd been a child the last time he set foot inside it.

Our plan was to go in silently, kill Gisborne, and get out as fast as possible. There was no time for anything else, not if we wanted to live. We pulled our hoods over our heads and followed Rob through a back entrance he'd once used when sneaking out to the forest as a kid. He said it was the best way to by-pass the guards. He took us straight to the staircase and up two flights of stairs to the master chamber. Gisborne's room. Rob really did remember everything about this place.

My heart pounded. This was it. The end of Gisborne, and therefore the end of everything that happened in my dreams.

Rob drew his sword slowly, barely making a noise, then pushed open the door. I craned my neck to see inside. Firelight lit the room and dim moonlight shone in through the window. The room contained an empty bed, two empty chairs and a desk.

And no Gisborne.

"Perhaps he's on his way," I whispered. The fire wouldn't be lit if the room wasn't in use.

Rob nodded. "Perhaps."

"Do we wait?" asked Tuck.

Rob's eyes went from object to object, as if he was rechecking Gisborne really wasn't here. He shook his head. "We can't wait here. If Gisborne and his guards walk through the door, it'll be us trapped in this room rather than him. I think we search for him. It's unlikely he'll be anywhere else on this level, he's probably still downstairs." Rob walked out without waiting to hear anyone else's thoughts, followed by Miller, Tuck, and then John.

They were a little ahead by the time I silently shut the door, and even farther after I paused to glance into the slightly open door of the room next to Gisborne's.

Eliza Thatcher sat at a desk, her back to me, working on something by the light of three candles. My heart jumped when I realized Gisborne could be with her. I shuffled across, looking around the door. She was alone. At least we were building up a picture of the places Gisborne wasn't tonight.

I started down the hallway, but she was suddenly there, gripping my arm. "Why are you spying on me?" She spun me toward her and pulled the hood off my head. Her mouth dropped open, and her eyes ran down my body, stopping briefly on my hands clasped in front of me before rolling back up to my face. "What the...? You're back?" She let go of my arm.

"Please be quiet," I whispered, thinking of the others. If she called for help, we were all screwed. "I'm not here to hurt you." The photo Tabitha gave me was still pushed into a pocket in my pants. Seemed like it could pass as a good reason to hang around outside her door. Or at least a reason she might believe. "I have a gift. From your sister." I fished in my pocket and held out the photograph.

She stared at it with disdain. "I don't want anything from you." She paused, then smirked. "Except Gisborne. And I already have him." Clearly, she was still confused as to whether I was Maud or not.

I flashed the photo at her, making sure she got a good look at it, then shrugged, moving to put it back in my pocket. "Your choice, but as I said, it's not from me. It's from Tabitha."

Her hand flew out and she plucked the photo from my fingers. "What is this?"

"It's called a photograph. It's so you can remember her." The two of them looked so similar that I was certain she could remember her sister just by looking in the mirror. "It's like a painting."

"She looks so real." Eliza's voice was soft as she ran gentle fingers over Tabitha's face, a soft smile lighting her own. She looked up suddenly. "Why couldn't you bring me this during the day? Why are you creeping around outside my chamber in the middle of the night? I should call the guards."

Good question. And one I needed to answer fast. I tilted my head to one side. "I have no wish to see Gisborne. I'm sure you know that. Seemed less likely to happen if I came here at night." Not bad. I was getting good at thinking on my feet.

She narrowed her eyes. "And you want what in return?"

"Nothing." Except for her not to rouse the guards and let everyone know we were here. I just needed her to let me walk away. "I promised your sister, that's all."

She considered this before nodding. "Very well. I'll escort you out."

That was the last thing I wanted or needed. "I'm fine. I got in here on my own. I'll get out the same way. Less chance of being noticed."

Her stare was wary.

"Enjoy the photo." I nodded at the picture in her hand, hoping the reminder would make her want to stare at her sister and forget all about me.

She dropped her gaze to the photo.

OUTPLAYED

I took two steps backward, my heart racing. I'd had to think fast to get this far. All I could do now was hope staring at the photo would be enough for Eliza to let me leave.

Finally, she nodded, eyes still on her sister. "Don't come back here. Ever. If I see you again, I'll call the guards."

I didn't need to be told twice. I turned on my heel and hurried along the hallway and down the stairs after Rob and the others.

I didn't think I'd been long with Eliza. Part of me expected Rob might come looking if he thought me missing. That he hadn't made me think they couldn't be far ahead.

There was no sign of them on the second floor, so I raced down the stairs to the ground floor and saw Miller disappearing through a door on the left of the hallway. I hurried after him, my feet silenced by the floor tapestries. The room we entered was large with a massive glowing fire to our left. Long tables surrounded with bench seating filled the space to the right.

The room looked empty. Just the tables, chairs and fire. It took a moment to see the reason we'd walked in here.

In a chair in front of the huge fire, his back to us, sat Sir Guy of Gisborne.

Eight

Rob didn't go for stealth this time when he drew his sword, the ringing metal echoing around the room. Tuck and Miller did the same. In five steps, Rob would be on Gisborne and Gisborne would be dead.

Gisborne turned at the sound, one eyebrow quirking. "I wouldn't do that if I were you, brother." His voice bounced off the walls.

"Seems like a sterling idea to me." Rob stepped closer to Gisborne, his boots tapping on the stone floor.

Swords scraping from scabbards sounded around the room. Soldiers I hadn't seen at first glance, at least four of them, moved out of the shadows around the hall, swords in hand. "Did you really think you could kill me in my own home?" Gisborne's mocking laughter made me cringe. "My own home. See what I did there? Because it's not yours anymore." He laughed again.

The hackles on the back of my neck rose. Gisborne wanted to goad Rob into a reaction. Or any of us, probably. Though I would have loved to stab him with my dagger, I, like everyone else, stood deadly still, waiting as Rob assessed our next move.

I looked over my shoulder, calculating the chances of us all turning and making a run for it before the guards caught us.

"You look thin, brother. Like you haven't eaten in a while." Gisborne pushed up out of his chair and stood with his back to the fire, smirking at us. "It seems living in the forest doesn't agree with you. Perhaps you should find yourself a real home. One with four walls and a roof. One like this." He laughed again.

Asshat.

Rob advanced on him, one hand gripped his sword, and the other was balled into a fist at his side.

"Rob." I warned him against doing anything rash. My guess was that Gisborne didn't think his guards could beat us, since he hadn't set them upon us yet. In a sword fight against the current guards, my money was on us, too. Rob could take two of them, as could Tuck. And if Gisborne wasn't at full strength, Miller could take him. We could kill them all without even using an injured John. But the moment they raised the alarm—and they would—none of us would get out of here alive. We needed to think carefully before we made our next move.

"Ah, Rob. Listen to your..." Gisborne's eyes moved to me, and his smirk turned into a snarl. "Listen to your whore. Even she knows attacking me is a bad idea."

"Rob," I warned again. Gisborne seemed to be itching for a fight and I was fairly certain Rob felt the same way.

Tuck moved his hand, indicating Miller, John and I should move back toward the door. I was with him. Given this confrontation included more guards than we expected, we should get out of here while we could, regroup and find a different time and place to kill Gisborne.

"You think I'm scared of your guard dogs?" Rob spat, eying his brother. "I'm not afraid one bit. The forest will be a better place without you around."

Gisborne shook his head slowly, clicking his tongue. "Always such a martyr, aren't you, brother?" His eyes moved from Rob, to Tuck, then John, the only indication that he might not be as at ease as he seemed. Another step, and Rob would be close enough to kill him. One more step and it would be all over for Gisborne.

Gisborne hadn't moved to take his own weapon. Nor had he commanded anything from his guards. Yet.

I glanced at Tuck, uneasy. Gisborne had a plan. Had to, or swords would be clashing by now.

"Before you raise your weapon, I have something for you to consider. Someone, actually. Someone you love more than you love yourself." Gisborne gave his brother a pointed stare, a message I couldn't interpret sent with every second they faced each other.

Rob's entire body stilled, which brought another smirk to Gisborne's face.

"You're bluffing." Rob shook his head. "I was there today. You've done nothing, hurt no one."

"I didn't say I had, brother. Just that I could. If you kill me tonight, it'll be a death for a death. I've left instructions."

Rob licked his lips. "You can't know…"

"Oh, but I can. And I do." Gisborne held up one hand, counting on his fingers. It could have been my imagination, but he seemed stiff. Perhaps he still wasn't recovered enough to pick up his sword. "Clipstone, Bligh, Overton, Hamilton. Should I go on?" There was another long stare between them. Another undercurrent of silent messages sent in a conversation I didn't understand.

I looked to John. To Miller. To Tuck. Tuck's nostril's flared and his fists balled. Whoever Gisborne was threatening was clearly someone that meant a lot to one of them. Likely Rob.

Gisborne clasped his hands behind his back. "In fact, I'm going to do it anyway. Teach you a lesson for daring to enter my home."

"You wouldn't. You're not that cruel." Rob shook his head, but he also took a hesitant step back.

Gisborne's smirk grew wider. "You know I would. And that I am. Particularly if it means hurting you." He shrugged. "And saving my own life."

"I could kill you now." Rob's threat sounded empty, especially when paired with the backward step.

Gisborne lifted a shoulder. "You could. But you won't risk it now you know what I know."

Rob's knuckles grew white around the hilt of his sword. "Doesn't family mean anything?"

"You, brother, are not family. And I would have thought you figured the answer out to that question six years ago when you were lying on the forest floor, gasping for breath."

Rob stared at Gisborne, and I could almost see the battle going on inside him. He gave a loud curse before turning on his heel and striding from Woodhurst Manor, the rest of us close behind.

We moved through the forest so fast I was almost running to keep up. Gisborne's guards didn't follow. I couldn't decide if it was because they expected to lose, or because they believed they'd already won.

"Who was he talking about?" I asked to the four backs striding through the darkness ahead of me, Gisborne's threat repeating in my ears.

Silence.

"Was it one of us?" I didn't think so. Gisborne's words had felt removed rather than pointed. Plus, he'd named a number of villages that had nothing to do with us.

More silence.

"Was it a threat to make you stop giving gold to the poor?" I waited a beat before adding, "Why won't anyone answer?"

Rob stopped, spinning to face me. "Don't pretend you care." He shook his head, his lips turned down in disgust, before striding away.

"Of course I care," I said to his back. Rob had never looked at me that way. Was he angry because I'd left him? Angry I'd returned?

John slowed to walk beside me. He ran a hand through his hair. "There are a few reasons we don't want to talk about it, but I suppose the one you'll understand is because we're not particularly proud of ourselves. If I had to guess."

"Why not? What have you done?" Now I was starting to worry. When I was here before, they'd done nothing to feel ashamed of. I was so confused. Were they becoming the villains the people of my time knew? Had my leaving changed history again?

No. That wasn't the problem. They still wanted to help the poor, so something else was going on.

Rob sighed, slowing his pace to walk on the other side of me. "Nothing. We've done nothing. And we'll continue to do nothing."

I frowned. "Meaning?"

He stopped in the middle of the track, the rest of us coming to a halt around him. "Meaning we had the perfect opportunity to kill my brother—*I* had the perfect opportunity—and like I've done for the past three months, I caved in to his threats." Rob's voice was hard, shaking with anger.

Tuck clapped his back. "For good reason, Rob. For good reason."

I looked to John. To Miller. Back to Tuck. Was all this anger about missing their chance with Gisborne? I didn't think so.

John licked his lips, taking pity and giving me an answer. "It's like Rob told you earlier, Maryanne. Gisborne convinced the Sheriff to put all his resources into keeping the forest safe. Anyone who gave information leading to our capture—Rob's capture, actually—would receive a trunk filled with gold. It made our offerings, a few pieces of gold, look meager. And it meant anyone might turn us in."

"No. It meant we valued our lives above everything else. And it meant no one got any gold." Rob spat the words at me, not meeting my eyes. No wonder Gisborne looked so self-satisfied. All the measures he'd put in place had worked. On top of that, he'd somehow made his brother leave tonight without laying a hand on him.

The problem was, Rob had never valued his life above anything else. Not ever. I'd seen him step into situations he shouldn't have simply because he thought he could make a difference. There had to be something else going on. "I don't believe you," I said, softly.

"Aye, it's true," said John. "There are too many soldiers around for us to stop carriages, even though the people would surely take our gold now, they've grown so desperate."

John misunderstood. I believed *what* had happened. It was the why that I struggled with.

Rob's voice was rough with anger. "The villagers have had to learn to look after themselves. We can't do everything." He picked a stone from the ground and threw it with all his might into the darkness before striding away, his pace brisk again.

Was I missing something? Why was he so annoyed? Because he couldn't help people? Because he hadn't *tried* to help them? Because he'd missed his chance with Gisborne tonight? Or because Gisborne had threatened someone close to him? I ran after him.

Tuck put out a hand to stop me. "Rob probably just needs a few minutes alone."

"And he can. After he's explained what's really going on." Something was amiss, and I wanted to know what. I fell into pace beside him on the moonlit trail. It was wide here, a rutted valley made by carriage wheels down both sides. We walked with one of those rugged strips between us.

"Talk to me, Rob. Tell me what's happening here." I wasn't sure if I meant with him personally, or with everything since I left. I'd settle for an answer to either.

He shook his head, his pace slowing a fraction. The others were far enough behind that we had some privacy. Rob walked in silence for a while, before finally speaking. "Like I said, things are different. Gisborne hunts me. At least, his men do. As soon as he's well enough to ride again, which will be soon, he'll be at it, too. It's been his sole mission since the day of the tournament. And then there's..." His voice trailed off.

So, it was the fear talking. I could deal with that. Could maybe even fix it. "It's okay, Rob. I'll help you sort this out. The forest is large, and Gisborne is only one person. We could—"

"No, Maryanne. We can't. You don't know what it's like here now." Rob's voice rose and he whirled to face me, fists clenched.

"Then tell me." He was right. I couldn't help if I didn't understand.

"I have. I am! You're not listening. Gisborne and the Sheriff, they're winning."

I shook my head. He was wrong. "They're not winning. You're still here. They only win when you stop doing all the things you want to do, like helping people, because you're too scared of them."

"In that case, they've already won. Because I'm too terrified to do anything to help our people."

He shook his head. "Don't worry about it. It doesn't even matter."

I stepped toward him, touching his shoulder with my hand to reassure him. "I can help you. Together, we can be what we were before the tournament."

He shrugged out of my touch and stepped away. "No. You can't. And you won't."

"I know you, Rob, and this isn't you. You're not scared because you fear for your life. No matter how many times you say it, I won't believe it. So, what is it? What's going on?" What was I missing?

A harsh laugh blew from his lips. "You're right. It's not my life I fear for. It's everyone else's. The way he wins is by killing the people I love and making me watch." He shook his head, his confession making his voice soft. "I can't do it. I can't look after everyone. You have to go home." He stared straight along the pocked trail.

"Pardon me?" I *thought* he'd just told me to go home. He couldn't have, though. I was going to be part of his legend. Maybe even *his* Marian. Right after I saved him from Gisborne's arrow in his back, that was. But that aside, we were a team. A bloody good one, too.

"You heard me." His voice was flat.

"I'm not asking you to protect me, Rob."

He swallowed, his jaw stiffening. "You need to go home."

"I'm not going anywhere!" My own voice rose as I realized he might be serious. How had we gone from an ecstatic greeting a few hours ago, to this?

He turned his back to me, running both hands through his hair. "Did you talk to John about his hand?"

"About how he burnt it on the fire?"

Rob let out a sound that was half laughter, half dismissal. "It's not a burn and it wasn't from the fire."

His tone made the hair on my arms rise. "Then what?"

"Gisborne." He paused for a long time, and I thought he was going to leave me to fill in the blanks. Eventually he started walking again, talking, too. "I'm sure you'll hear a different version when you get sick of being out here, but for the sake of balance, I'll tell you John's version."

He licked his lips. "Gisborne's men caught John, out here on the trail while he was hunting. They had him for weeks, Maryanne. Weeks." His eyes in the moonlight asked if I understood what that time without his best friend had done to him.

I couldn't know, not for sure. But I could guess. And every guess told me that time without John had been horrendous.

"I didn't sleep because each time I closed my eyes, I found a new way to imagine his death. I didn't eat, because I felt constantly sick about what could be happening to John. And I spent every single day searching the forest for him." He drew a deep, shuddering breath. "For his body."

His imagery was too vivid. It made the hair on my arms stand on end. "Oh, Rob." I breathed out his name, because I could think of nothing else to say.

"I was searching near Woodhurst Manor about three weeks back, hoping to find him, when this kid came running up to me. Told me he'd heard that John would be going through Hidden Bend that afternoon." He ran both hands through his blond hair again. "I wanted him back so much that I didn't think. Which was probably good, in the end. It could have turned out so much worse if I'd brought Tuck or Miller with me."

He walked a few steps away, head down and hands gripping the hair at the base of his neck.

I wanted to strangle Gisborne for making Rob feel this way. I couldn't begin to guess where this story was going, except somewhere bad. It was plain to see that whatever he was about to tell me had screwed Rob up big time.

"I went alone and waited near the rise on Hidden Bend." He glanced my way like he was checking I knew where he meant.

OUTPLAYED

I nodded. Hidden Bend was where we'd once stopped Bridgette Sutherland's carriage.

"I sprinted there, arrived out of breath. I hid in the bushes and waited. Had all these plans racing around in my head. Like how, if John came past in a carriage, I'd shoot the driver then his guards before dragging John to safety. Or, if he was on the back of a horse, I'd shoot everyone I could, then come at the rest with my sword." He shook his head. "In the end, none of that mattered because he didn't come past at all."

He turned back to face me, his eyes shining in the moonlight. "I heard him scream out in pain. That sound is forever etched into my bones." A shiver went down his spine and I had to stop the one attempting to run down mine.

"He wasn't on the trail, but he was near. I sprinted in the direction of his scream, yelled out his name, told him I was coming. He yelled back at me, told me…" He looked over my shoulder and swallowed deeply. There were tears sitting on the bottom of his lashes, ready to fall. But he held them back. "Told me to stay away. Screamed that it was a trap." Rob shook his head, his voice losing all its strength. "He would have died, rather than let Gisborne's men find me."

I touched his arm. "We all would." And Rob would do the same for any of us. It was what I loved about him. About them all. They were family. And they would look out for each other until they took their dying breath.

Rob jerked his arm from my grasp, his glare saying no one should do that for him.

"I didn't listen. Pushed through bracken and bushes, clambered over logs and rocks, sprinted toward his voice. Didn't care how much noise I made. Didn't care he shouted it was a trap. I'd already decided. If my brother was there, I would kill him." His voice shook with anger and I had no doubt Gisborne was not there that day, otherwise he'd already be a dead man.

"John screamed out again, sounded like they were killing him piece by piece. I yelled his name, sprinted harder. He went quiet and I thought I was too late but kept running anyway. I reached the clearing and drew my sword, ready to kill anyone who got in my way. But they were gone. The soldiers. They'd left. All but John. He was curled around himself on the ground, trying not to make a sound while blood poured from his hand."

An invisible vice clamped down on my chest and squeezed until I couldn't breathe. I'd seen John in my dreams lying on the ground with blood coming from one hand. "What had they done?" I whispered.

"Cut off two of his fingers." Rob resumed his pace along the trail.

I raced after him. How had I not connected my dream and John's hand? How had I not realized he was lying when he'd agreed that he'd burnt his hand on the fire? "His...fingers?" John should have corrected me. Should have told me what happened.

Rob nodded, blowing out a deep breath and rubbing a hand across his eyes. "The soldiers came back before I could do anything for John. Fired arrows at us from just outside the clearing. They mustn't have been very close, because they didn't hit us. I don't even know if they could really see us. I waited with my sword ready, expecting them to charge. When they didn't, I risked putting it down a moment to ready my bow. Fired at them a few times. When I hit someone, they left us alone." He licked his lips. "Thought about it afterwards. We were sitting ducks. If they'd wanted us dead, it would have been so easy."

The attack had been designed to terrify rather than kill and it made me feel physically ill. "Is he okay?"

Rob raised his palms. "After they left, I built a fire, then heated up the end of my knife and pressed it onto his skin to stop the bleeding. Been keeping it wrapped up since then. I guess he's in pain, but he never says. And there doesn't seem to be any infection, so...I guess he's okay." His voice was resigned.

Physically, at least. Mentally, I doubted either one of them would get over that in a hurry. "At least he's alive." Because surely it would be so much worse if they'd killed him.

"There is that," he said quietly.

"But...?" It seemed as if he was holding back what he wanted to say.

He sighed. "Apart from John not being able to hunt, and the fear that never leaves me that his hand might become infected, Gisborne had his men do that on purpose. As a warning. He knew I'd come. He'd arranged everything so I'd be there. He could have captured me that day, taken me to the Sheriff, had me hanged. Hell, they could easily have shot an arrow through my back and left me to die in that clearing."

A shiver ran through me. That was a scene I'd watched too many times these past months. "Maybe he's...maybe he's not as bad as you think. Maybe that's not what he wants anymore." Even as I said it, I didn't believe it. Rob was right. Why else would Gisborne's men leave Rob when they could have taken him in?

Rob blew a quick breath out his nose and shook his head. "I publicly embarrassed him, as you well know. His revenge will come from hurting me. From hurting the people I love. And once he's brought me to my knees that way, and only then, will he kill me."

The nausea returned and I swallowed deeply. I'd seen everything he spoke of in my dreams, so I couldn't dispute it. John's hand. Miller with a face so bruised it was almost unrecognizable. Rob siding with Gisborne rather than helping the people in the forest. And finally, Rob dying. An arrow in his back.

"Maybe we should keep out of his way? Just for a while." I'd planned to suggest it anyway, even without knowing any of this. It seemed like the best way to keep Rob safe from Gisborne. To change that little piece of history I'd come back to fix.

Rob nodded. "That's exactly what I've been trying to say." Relief filled my veins for just a second, until he said, "So you agree? You'll go home?"

Wait, what? That wasn't what I'd suggested at all. "I'm not going home, Rob."

"You are. You cannot stay here." His jaw stiffened. His entire body stiffened.

"Yes. I am." I glared at him. "I came back knowing it would be hard. I can deal. I don't expect or want your protection. Miller can keep teaching me to use a sword. I have my bow. I can look out for myself." My voice grew louder with each word. I didn't want to sound like I was pleading. I wasn't. There was no decision to make on my part. Even if I could go home, I wouldn't. This was where I belonged.

Rob stared at me; lips pursed. "I'm glad you have a plan for yourself, because whether you stay or not, I won't be around anymore."

What the hell did that mean? "Why not?"

He looked away and shook his head. "Places to be."

"On your own?" My voice rose further. I didn't understand what was going on with him. Apart from those first few minutes together, he'd acted strangely since my return. This wasn't how he did things. The other boys were his family, he would never head out on his own and leave them to it.

"No. Not alone. And not with you, either. There are other people who need my protection more." His lips formed a tight line, and his eyes focused somewhere in the distance.

Oh.

The tone of his words made something click into place in my brain. I'd been gone for months. We'd never made each other any promises, had kissed only once. I'd never even thought to ask if there was someone else. I'd assumed I was the

Marian of legends, so therefore there must be a Rob and me. But he was saying something else. "By other people, you mean you're going to look out for your girlfriend."

His jaw stiffened further. He closed his eyes. "Yes, Maryanne. That's exactly what I mean."

Nine

"All right?" John asked, coming to a stop beside us. He looked from Rob to me, then back.

"Perfect." Rob folded his arms across his chest, his voice short.

I felt a little like doing the same, but instead took a deep breath as if I hadn't just had the wind knocked out of me, and smiled John's way. "We're good."

John looked between us both again, as if trying to decipher a code. With a nod, he put his good hand on my back and directed me off the wide track and on to a narrower one I hadn't noticed. He glanced over his shoulder at Rob. "I'll take care of Lady Maryanne. You go do what you need to do."

OUTPLAYED

It was John's words, rather than Rob's, that bit into my heart. Until then, I'd thought, maybe, Rob was pretending. Saying something to hurt me so I would do as he wished. Gisborne had said there was someone else Rob needed to look out for. Someone I knew nothing about. And he'd called me Rob's whore. But until John spoke, I'd hoped the other person wasn't really a girlfriend. There could be hundreds of people Rob loved more than himself; aunties, uncles, cousins.

Or a girlfriend.

For a moment, I couldn't breathe. John's hand on my back propelled me forward, and even without air, I made it to the base of the hill, then up it to sit in front of an almost extinguished fire outside the cave. I'd like to say I didn't see Rob again. I'd like to say I wasn't aware of him standing at the edge of the light, watching for a few moments before he left for who-knew-where. I'd like to say him going off to someone else didn't make my breath freeze in my lungs, that it didn't bother me a bit. But it would be a lie, and damned if I'd let any of them see that.

"Anyone want presents?" My voice was falsely bright. I was too amped to sleep and needed a distraction. With any luck, my beaming smile suggested I wasn't bothered by Rob's sudden departure. I fished in my pack. "I brought you all presents. You know, since I missed Christmas and everything."

Miller's eyes widened. "Presents?"

I nodded and handed an item to each of them. There was another present in my pack, but the recipient wasn't here. Perhaps it'd be a present for me, instead.

I'd wrapped the gifts in plain brown paper, but after bouncing around in my pack the last couple of days, they weren't looking quite as good as they once had. The boys didn't seem to notice.

"Can we look inside?" Miller was both buzzing and trying to play it cool. He acted so much older most of the time, it was good to see a glimpse of the child he usually kept hidden.

I nodded.

Miller ripped into the paper and gasped, drawing his hands away. He frowned. "A book?" It sat on his lap, the paper still beneath it. He hadn't so much as touched it. Maybe I'd chosen the completely wrong gift. "But...I can't read. And no one just carries a book around with them." His eyes were on the book, like he desperately wanted to touch it but was too afraid.

"You don't need to be able to read for this one, Miller. Turn the pages." His gift had been the easiest to buy, after Rob's. I'd known exactly what

I wanted Miller to have, but his reaction made me doubt myself.

He brought his hand to the edge of the hard cover and turned the page, his fingers gentle. He sucked in his breath. "Weapons."

"For now, you can look at all the pictures. When you're ready, I'll teach you the words." The book was an illustrated guide to weapons through the ages, including modern weapons, like guns. I had the feeling Miller would get a kick out of it.

"You will?" He breathed the question.

"In exchange for sword lessons? But even if not, if you want to read, I'll teach you."

"I do! And I also want you to learn to use a sword." He held up the book, turning it to show John and Tuck, a huge smile on his face. "Are you going to open yours?"

Tuck and John's presents rested on their laps. "Is this a bribe?" Tuck's eyes ran over my face, stopping at my hands resting in my lap.

"A bribe?" I laughed. Tried to, at least. It probably didn't sound too much like laughter because Rob's departure was still on my mind. "What reason would I have to bribe you?"

Tuck's shrug was exaggerated. "I don't know. Perhaps you should tell us."

That weird vibe I felt earlier was back. I looked to John for an explanation.

He stared at the single flame in the fire like he wasn't going to answer. When he spoke, his voice was gentle. "Are you trying to make us ignore the pain you're bringing our way?"

The pain? Oh. They thought I was going to leave again. John had told me once before that he was worried I'd hurt Rob. Leaving had probably done exactly that. Maybe they'd all felt a little hurt by it. I reached over and squeezed his arm. "I'm not going to hurt you. This is just a gift to say how happy I am to see you all again. Please accept it."

Miller closed the book, his eyes going to John for guidance. He pulled his hands back from his gift as if he shouldn't touch it because he might not be allowed to keep it.

John must have seen his movements, too, because he sighed. "Okay. Thank you, Maryanne. Your gifts are very generous."

Was it just me, or did that sound overly formal? I ran my hands down my face. I was being stupid. It was late. I'd walked all day and a lot of the night and had barely slept last night. I was hearing things that just weren't there. "You're welcome."

Both John and Tuck were more cautious with the paper when they finally pulled back the tape, carefully trying not to rip it, then folding it neatly to, apparently, keep for later.

OUTPLAYED

For John, I'd brought a selection of dried herbs and spices plus salt and pepper for adding to our meals. Once I'd explained what they were, he gave me a beaming smile before jumping up and hugging me.

Tuck had been the hardest to buy for, but in the end, I settled on a new copy of the bible in a waterproof case. The little one he carried everywhere was tattered and torn. His reaction was a genuine smile, something I didn't see often—or ever—from him.

An awkward silence fell around the fire. "How long will Rob be gone?" Because I had exactly that long to convince the rest of them to let me stay.

John gave Tuck a glance I couldn't read. "He's not coming back. Not for a long while, maybe not ever."

John's answer bit into my heart. Never coming back? He had to. He was Robin Hood. He belonged here, with us. How could I keep him safe from Gisborne's arrows if I didn't know where he was? "He wants me to go home." Might as well put it out there.

John nodded. "I heard."

I sighed. We had raised our voices, but I didn't think the boys had been close enough to hear us. "I can't get back home. And even if I could, I wouldn't go." I might not have pleaded with Rob earlier, but I was pleading now. I didn't want to be tossed out into the forest on my own.

"Didn't think for one moment you would. You're always welcome here." John smiled. "No matter what Rob says."

His smile eased some of the tension which knotted my shoulders. I'd missed Rob in the months I was home, but I'd missed the others almost as much. It was good to hear they wouldn't get rid of me, even if Rob said he wanted me gone.

The dreams returned that night. Maud said they'd be with me until I did something to stop Rob's death. I'd stupidly hoped they might be gone for good, and that just coming back here would be enough to keep Rob alive. Instead, I watched him die again with an arrow in his back, the same as he had over and over when I was home. I woke screaming his name, and woke the others, too. Somehow, it was worse to watch him die here, than it had been from eight hundred years away.

By the third consecutive night, I had the screaming under control. It wasn't even close to morning, but the hole in the roof of the cave let some moonlight in. I got up from my straw mattress—a bonus of the cold months and living in one place—and picked my way over sleeping bodies to sit at the cave entrance. I was soaked in sweat and would soon be shivering in my clothes, but for the moment I felt hot and sticky. I drew in deep lungsful of cold air and waited for the last of the dream—horses' hooves and Gisborne's laughter—to fade.

"Are you all right, Maryanne?" John's voice was low, and I turned to find him sitting up on his mattress.

Yes. Maybe. Not at all. Since the dream returned that first night, I'd tried to discover where Rob had gone, so I could work out if it was the place I kept seeing. The boys either didn't know or were determined not to tell me, and I had no further information about where he was than I'd had on the day he left. I was beginning to feel like time was running out. "I think Rob's in trouble," I blurted.

John watched me a moment, then stood and walked over to sit beside me. "Rob's been in trouble since the moment he marched down the hill at Edwinstowe and Gisborne saw his face." The moment Gisborne learned his brother was still alive.

I glanced at Tuck. His chest rose and fell in the gentle rhythm of sleep. If he was awake, he'd likely have said the next words. Because he wasn't, I spoke for him. "Before that, probably." I'd had many heated conversations with Tuck about the first stupid thing I did when I arrived here and how it had probably ruined Rob's life.

John watched me closely. "Your worry for him is about more than him not being here, isn't it?"

I nodded. Knowing what I'd seen was going to happen unless I found a way to stop it made a ball of dread form in the pit of my stomach. I couldn't forget the dream of John lying on the ground and screaming in pain as blood poured from his fingers. I glanced at his hand, the white of the bandage bright in the moonlight. Rob's description of that day had been exactly like my dream.

I ran a hand down my face. How did I explain this in a way that would make him believe me and not think I was a crackpot? "There's this place. I've never been there, so I don't know if it exists. But if it does, I think Rob shouldn't go there." Yeah, that didn't sound crazy, at all.

John looked at me sideways. "Because...?"

How much was I allowed to say? "Because something bad will happen." I wanted so much for him to believe me. But I still felt as if they thought I might leave at any moment, and that lack of trust meant it could be a while before he believed me without question.

OUTPLAYED

He licked his lips, slowly, like he was thinking something through in his head. "That's very vague."

I nodded.

"Can you give me something more to go on?" His brow furrowed, like he was silently pleading for me to give him what he asked for.

But I couldn't. "You don't believe me." I sighed. Of course he didn't. Why would he when I hadn't really told him anything?

"I want to. Does that count?" He tilted his head to one side, eyes roaming over my face.

"Then believe. I'm still the same person I was a few months ago. I want to keep Rob safe. To keep all of us safe." I wasn't going to skip out on them without saying goodbye again, but I'd told John I wouldn't leave once before, and I had. No wonder he was having trouble trusting me.

"What place?" Tuck was so still, had he not moved one arm to rest over his forehead as he lay on his back, I might have convinced myself he hadn't spoken at all. "What place can't Rob go?"

I drew in a deep breath, my skin going tingly as I thought about the dream again. "It's a huge grassy field. There's forest all around, but far away, too. And water. Not close enough to see, but perhaps close enough to hear."

Tuck sat up. "Anything else?"

"The field slopes downhill, toward the forest. It's peaceful and pretty."

The sky was beginning to lighten, and I caught a worried glance between John and Tuck.

I waited for one of them to speak. When neither did, I asked, "You know where it is, don't you? You know the place I just described?"

John nodded but offered no further details. It didn't take a genius to figure out why. "Is Rob there now?"

John glanced down, his eyes falling on my hands, which I'd gripped tightly together while I waited for his answer. He nodded again.

I jumped to my feet. "Let's go, then. Let's get him to leave." As I was saying the words, I heard how they sounded. If I were them, I'd think I was looking for any excuse to find Rob and bring him back. Worse still, it sounded like I was hoping to drag him away from the life he was happily living.

Tuck shook his head. "Can't." The edges of his lips pulled tight, and I couldn't help but feel pleased. If he was worried because of something I'd said, he was more likely to do something about it.

"Can't? What sort of answer is that?" Urgency to get Rob to safety had me wired. It might be just before dawn, but we had to go now. We had to get to Rob before Gisborne did. My desperation may also have made my tone condescending, which was never the right way to talk to Tuck.

His nostrils flared. "What, exactly, is Rob in danger of?"

"Gisborne, of course." Then, I added, "I think." Because I didn't want to lie, and I'd never actually seen who shot the arrow at Rob.

"You think?" He shook his head. "Seems like this is just some stupid-girl way to bring back someone who doesn't want to be here. If you're so worried, why didn't you tell us sooner?"

Because mentioning the dream meant I would die. And I wasn't ready to martyr myself just yet. "Stupid girl?" If Tuck understood the danger, he'd be as eager as I was to get Rob out of there. The trouble was making him see it. I stood up. "Better a stupid girl with all her friends alive than so closed off to possibilities that you no longer have friends." I pointed my finger at him, and to make sure he didn't miss my meaning, added, "Because they're all dead."

"Maryanne, sit down," John said softly. "The reason no one is moving is not because we don't believe you." He leaned forward to look around me and give Tuck a pointed stare. "It's because Rob doesn't want us there. Any of us."

"He…what?"

John shook his head. "He was firm. None of us are to go to him. For any reason."

"You're kidding, right?" There were reasons, and there were Reasons. Rob would want to know if the place he was staying was dangerous. Surely keeping him safe was a bigger concern than whatever rules he'd made. Unless. "You really don't believe me," I whispered. Somehow, I'd never considered they might feel this way. I thought I could convince them. Or that they'd just believe what I told them.

John swallowed. "Of course, we do." It was a lie.

"Rob's just trying to keep everyone safe." Miller's voice was morning croaky. "It's for the best." He was a worse liar than me. It didn't sound at all like he thought it was for the best.

"Everyone except himself." Frustration welled inside me. "Gisborne said the other night he knew where...where the place is." Gisborne was already a step ahead of me. He knew more than I did. "Surely you can see that makes him a target." I couldn't believe I hadn't thought of this sooner. There was no way Rob should be staying in the place that Gisborne talked about.

"He's no longer there." Tuck's tone said I was stupid for suggesting such a thing. "They've moved on."

"How do you know?" I spat.

John threw a glare at Tuck. When he turned to me, his smile was weak. "He had a plan. In case something like this ever happened. And I checked yesterday. They're no longer in the village Gisborne threatened."

I let out a breath. Good. Although the word *they* drove a stake into my heart. "So, they've moved away from the place in my…the place I described?"

John looked at Tuck.

Their pinched expressions made it clear where Rob had gone. "Or to it?"

"To it." John sighed.

"Then, please can you warn him? It's stupid to think he wouldn't want you to tell him about this."

"Tell him what exactly?" snapped Tuck. "That you miss him and want him to come back? Because, that won't make a scrap of difference to him anymore."

I ran my hands down my face. I could totally hear how it sounded, and it was exactly the way Tuck described.

"How do you know all this, anyway?" Tuck demanded.

I shook my head. "I…I can't tell you."

"Why not?" Tuck was restless and growing angrier by the second.

"I just...can't." Not yet. Maybe not ever.

John tried to smile. "Rob has his reasons for making it this way. We all agree with him."

"But do you really agree?" Because that half-hearted smile said he didn't.

John lifted his shoulders. "It doesn't matter. You know Rob. Once he's made up his mind..."

I stared from one to the next. "So, after everything you've all been through together, you're just letting him go? You don't even want to give him the option of choosing to leave? Of choosing to live?" No one met my eyes. There was some other reason they didn't want to listen to me, and I didn't have a clue what it might be.

Fine. I'd try a different way. "Miller. Don't you care about Rob enough to try to keep him alive?" It was a low blow. The pedestal Miller put Rob on was a high one.

Miller's head shot up. "Are you saying I don't love him? Because you're wrong." His voice shook with emotion.

"Then do something! Warn him. Tell him I think he's in danger. If he moves on to another village from wherever he is now and I'm wrong, where's the harm? If he doesn't and I'm right..." I let my words trail off. Miller would get the picture. They all would.

OUTPLAYED

Miller squeezed his eyes shut. When he opened them and spoke to Tuck and John, he sounded far older than fourteen. "She's right. You both know she is. We have to tell him that Maryanne thinks he's in danger. He can make his own decision about what to do, but we shouldn't keep this from him."

Once I had Miller onboard, it didn't take long for the other two to give in. I seemed to be the sticking point. They were adamant I couldn't go into the village where Rob was staying. If that was their problem, they should just have said so in the first place. We could have sorted this out far quicker. I was fine with not going all the way with them—they didn't want to leave me alone at Kings Cave, so were taking me part of the way—so long as they promised to make Rob understand he was in danger.

Tuck decided he wouldn't come with us when we started out later that morning. He thought it was just as important to continue talking to his contacts in the nearby towns in the hope of finding out what the Sheriff or Gisborne were planning to do next. He would meet us at Bob's Cavern, the place I would wait for John and Miller, and where we would stay tonight.

Still, they kept the name of the village where Rob was staying to themselves. Goodness knew what they thought I might do with that information. Go running to him to declare my undying love? Probably.

Tuck pointed a finger at me as we left. "You make sure you do what's expected." Meaning, don't go near Rob.

I got their message, loud and clear. "Don't worry. I want to go there about as much as he wants me to." I had zero desire to see his new life. Seeing Rob—and *her*—would hurt more than I was ready to deal with.

Ten

WE walked in silence along the trail. I wasn't sure if John and Miller were quiet because they didn't want anyone to hear us, or because they weren't in the mood for words. Or, because they were worried for Rob. Any of those things seemed like a good reason for silence, and I didn't feel particularly like talking either. What if we were too late? Rob's death in my dreams always happened at dawn. What if this morning had been *the* morning?

I supposed it didn't matter. Rob was either already dead or he wasn't. If it had happened already, we were too late to do anything, and if that were the case, I'd deal with it once I knew for certain. If he was still alive, there was no rush. We still had until at least tomorrow morning to get him out of there.

John put his hand up to stop us walking and pointed down the hill to a larger trail where a carriage rumbled past. Soon it would make a turn away from us and around the base of the hill. I nudged John. Some habits die hard, but even with Rob's absence, there was still a legend to protect. "Let's go," I mouthed. No need for me to explain what I wanted to do. We could beat the carriage to the other side of the hill by scrambling over the top.

He shook his head.

"Come on. There are no soldiers traveling with it." We had a good view of the trail from both directions up here. "It'll be fun." And totally reckless. But if Rob wasn't going to look after his legend, I would do it.

John held up his bandaged hand. This morning I'd washed it and smeared it with the antiseptic cream Mom had stuffed into the little first aid kit I'd brought with me, before bandaging it again. Still no infection, thank goodness. "Ain't a thing I can do if it all goes wrong."

Hadn't thought of that. I turned to Miller. "You're game, right? You'd like to bring some joy to the less fortunate, wouldn't you?"

OUTPLAYED

Miller eyed the carriage warily, then glanced in both directions along the trail. "Maybe. So long as there are no soldiers over the other side of the hill."

I turned back to John. "Nothing will go wrong. Hold your staff in your left hand. Keep your other hand hidden in your cloak. They'll never know you're injured." He watched the carriage take the corner with his lips pursed. Not an immediate *no*. That was good. "You could take the gold with you when you go to Rob. He'll be less annoyed with you for going to him when he sees how happy the villagers are."

John looked at me from the corner of his eye, a faint smile on his lips. "You're very persuasive when you want to be."

"Is that a yes?"

He rolled his eyes. "I guess so."

We jogged over the top of the hill and back down the other side. From here, we had a better view of the trail in both directions and there were no soldiers lying in wait, not another soul around. Miller started to hand me his bow, a reflex from other times we'd done this. I shook my head. "I've got my own, remember. Anyway, I'm coming with you."

"Like hell." John was about as serious as I'd ever heard him.

I shrugged. "Try to stop me." I stepped around him and ran the final few paces down the hill and onto the trail.

"I don't like this," John murmured, following.

There was no point in answering. I was going out on the trail with them and that was that. "You take Rob's place. Miller and I will back you up." It would sound far more commanding to have John demand gold, than a woman or a fourteen-year-old. "Just try to sound authoritative."

The carriage bumped around the corner. John held up his hand and the carriage slowed. "We're going to need some gold to let you past."

The coachman shook his head. "We have none."

John's laugh was forced. "You expect us to believe that when you're riding through the forest in a fancy carriage rather than traveling on foot like the rest of us." He shook his head. "Hand it over."

Miller drew his sword, the metallic echo ringing around the forest. The coachman jumped.

I took an arrow from my quiver, nocking it and pulling the string back until the fletching brushed my cheek. The coachman's eyes widened, and he banged a hand on the carriage, sending a message to the occupant. It may have been a few months since they'd robbed anyone, but the rich still knew the stories well enough to be worried.

OUTPLAYED

The door opened a sliver and an old man's hand poked out; a coin purse gripped between his wobbling fingers. John took it, weighing it in his hand before nodding. "Thank you, milord." John gave a low bow, then strode off the track, the gold jingling as he walked.

Miller and I followed, sprinting up the hill until we couldn't breathe. When we finally stopped, far from the trail, John and Miller looked at each other and, in unison, let out a huge whoop. That was a rush. No wonder they'd loved doing it so much. I couldn't stop the smile pulling at my cheeks.

"So much for keeping quiet to avoid soldiers," I mumbled.

John picked me up and swung me around. "No soldiers nearby. It's been too long since we did that." He placed me back on my feet. "And don't pretend you're not as high as either of us. I can see the smile bursting out of you."

It was. I giggled. "That was so much fun!"

John held up the coin pouch. "And it'll be even more fun giving this to the villagers." He grinned, then threw me an apologetic glance. "Sorry, you won't get to do that."

I didn't care. If they were handing out gold, they were continuing the Robin Hood legend. It was better than letting Gisborne stop us doing all the things we wanted to do.

The wait alone at Bob's Cavern felt like forever. I told myself it would take time to talk to Rob and hand out the gold, but I couldn't sit still. Instead, I walked around the outside of the hollow base of the tree that was Bob's Cavern, reminding myself this was why I'd come back. I was saving Rob's life.

It was mid-afternoon when they returned. Apparently, the villagers were ecstatic, but Rob refused to move on.

"Did you tell him what I said?" I demanded.

"It's not that he doesn't believe you, milady." John shrugged. "He thinks Gisborne will find him wherever he is. He thinks his current residence offers the best chance of escaping, if it comes to that."

"There's no escaping. The only escape is if he's not there." Panic built inside me and my words spilled out on top of each other. I should have insisted I go with them. If I'd been there, I could have made Rob see how important this was, rather than him hearing it second hand.

John shook his head. "We tried. There's nothing else we can do."

There was. I just hadn't thought of it yet.

Tuck didn't turn up that afternoon, the way he was supposed to.

I asked Miller for a sword lesson to fight the boredom and niggling worry, but John quickly quashed that idea. We were too close to the trail into the village where Rob was staying—which I now knew as Oxham after Miller let it slip—and someone might hear us. We weren't close at all, but his caution was sensible. Instead, Miller and I went fishing in the river that passed by the back of the hollow tree that would provide our shelter tonight. We even caught a trout that tasted pretty darned good when John cooked it up for dinner.

The following morning as we ate breakfast around the fire, heavy footsteps pounded toward us. I reached for the dagger in my sock. John and Miller were already on their feet, with their weapons in their hands when Tuck appeared, out of breath.

"Rob..." he panted.

I stood, my mouth going dry.

Tuck bent over, resting his hands on his knees.

"What about Rob?" Miller asked, before I had the chance.

"Is he okay?" Tuck wheezed. "Did you get him out of Oxham?"

John shook his head. "He wouldn't leave."

Beneath cheeks reddened from running, Tuck's skin paled. "Are you sure?"

Both Miller and John nodded.

"Get your weapons. There's something you all need to see. You too, Maryanne."

Eleven

We sprinted after Tuck, one-by-one down a narrow trail that led to a wider one. I already knew why Tuck was so distraught. Saw it again and again in my mind as we raced along the trail toward the village. Soldiers had attacked. He didn't need to say it. His reaction made it clear enough.

My fault. I should have tried harder to make Rob leave.

Best I could hope was that Rob was lying on the ground injured. It was that thought that drove my feet to run even as I was out of breath. The next best option was that he was alive but captured—we could do something about that, too.

The final option, the one where he was already dead, stayed pushed to the back of my mind.

The tang of blood was heavy in the air and obvious before we saw the village. The hair on my arms stood on end, and I wasn't sure if my difficulty breathing was from running, or fear of what I was about to see.

Tuck led us between two huts, turned left and sprinted down a pocked road to the hut farthest away. Bodies scattered the ground, lying where they'd fallen, blood already dry on the dirt beneath them. I followed, scanning for a brown cloak with a fur-lined hood like Rob's, or his bow lying on the ground. I saw neither of those things.

Tuck raced into the hut, then tore back out. "Not there," he panted. I guessed that was where Rob lived.

Miller and John seemed to take that as an instruction, turning back the way we'd come and stopping to check each body, all without uttering a single word.

Checking for Rob.

"I'll go and look inside the other homes." I doubted Rob would be cowering inside, but I didn't think he was among the dead we'd already passed either, and I had to do something.

"Me too." Tuck nodded. "I'll take this side, you do that side?"

OUTPLAYED

I started running before he finished speaking. I sprinted from home to home, opening doors that were shut, barging through those that were open, hoping not to find Rob, but expecting to see him lying on the ground bleeding, anyway.

The homes were empty. All of them. Everyone who had been here was either lying on the ground outside or they'd fled.

Tuck fared no better on his side.

"He's not here," said Miller, as we met in the middle of the village, beside the church. He kept moving on the balls of his feet, even as we stood still, his gaze never lingering in one position for long. "We've checked every single body on the ground."

"They must have bolted when they heard the soldiers coming." John ran a hand through his hair.

Tuck let out a deep breath and loosened his shoulders, but I couldn't relax. Something didn't feel right. Rob wouldn't have run away from the village that had hidden him, leaving them alone against the soldiers. He'd have stayed and fought.

I walked back up to the first home Tuck had brought us to—Rob's home—and pushed the door open.

There were straw mattresses on the floor and the fire in the middle of the room was cold. I turned in a slow circle, taking in the near-empty room Rob shared with the faceless girlfriend.

I grinned and sprinted back out the door, almost running into John as I did. "He's not here!"

John looked at me sideways. "I thought we'd already established that."

We had, but I'd had questions. "He didn't run. Not from the soldiers. There's nothing of his inside that house. He must have packed up and left after you and Miller were here."

Tuck pushed past us to look in the hut. "Huh," he said, as he came back out.

Miller looked at Tuck. "Well?"

"She's right. He's gone." He scratched the back of his head. "Didn't notice in my rush to find him."

"Thank the Lord," said Miller, a slow smile spreading on his face.

"Couldn't have said it better myself." Tuck gave a shaky laugh before his face grew serious once more. "There is something else you all need to see, though."

Tuck led us to one of the homes he'd checked, opening the door and entering with a beckoning nod for us to follow. Muffled moans escaped the room as I stepped over the threshold with a measured stride.

OUTPLAYED

Inside, four people lay on the straw mattresses on the floor; two adults and two children. One adult had a bandage wet with blood covering his eyes. Another had blood, dried now, dribbling down her chin and over the center of her clothing. The two children were crying softly, and their hands were wrapped in bandages. I glanced at Tuck for confirmation.

He nodded.

The soldiers hadn't just killed this time, they'd maimed, too. Eyes, fingers and a tongue. Worse still, was the blood each of them had on their left cheek, because beneath it, cut into their skin, was a letter G. Carved with a knife.

I pushed my way between John and Miller, back out the door, and emptied the contents of my stomach onto the ground.

I'd seen this. Or I'd seen something like it. Not the carving. But the damaged eyes and tongues and hands. A second wave of nausea rose, and I couldn't keep it inside. This was a message from Gisborne. More people were suffering because of us. Because Rob had lived here. Because he'd left before Gisborne could get to him Or, perhaps, because they'd been the recipients of the stolen gold.

I wiped my chin with the back of my hand and got to my feet. Tuck had brought us here to help. It was the least I could do.

John and Miller were still standing in the doorway where I'd left them, mouths partially open, faces a pale shade of green, while Tuck had pulled out his bible and was praying.

"Is there anything I can do?" I asked, looking inside my pack. I had a few first aid supplies with me. I could leave a tube of antiseptic cream with this family—not that it would help the missing tongue, but at least it was something.

Tuck stared pointedly at his bible, the words falling from his lips without pause.

"Anything practical?" I searched for cloths to clean their injuries. There were none, so I settled for ripping a strip from the bottom of my tunic. As Tuck continued to pray rather than answer me, I cleaned the wounds and applied the cream.

As I worked, Tuck said, "Miller's going to go to Mansfield and get a healer, aren't you, Miller?"

It sounded more like an instruction than something they'd discussed, but Miller nodded, already backing away. I got the feeling he couldn't get out the door fast enough, and I didn't blame him.

"Meet us at Kings Cave, once you're done," Tuck called to his back.

Miller nodded again, leaving without another word. I watched him trot down the street and duck into the forest before turning to Tuck. "I hate to say this, but…"

"We should be going?" He glanced up from his bible.

I nodded. "If Gisborne wanted to kill these people, he would have done it already. I don't think they're in danger." But we very well could be.

He got to his feet. "Wouldn't surprise me if Gisborne's men were to come back, looking for us."

My mouth dropped open. Tuck and I were thinking along the same line. There was a first time for everything.

We left water in easy reach of the family and told them a healer would arrive soon. It was all we could do, and it wasn't nearly enough. To take them with us would slow us down, possibly put us in the path of soldiers, and put them at a higher risk of their wounds becoming infected.

I wasn't sure exactly how I made it back to Bob's Cavern. I felt dazed and broken. Gisborne had left those people alive as a message. A message that could only be interpreted as *I am in charge.* He might easily have killed Rob, too, had Rob not listened to John and Miller and left. Instead, other people died because of him. It terrified me that Gisborne had come so close to getting what he desperately wanted, and I couldn't even celebrate the fact that Rob escaped.

We packed our things and left the cavern. No one spoke. I imagined everyone was having much the same thoughts. Feeling the same guilt because we were all pleased Rob wasn't dead, even though so many others were.

I didn't remember the walk to Kings Cave, I just put one foot in front of the other and eventually arrived. I dropped my pack on the ground and lay down beside it. I was cold and sweaty at the same time. The idea that I might be to blame for those deaths had crept up on me as I walked.

"All right, Maryanne?" John placed his pack beside me.

"It was all my fault," I blurted.

He frowned. "Your fault Rob is safe?"

I shook my head. "If I hadn't insisted we stop that carriage and take the gold, and if we hadn't given it to the people of Oxham, Gisborne wouldn't have attacked them." I should have listened when the boys said they couldn't stop carriages anymore because Gisborne would retaliate. Instead, I'd focused on the legend, and my place in it. My foolishness had cost lives and left people maimed.

"Yeah, well, you're not the only one who knows how to do stupid. We all make unwise decisions from time to time." He sat heavily on the ground beside me.

I'd been expecting sympathy not whatever that was. "Not you. You always think before you act."

"Sometimes too much." He leaned forward until his elbows rested on his knees, then put his hands in his hair. "I've been so, so stupid. We might all have been grieving because of my foolishness." His voice dropped to a whisper and sent goosebumps up my arms.

I sat up. "What's happened?"

"Nothing." The word came out like a sigh. "Thank goodness." He shook his head, as if he was clearing it. "And what happened today was in no way your fault. Gisborne couldn't have known about the gold that quickly. He might have heard about the robbery, but he had no way of knowing what we'd done with the gold. None of that is your fault. Okay?"

I nodded. Logically, it was likely true, it just didn't feel that way at the moment.

Twelve

Miller didn't return that afternoon. Or during the night. Tuck and John spent the following morning either pacing across the small entrance to the cave, or clambering around the ledge at the side of the cave to climb to the top of the hill to see if anyone was coming. Not that it helped. The forest was too thick. I guess they just needed to feel as if they were doing something.

"We should never have sent him." John marched past, mumbling loud enough for me to hear.

"Who should we have sent, then?" I asked, as much to fill the silence as to hear his answer. Rather than sit around and idly wait for him yesterday afternoon, we'd robbed another carriage and handed out the gold at the nearby villages of Huxley and Clipstone. The people had been among the most grateful I'd ever seen at any village, even agreeing when we suggested they melt the gold down so Gisborne couldn't link them with the carriage robbery. I couldn't shake the sense of déjà vu I'd gotten from Huxley, even though I'd never been there before. There was no reason for it; I hadn't seen the village in my dreams. But still, it was there.

Today though, we were in no mood for carriages. We were in no mood for anything other than Miller returning.

"Me," said John.

I glanced pointedly at his hand. He still couldn't use a bow and his staff was more about decoration these days.

He caught my glance and huffed out a breath. "Fine, then. Tuck."

"You think I don't know that?" called Tuck, from somewhere above us. "Do you think I haven't wished I went instead of Miller every moment he's been gone?" Tuck jumped off the overhang to land on the thin strip of flat rock just in front of me. "I think we should leave Kings Cave. I don't think we're safe here."

I shook my head. He couldn't be serious. "We can't leave. This is where Miller is meeting us. This is where he'll come as soon as he can." If we left, he wouldn't know where to find us.

"If he was coming, he'd be here by now," Tuck snapped.

"So, after just one day, you're giving up on him? I knew you were cruel, Tuck, but this..."

John didn't give me the chance to finish. "I agree. We can't stay here."

I shook my head, imagining how abandoned Miller would feel if he turned up at the meeting point to find us gone. I couldn't do it to him. "We have to."

"What if he's hurt, Maryanne? What if he can't get here?" John's mouth was a thin line. He wouldn't abandon Miller unless it was necessary, I knew that. It still didn't make the decision any easier.

"He's only fourteen. We can't just leave him all alone!" Except, we could. Because by twelfth century standards, he was all but grown up. If he was living in a village, he'd be engaged, possibly married by now.

"He's old enough to look after himself. Just like we need to look after ourselves."

I eyed John. It wasn't like him to suggest such a thing, especially where Miller was concerned.

"Are you feeling all right?" He'd been out of sorts since his visit to Clipstone yesterday, after seeing his sister.

"Not really." He shook his head. "I'm worried for Miller and I miss my family. Even if I can't be with them every day of the year, I don't intend to die and leave them with no one to look out for them, either."

"You're not going to die." There was no reason to think that.

"What would you know?" John snapped before scraping his hands up his face and through his hair. "Sorry, Maryanne. I didn't mean to bite. It's just I saw Luke, my nephew yesterday. He's almost two now. Has this beautiful head of white-blond curls. Reminded me of my little brother at the same age." He let out a deep sigh. His little brother died along with John's mother the day soldiers attacked John's village. "He's the most beautiful kid I've ever seen, and…" He shrugged. "With his father dead, I need to look out for them, even if I don't ever get to spend any time with him. If Miller leads Gisborne here, he and Josephine will have no one." He shook his head. "I won't risk it. We have to leave."

"We'll search for Miller," said Tuck. "Just not while we're based here." His voice had taken on a don't-question-me tone.

I didn't care. I'd question him all day on this, no matter what tone he used with me. "You're both walking out on him?"

A rustling noise had us all searching the edge of the forest, hoping to catch sight of Miller. Instead, Rob stepped, huffing and puffing, onto the now crowded area in front of the cave. His blond hair fell loose. I hadn't heard him come up the trail. Must have been too focused on fighting for Miller. I let out my breath. Rob would take my side. He'd never leave Miller behind.

Rob looked between us, a frown on his forehead. "What's going on?"

Tuck gave Rob a quick rundown of the last twenty-four hours.

"He should have been back by now," said Rob, his frown growing heavier. "I've seen no sign of Gisborne or his men in my travels. The forest seems extra quiet today. If they have him, they've likely gone to ground."

"I agree," said Tuck. "And I think continuing to stay here at the cave is unwise."

Rob nodded. "I think so, too."

I jumped to my feet. What was wrong with him? The Rob I knew would never walk away from a friend. "What the hell? How can you agree with this?"

OUTPLAYED

Rob's eyes ran slowly over my face before he blew out a breath and turned away. He lifted one shoulder and I thought he'd dismissed my question out of hand until he said, "Gisborne is going to hurt Miller to find out where we are. If Miller can't handle it, this is the first place soldiers will come."

I didn't understand how they all thought Miller would give them up. "But, this is Miller."

Rob shook his head, and his jaw stiffened. "It isn't up for discussion. For your own safety, you need to leave. And you need to leave now."

I met his eyes and lowered my voice. "And what will you be doing, Rob?" The distance between us was growing by the second. Everything he'd done since I came back was at war with the way he'd behaved when we first met, including forcing us to leave Miller behind. Yet, I was still hopeful. Hopeful there was still some of the guy I thought I knew inside him. Perhaps he'd ask us to leave but would wait here for the friend he treated like a brother.

"I'm leaving, too. None of us should be here. It's not safe."

"But—"

"Enough, Maryanne. You all leave. Now."

John moved to stand beside me, his voice gentle. "If Gisborne has him, and be honest, it's what we're all thinking, then he'll be doing everything he can to make Miller tell him where we're staying. Everything. It's what he did with me."

I glanced at his bandaged hand. *It's what he did with me.* "But you didn't tell him."

He shrugged. "Two fingers aren't too high of a price to keep my friends safe."

The thought of Miller losing part of his body made me feel physically ill, but I also knew how much Miller wanted to be like the rest of them, and how far he'd go to protect them. "Why don't you trust him? He won't tell Gisborne where we are." There was no way Miller would put his friends in that sort of danger.

John dragged a hand through his hair, and it stuck out in every direction. "It's not that we don't trust him. I don't want Miller to have to make the same choice as I had to make. He knows, Maryanne. He knows we'd rather he keep himself safe and give up our location. He knows we'll move on and we'll find him when we can."

Rob let out a breath, sounding more like himself than he had since Woodhurst. "I don't like it either, Maryanne, especially since Gisborne seems to have the upper hand again. But we can't help anyone, let alone Miller, if we're dead. Which is what I think will happen if you all stay here."

OUTPLAYED

Gisborne had somehow managed to tie our hands and our feet. "I can't sleep knowing Miller isn't safe," I whispered.

"Do you think any of us can?" asked Tuck, with just enough edge in his voice to sound harsh.

"We're not giving up on him," said John. "We're just helping him from a different place."

Rob straightened his bow on his back. "So, it's settled? You're leaving?" He looked from John to Tuck, both of whom nodded. "I'll find you in a day or two. Sooner if I have any news." Without a backward glance—or even a glance my way—he turned and disappeared into the forest. Back to the girl who meant more to him than the friends who'd once been like his family.

We moved from Kings Cave to a tiny cave they'd never taken me to until now. It was farther from Kings Cave than I would have liked. They called it Black Hole, and although the ceiling was higher than Kings Cave, the rest of the cave was smaller. The ground was rough and uneven, and places to stretch out and sleep were limited. Plus, there was a stream running through it that made the cave constantly damp and cold, even after we lit a fire. Still, it was better than being out in the open with such low temperatures at night, something Miller might not have the benefit of.

The following day, John and Tuck went out searching for Miller, like they'd said they would, while I waited at Black Hole, in case Miller turned up.

I sat at the mouth of the cave for half an hour before I decided I wasn't sitting around waiting at this place. Miller would come to Black Hole only after he tried Kings Cave and found us gone. I should be waiting there. As for him leading Gisborne to us, I wasn't worried at all. Miller would never. And if he did, I'd have my bow and the element of surprise.

I'd watched Rob die in my dreams again last night. Same as always, an arrow in his back at the edge of the forest. Hadn't been able to do a damn thing to stop it. The powerlessness felt far too similar to what was happening with Miller, and I didn't know how to fix either problem. I just knew that Kings Cave was where I needed to wait, no matter what anyone else said.

When I arrived, I searched the cave, then tucked myself cross-legged onto one of the mattresses. No one had been here since we left, which was both good and bad. Good because I hadn't missed Miller, bad because he hadn't been here. I wasn't worried about soldiers and their swords. The ceiling was too low to fight in here. Plus, from the darkness of the cave, I had a full view of anyone who stepped inside and would fire on anyone who wasn't Miller.

Miller didn't come that day. Or the next. Each evening I went back to the cave at Black Hole, arriving before Tuck and John and hoping someone had found him. No one had.

Rob never came back either and it pissed me off. Miller should be more important than his girlfriend.

I sat on a mattress at the back of Kings Cave, fishing around in my pack for something to eat and instead finding the present Josh gave me at the airport. Somehow, in all the excitement and terror of the past week I'd forgotten all about it.

I ran my fingers over the wrapping paper, blinking back the tears that attempted to form. I'd walked away from my little brother and returned to a place where nothing was as I'd expected. I already missed him. It was worse knowing I might have made a terrible mistake in coming back here. Rob was barely talking to me; Tuck and John were always angry, and Miller was missing. It felt as if everything was falling apart.

The package was just larger than my hand and reasonably heavy. I moved into the light cast by the small hole at the top of the cave and opened it slowly. At home, I was more of a tear-up-the-paper sort of present-opener. Today, I drew out the anticipation. It made me feel closer to Josh to be touching something he'd lovingly wrapped not so long ago.

With the final piece of tape undone, I removed the paper and placed it to one side. Two large blocks of milk chocolate sat at the top of the parcel. My favorite. And possibly the only chocolate I'd ever taste again. I put them back in the bottom of my pack for later.

Beneath the blocks of chocolate was a photo album. The type that was the size of a single photograph and contained about twenty photos in total. I flicked through the pages fast, strange noises coming from my throat as I saw the pictures he'd chosen for me. I couldn't get enough of seeing my family again, and twenty photos didn't seem like nearly enough.

I flicked back to the start and looked through them slowly. The tears I'd blinked away moments ago blurred my vision. Josh knew me well. There was nothing he could have given me that would have been better than this.

The first few photos in the album were some we'd had taken in a studio for Mom and Dad's wedding anniversary last year. Josh was in a suit and tie, Carrie in a rainbow-colored sundress, and I wore black jeans and a black T-shirt. We were all smiling but none of us looked happy.

I hadn't realized it then, but now I knew none of us had been.

He followed those with older photos; all of us with the snowman we'd made in our back yard when it had unexpectedly snowed in spring a few years back; Carrie and I eating ice-cream on the beach with our arms around each other's shoulders when I was about six; Josh and I cuddling our pet cat who'd long since passed on, and some photos we'd snapped in the days before I came back here. And finally, a photo I hadn't known existed. Our family on the beach, posing together moments before my sunhat blew from my head and I chased it down the beach. Dad had always kept the other version of this photo—the version where I didn't feature—in a frame on his desk. There was a sticky note attached to that photo, written in Mom's hand but from Josh.

MA

Stole this from the album Dad keeps in the top drawer of his desk. Hope you like it.

J

I smiled. I hadn't even known Dad had an album in his desk. I wasn't sure how Josh knew, unless Mom had helped him, which was likely.

Thanks, Joshy, I whispered. *I love it.*

Something outside caught my attention. I didn't know what it was, just knew I was on edge. I shuffled backward, away from the light, and carefully picked up my bow.

Had it been someone drawing a sword? Gisborne's soldiers? I cast my hearing wide, but the sounds were ordinary now. Just birds chirping and wind in the trees. Perhaps there had been no noise. Perhaps I was jumping at shadows.

Another noise, down the hill. A stick breaking? No. That would have told me for sure someone was here. Footsteps on the ground, maybe.

I climbed onto my knees and nocked my arrow, tilting the bow sideways to avoid the ceiling. I hoped Miller was out there, though I doubted he was. He'd have run up the hill and sprinted inside. Wouldn't he? He wouldn't have made this slow march up the hill, that whoever was out there was currently making.

I pulled the bowstring back. The moment I saw anything burgundy or gold, I would shoot. Then I'd nock another arrow and shoot again.

There was no movement outside the cave. No other sound that seemed out of place. Maybe I'd imagined it. Maybe it was nerves talking.

"Drop your weapon."

The voice came from the edge of the entrance, like he'd come up the steep side of the hill to avoid being seen. Like he knew this place well.

Thirteen

"Rob?" My hand on my bow shook. It sounded like him, but I wasn't dropping my weapon until I knew for sure.

"Maryanne?" Rob stepped into the entrance of the cave.

I let my bow slide from my hand. It clattered onto the stone.

It was just Rob.

Not some soldier about to gut me alive. Or chop off my body parts the way they had with John.

"What are you doing here?" he asked. "I thought I said—"

"I know what you said," I snapped, the adrenalin pumping through me making me short. "I disagreed with your command." Also a snappy response, but this one wasn't entirely due to the adrenalin.

"Well, there's a surprise," Rob muttered, bending to enter the cave.

I folded my arms over my chest. "You obviously disagreed with yourself." Since he was here. Not…wherever else he'd been hanging out this week.

"I thought I'd come by and check Miller hadn't been here. I didn't intend to camp out here until he returned." His voice was gentle and far from accusatory, but that's not how I took it.

"I'm not camping out. I'm waiting. And I go back to Black Hole every night. Like a good little girl."

Rob was on the other side of the light coming from the roof. His eyebrows lifted. "I'm guessing Tuck or John don't know you go anywhere during the day?"

"Why? Because if they knew, they'd have run to you." Where was all this anger coming from? I knew I was upset about leaving Kings Cave, but the words coming from my mouth were more than just anger.

He pressed his lips together, not even bothering to deny that he did expect John or Tuck to tell him where I'd been, had they known.

"At least I'm doing something. It might not be much, but it's better than swanning around with my new girlfriend and forgetting the people who've been my family for the past few years." That was it. The reason. I was disappointed and annoyed he'd chosen someone else over Miller. Especially when that boy looked at Rob like he was a superhero.

"Is that what you think?" he asked quietly.

"What else am I supposed to think? You haven't been near us since we moved to Black Hole. You wouldn't have a clue whether Miller was back or not!" I felt so helpless with Miller missing. He could be anywhere in this huge forest. He might be dead and I couldn't fix it, but I expected Rob to. Unfair, and I knew it. But he wasn't trying nearly hard enough to make it better.

He sank down onto his butt and I realized we'd been face-to-face, arguing on our knees. I copied.

His eyes ran over me, and he pulled his hair from the tie at the back of his neck, retying it before speaking. "I can't be everywhere."

"Some places are more important than others."

"And you think you get to decide what or who is most important in my life?" That was a reprimand and I deserved it.

Only he could make that decision. And I guessed he had, because it wasn't us. My heart was broken, but it was up to me to live with it. "Sorry." I sighed, because I really was sorry. "I guess we're so used to having you in our lives that it hurts a little..." I drew in a deep breath. "...okay, a lot, when you choose not to be with us any longer. But you're right. How you live your life should always be your choice. Not mine. Not anyone else's."

There was a long silence where he watched me in the dim light while I focused on my hands in my lap. I'd gone too far, anger making me say things I would usually keep to myself. Now I was embarrassed for saying too much.

"I've been splitting my time," he said, finally. "Between searching for Miller, checking he's not already back with you—usually in the middle of the night when you're all asleep—and..."

"Her." I finished his sentence for him.

He nodded. "I'm doing the best I can. I want to find Miller as much as anyone. Possibly more. I have other responsibilities, too, with..."

"Her," I said, again. *Ask her name.* It was the polite thing to do, and I probably owed it to him, but my lips clamped shut.

He *was* trying to help us. Knowing it made me feel worse for how I'd acted. "I take it you've found no sign of him?"

Rob blew out a deep breath. "Not one. It's like it was with John all over again. I've looked in all the places John suggested." Rob's voice caught.

I remembered how he'd talked about the time without John, how he'd hardly slept. Now he was spreading himself so thin, that I imagined the same was true again. "Are you sleeping?"

"Barely. But—"

"You'll be no good to Miller if Gisborne catches you because you're too tired to notice him coming." I nodded to the mattresses behind me. "Lie down. Rest for an hour or two. I'm staying for a bit. I'll look out for you both." It was the least I could offer after the way I'd just spoken to him.

Rob rested. I listened to his breathing grow slow and even, and allowed myself to think about the dreams. Obviously, I hadn't done enough to stop Rob's death. At home, the answer had seemed so simple—don't let Rob return to Oxham. But maybe I was missing something. Perhaps where it happened didn't matter, just that it would. Perhaps I couldn't actually change the future the way Dad and Maud thought. Perhaps coming back to the twelfth century meant I'd have to watch it happen in real time as well as while I slept.

No. I wouldn't accept that. I was going to stop it. Even if I had to figure out how as I went along.

Rob woke quickly. It seemed as if I was listening to his heavy breathing one moment, and the next he was sitting beside me, rubbing the sleep from his eyes. "Thanks," he said, voice rough. "I needed that."

"You should've slept longer."

He shook his head. "Can't. Got to get back."

I sighed inwardly. "Just…make sure you don't go near Oxham, okay?" I'd keep asking him this day after day, if I had to. For now, it was the only practical way I could keep him safe.

"You know the threat is likely gone from there now? Gisborne knows I've left. He won't send his men back."

I didn't agree. I turned to him, hoping he'd see in the dim light exactly how much I needed him to hear what I was asking. "Just humor me, would you?"

His eyes narrowed. "Why? Do you know something?"

I shook my head. Nothing I could share with him without dying myself. And I wasn't quite desperate enough to allow that to happen.

Silence returned between us. And not the comfortable sort, either. It didn't take much these days for our conversation to become stilted.

Probably because I felt like I was hiding things from him. Maybe I needed to try harder. I took a deep breath and spat out the words I didn't want to say. "What's her name?"

Rob looked at me with raised eyebrows. "Her name?"

Okay, then Rob. Make me spell it out, why don't you. "Your girlfriend."

He licked his lips.

"Or…boyfriend?" I held up my hands. "No judgement here, whichever it is."

The corner of his lips quirked. "Not a boyfriend."

We lapsed back into the same uncomfortable silence. I tried again. "So, her name?"

He shook his head. "Why would you want to know?"

I didn't. Was just making conversation. "Because that's the sort of thing friends tell each other, and we used to be friends once." Back when talking was easy.

He turned to me. I couldn't read his expression. Regret, perhaps, but more likely, that was wishful thinking on my part. "Are we not friends anymore?"

"Doesn't feel like it."

"Friends fight."

Rob and Tuck certainly did. I'd seen it. I wasn't sure this was a fight. Yes, I'd said some things earlier, and I was keeping the details of my dreams from him. Perhaps I was being selfish—telling him would bring about my violent death which would in turn save his life. It was one solution to the problem, but I was certain there was another. One where both of us came out of this alive. I just had to find it. Maybe it would come at the expense of our friendship, because it was feeling more and more like we'd grown apart. "Are we fighting?"

He shrugged. "I don't know." He ran his hands down his face. "I'm a fool for even trying to have this conversation."

"It was always going to be this hard when one of us moved on," I said, my voice soft.

"Have you? Moved on?" For a moment his eyes were eager, then they hooded over and I could no longer tell what he was thinking.

"I don't want to answer that," I said, faster than I should have. What did it matter anyway? He had, and that was part of the problem. We could never talk and laugh the way we had in the past now that he had someone else. He shouldn't even want to.

Unless.

I glanced at him. What if I wasn't the only one keeping secrets? He was cagey when talking about her. Maybe there wasn't a girlfriend at all, but some other reason that was taking his attention. In the back of my mind, I knew it was a stupid thing to say, wishful thinking, but that didn't stop the words coming from my lips. "You know I don't believe you."

"Really?" he asked, pulling his knees up and wrapping his arms around them. "About what?"

"Her."

Beside me, he stiffened. "Why not?" His question was careful, like he didn't know the right way to ask it. Or didn't want to talk about it.

The answer to that was easy. It was because I wanted with all my heart for there to be no *her*. I'd never tell him that, though. "You don't talk about her. You come to see us reasonably often, never with her. If I was her, I'd want to know your friends. I'd want to come with you."

There was a pause before he said, "Maybe she's just more secure in our relationship than you would have been."

Ouch.

Maybe. "She should still want to know your friends, your family, the most important people in your life."

"Like you did?" he said, meeting my gaze. Getting to know his friends had come hand-in-hand with knowing him a few months back.

OUTPLAYED

Something in his eyes stole my breath and I had to look away. "We're not that difficult to get along with. Most of the time. Which just makes me think..." I shrugged. "Well, is she real?"

Rob ran his hands down his face. "Say I answer that question the way you want me to, what will it achieve?"

Well that was a no-brainer. If there was no girlfriend, then it meant only one thing. "You'll come back to us." And maybe the two of us could learn to have more than a stilted conversation.

He stared straight ahead, the muscles in his jaw working, his eyes fixed on something outside the cave.

"But you won't, will you?" I asked. "Whether you have another girlfriend or not, you're not coming back." If there wasn't a girl, I'd expected him to return to us as soon as whatever was keeping him away was resolved. The sadness in his eyes told me it wasn't going to happen, and it was like a punch to the gut. I hadn't seen it coming.

He picked up his bow and sword from the ground and scrambled out of the cave. "I have to go."

I followed him out. "Sorry." Seemed all I did was apologize to him lately. "I shouldn't have pushed so hard."

With his back to me, he released a sigh, his shoulders drooping. "You should have. You were right to." He started to leave, stopping to look back up at me. "And you're right about the girlfriend. There isn't one. I'm sorry I lied." He continued down the hill and disappeared into the forest before I could react.

I watched him leave then headed back into the cave. Rob's admission hadn't made me feel as good as I expected it would. He didn't have a girlfriend. But he still had another reason to stay away from us. Something he couldn't, or wouldn't, share with me.

I flicked through my photos, taking my time before putting the album into my pack. It would soon be time to head back to John and Tuck.

I was just pulling my quiver over my shoulder when the cave entrance darkened. Someone was there. They'd arrived so silently, I hadn't heard them approach. I picked up my bow.

Not a soldier. No chainmail. No burgundy and gold cloak.

I drew an arrow from my quiver, readying myself to shoot.

The figure crouched, his movements awkward as he entered the cave.

"Miller?" I whispered, already crawling toward him.

Fourteen

Miller backed out when he saw me, standing and waiting in the long afternoon shadows beneath the rocky overhang at the cave entrance. The moment I reached him and before I could say a single word, he wrapped his arms around me and tucked his head into the crook of my neck, sobbing.

"Miller. It's okay." I rubbed his back while trying to do a visual inventory of all his body parts without pulling away to do so. "You're okay now." His sobbing continued no matter what I said, his whole body shaking. I whispered words that meant nothing in his ear and let him cry until he was done. Finally, he stepped back and looked at me.

I put my hand over my mouth when I saw his face. "Miller? What happened? Are you all right?" He wasn't. Clearly. Apart from the crying, his entire face was purple and swollen. One eye was shut, the other was almost. There were cuts on his lips, and his cheeks were so tight, they were shiny. "Can you talk?" It didn't look like he could move any part of his face.

He nodded, still quiet.

I moved to take his hand, wanting him to know that I was here for him and I'd do my best to make everything all right. He pulled back before I could touch him. Then he held his hand up, an apology in his semi-closed eye. His little finger and the one beside it were sticking out at odd angles. Broken.

"Gisborne?" I asked.

He nodded.

Cold fury washed over me. I was going to kill that man. Though, I suspected I might have to stand in line once Rob, John and Tuck saw Miller. "The others have gone."

He nodded, like he expected it. "To Black Hole?" His voice was raspy and unused.

"They think it's unsafe here."

"It's not," he whispered. "No one followed me." His eyes, what I could see of them, had lost their spark, and it hurt my heart to see it. I wanted to

OUTPLAYED

ask what had happened but couldn't make him relive it. Not yet, at least.

"Can you walk there? Or do you want me to go and bring them here?"

Miller straightened his spine. "I'll walk."

He was probably the bravest person I knew. Terrified and three years younger than me, he should have wanted nothing more than to curl up in a ball and close his eyes. Instead, he chose a slow and probably painful trek through the forest.

I had the feeling Rob might return to Kings Cave later, to check I'd gone back to Black Hole. I scribbled two words on the cave entrance using a burnt stick from our old fire, just for him. *Got him.* It was all I needed to say. If Rob read it, he'd understand.

John and Tuck were still out when Miller and I reached our camp. I sat Miller down inside the cave next to the cold fire, while I went to fetch some water and wood. Once the fire was roaring, I began to clean up his face, wiping away the dried blood with a cloth and water.

A noise I didn't hear had Miller on his feet. "Get behind me." With one hand, he urged me back, with the other, injured, hand, he drew his sword.

I picked up my bow from where it leaned against the cave wall and nocked an arrow before stepping around Miller. Damned if Gisborne was getting him again. Damned if he was getting either of us.

Miller dropped his sword, and it clattered against the stone floor of the cave.

"Are you okay?" I whispered.

He nodded, pointing to a place where the trees thinned. "It's Rob."

I kept my arrow ready, pointing out the cave door until I could confirm with my own eyes what Miller had already seen.

Rob stepped out of the forest and looked between the two of us, then raised his hands. "I know you're not happy with me, Maryanne, but there's no need to shoot." He crossed the three steps to Miller and wrapped him in a hug. Miller leaned into him and cried again. Rob looked over his shoulder at me, questions in his eyes. I shrugged. I knew as much as he did.

When his tears stopped, I continued to clean Miller's face. It didn't make him seem any less hurt, only less dirty.

"Gisborne's a dead man," whispered Rob through clenched teeth. He placed some small sticks on either side of Miller's fingers, then wrapped them in cloth, tying the ends so the bandage remained secure and his fingers could heal.

OUTPLAYED

Before I could agree, Tuck and John arrived back. There were more hugs and fewer tears, and when Miller began to talk, we all sat down to listen.

"They were waiting for me. Gisborne's soldiers. Outside Mansfield. I think they left that family alive hoping one of us would go for a healer. They had a camp just outside Mansfield and that's where they took me. To Gisborne."

Rob shook his head. I imagined his thoughts were similar to mine. If we'd acted sooner, we could have gotten to the soldier's camp and got Miller back before any of this happened. Instead, we'd given him the benefit of the doubt, had thought he'd just been held up, and had passed our time robbing a stupid carriage.

"They want..." He shrugged. "He wants exactly what we've always known he wanted. Rob. Maud. He expected me to tell him where you both were."

I looked at the ground, feeling ill. Another person hurt because of me. It stung even more this time because it was Miller. Because I felt a sense of responsibility toward him.

"I refused, of course," Miller continued. "So, they hit and kicked and beat me, to force an answer."

"Miller," I whispered, looking at his misshapen face. "You shouldn't have done that for me."

"Had to," he croaked. "You still don't know how to use a sword well enough for us to let you loose on Gisborne."

I smiled even though it was the last thing I wanted to do. "Well, I'm glad you're back to give me the rest of my lessons." More glad than I could even say.

"Me too." He drew in a wobbly breath. "The beatings got worse each time I refused to answer. Sometimes I passed out from pain. It got so bad that I'd decided to tell them what they wanted to know the next time they asked, because I couldn't bear it anymore." He glanced at Rob. "Sorry, Rob. I wanted more than anything to be like you, and I failed. You'd never have bowed to Gisborne's demands. You would never have considered telling him what he wanted to know." His voice broke and it brought tears to my eyes.

Miller wasn't the only one bowing to Gisborne's demands. Rob was, just by living elsewhere. And if the rest of us weren't so scared, we'd be stopping more carriages, handing out more gold. It felt as if we were only half fighting, and fully loosing.

"So, you told them?" Rob asked, his voice gentle.

Miller shook his head.

Rob's eyebrows rose, his surprise mirrored on the rest of our faces. "Good for you."

"When I woke up after that last beating, the rope around my wrists felt looser. I wriggled my hands and they came free. No one was watching me. They were drinking whiskey around the fire, so I untied my feet and ran."

"Good job," smiled John. "You're so much braver than you realize."

Miller shook his head. "I'm not. I'm stupid." He looked at the ground. "It was too easy, a trap. And I nearly fell in headfirst. Would have, had I not heard one of them following behind me. They weren't drunk. They'd loosened my ties on purpose, so I'd escape and lead them to you." He huffed out a laugh. "Once I knew they were there, I led them all around the forest, but never near any of the places we stay. Then two nights ago, while they slept, I ran. Kept checking they weren't behind me. They weren't, but I stayed away another night just to be sure. Haven't seen them since."

We stared at him in stunned silence. He might be just fourteen, but he was as clever as anyone else sitting around the fire. Not that he cared. There was only one person he wanted to emulate. It wouldn't hurt him to hear he'd done well. "You know, I think you did as good a job at losing them as Rob would have done."

John smiled. "She's right, Miller."

Miller glanced at Rob, then at the others. "Are you serious?"

I nodded and a small smile came to Miller's beaten face. It was the best thing I'd seen all day.

Early the following morning, just as dawn was breaking, I woke to find Rob sitting in the cave, watching me. We'd taken turns staying awake and watching for soldiers last night, just in case they found us. All except Rob, who'd disappeared straight after Miller's story, and Miller, who needed to sleep. Whose ever turn it was now had failed. Or Rob had taken over from them. "Kind of creepy," I whispered, sleepily.

"You love it," Rob whispered back. He beckoned with his head and waited for my response.

I hesitated.

"Come on. I just want to talk."

I was lacing my boots before I'd even nodded in agreement. We left so fast that the only thing I took was my cloak. And the dagger that lived in my boot.

"Should I ask why I woke to find you watching me?" We sat on a log just off the trail, far enough from Black Hole that we wouldn't wake anyone as we talked. The morning was cool, dew settling on every surface, and I pulled my cloak around my body, my hood over my head.

"Because I like the view."

The correct response to that would have been to tell him his comment was inappropriate. I was obviously all out of correct responses. "Do you do it often?" Because, super-creepy. And perhaps a little hot.

His intense green eyes homed in on my face and he shook his head. "Less often than I'd like."

Okay, I really couldn't let that one go. "Rob." I stretched out his name like the warning it was supposed to be.

He held up his hands. "I know. I know. Sorry." He shuffled back a few millimeters and stared silently at the silhouettes the early morning light made of the trees.

"Is there a reason you're, you know, hanging around here watching me sleep like a crazy stalker?" My heart rate had increased the moment his eyes ran across my face and hadn't slowed since. I was so glad he couldn't hear it. With any luck, one day I'd get myself under control around him. Clearly, that day wasn't today.

"Maybe because I am a crazy...whatever you just called me. When I'm around you I definitely feel crazy."

"Rob." I shook my head. He couldn't say things like that. The closeness we'd shared before was gone. We both had things we refused to share which created a wall between us.

"You're angry with me."

A little. But that's not the reason I wanted him to stop. If we were ever going to get back to the easy friendship we'd once shared, we first needed to have a proper conversation. About proper things. "We can't—"

"I know. But you're still angry." He stared at me, waiting.

Fine, then. I was. And since he'd asked, I'd tell him. "You chose someone else, something else. Over them. Over Miller! I know it's not up to me, who you spend your time with, but I just don't understand. Miller was always so important to you." They all were, but the bond between Rob and Miller had been particularly strong.

"Miller *is* still important to me." He shook his head. "And it might look like I have a choice, but I don't. Things have changed, Maryanne. The others understand. I know I haven't given you a reason, but I just need you to trust me. I'm where I need to be. Please don't ask me to explain more. I don't have the answers you want to hear."

I stared off into the distance, debating whether to push him further. In the end, I couldn't let it slide. "Fine. Don't explain to me. But don't fool yourself into thinking everyone else is good with this arrangement. Don't you think it hurts the others to see you choose something else—whatever it is—over them?"

His jaw stiffened. "I imagine it does. Just as it hurts me every time I have to walk away from you all. But this is the only way to keep everyone safe."

"So you keep saying. But Miller wasn't safe. You weren't safe at Oxham. John wasn't safe."

He sighed, looking past me again, his voice softening. "We can't all be like you."

"Meaning?" Because I really had no idea.

"Meaning..." He shrugged. "You inspire me. You're confident, brave and not scared of anything. I'm scared. All the time. I'm running myself ragged trying to do all the things I need to do and failing at every one of them. But you, you went and waited for Miller in a place you knew was dangerous, just because you wanted Miller to feel safe when he came back. You got the others to start robbing carriages again when we've been terrified of the consequences for months. It seems like you just go out there and do whatever you think will upset Gisborne the most." He shook his head. "God. I want so much to be that person, but I'm terrified of who I might lose if I am."

We were all in the same situation. We all felt the same pain when Gisborne hurt one of us.

"They understand the risks, and they think you're worth it. That what you're fighting for is worth it. We all do."

"If Gisborne kills any of—"

"Don't." I put up a hand to stop his words. "You can't think that way, you'll destroy yourself. If it were up to Miller, John and Tuck, you'd never lose them. They'd always be there for you, no matter what." They'd proven that enough times that Rob should know already, but I guessed everyone needed reassurance from time to time.

"And you, Maryanne? Will you be there, no matter what?"

"Does it matter?" The words slipped out before I had a chance to censor them. I wanted to support Rob and his choices. That's what friends did for each other. But somewhere along the way he'd decided he couldn't trust me and that it was easier to lie, to tell me he had a girlfriend, or not tell me anything at all. I clearly wasn't important enough to be privy to that information, and it stung.

He twisted to face me, his knees bumping against mine. "Oh, it matters. It matters more than you'll probably ever know."

Trust in Rob. That's what Mom said to me the day we walked along the beach together. Perhaps it was time to start doing exactly that. "What does that mean?"

"Nothing." His gaze went to my hands cradled in my lap. "It means nothing." He swallowed deeply. "You're right, though. I did come here for a reason. There are some things I need to tell you. And other things I need to ask."

Sticks cracked in the distance. "No! Stop!" A child's terrified voice rang through the forest, followed by the booming voice of a male saying something I couldn't hear. The child cried out again.

I jumped to my feet, torn between hearing whatever Rob was about to tell me and checking the child was all right.

Rob had no such concerns, pulling me back down onto the log beside him. "What are you doing?" he whispered. "There are soldiers out there!"

I dragged my hand from his grip; my decision suddenly easy. "What do you think? There's also a terrified child out there. I'm going to see if he needs help."

"Maryanne." Rob shook his head. "Whatever is happening, it's nothing to do with you." His face was grim, and his hand hovered over me like he wanted to hold me back.

This wasn't the Rob I knew. John and Miller's kidnapping and mutilation had hit him hard. Understandably. I was going to sound harsh, but he needed to move past it. "You've got to stop being terrified of shadows. You're not the only one who has a lot to lose should Gisborne ever find us. Every one of us does. You're just the only one who's chosen not to fight back against all the horrible things he does." I stared at him, hoping he'd jump to his feet and go look for the child. He remained seated on the log.

I shook my head, not caring that he could see how disappointed I was in him. "I refuse to let Gisborne rule my life and then feel guilty afterward because I didn't try. I don't want to keep thinking about what I might have been able to do after the fact." I pulled my dagger from my boot. "And if there is a soldier out there with that child, all the better. After what they did to Miller, I'm in a stabby kind of mood." I stomped away. He could sit there and hide, but I was going to check it out. Children didn't roam the forest alone, not this early in the day, at least. If everything was innocent, I'd leave it as it was. Judging by the child's screams, I doubted that was the case.

The commotion grew louder the closer I got. The child, a boy of about twelve, was crying. There was an older woman with him, probably his mother, pleading for his life. I watched from behind a tree at the side of the trail. Two soldiers, their burgundy and gold cloaks tickling the leafy floor of the forest, stood with their backs to me. One had his sword drawn, while the other was trying to lay the struggling child's hand across an overturned log. Behind the boy, the woman screamed. "No! Please don't. I'll do anything, just please don't take his hand!"

The child bucked and kicked while the soldier fought to hold him.

"Elton's the only one in our family who can work. My husband died. We'll starve if you take his hand." Tears rolled down her face and I sensed her hopelessness. She had no way to fight the soldiers. There were two of them and just one of her, and even if she knew how to use a weapon, they were stronger. There really wasn't anything she could do for her boy.

Branches rattled beside me and Rob stepped onto the trail. His hood was high, his sword hidden beneath his cloak. And the bow I rarely ever saw him without, was nowhere to be seen. "What's going on here?" He stopped behind the soldier in charge.

I smiled. This was the Rob I knew. The one who could put every bit of authority there had ever been into just four words.

The soldiers turned to face him, and my smile disappeared. I took a step back.

Gisborne.

Rob was looking at Gisborne.

 FIFTEEN

I REACHED over my shoulder for an arrow from my quiver. I'd kill the bastard now. My hand came away empty. I'd left so quickly when Rob woke me in the cave this morning that my bow was lying beside my mattress, where I'd left it last night. All I had with me was my dagger.

"Not that it's any of your business, but this child attempted to purchase wheat using stolen gold." Gisborne's sneering voice sent a shiver up my spine. I'd heard his laughter so many times in my dreams these past months, last night included, that it was like putting the dreams on replay.

Rob's shoulders stiffened at the sound of Gisborne's voice. I could almost see him calculating whether he could unsheathe his sword before Gisborne, who was already holding his, cut Rob to pieces.

With his arms relaxed at his sides, Rob said, "Is that true, boy?"

Elton shook his head, hard and fast. "No! I never stole a thing in my life!"

Rob nodded to the guards. "Says he didn't. You should let him go."

"He didn't!" cried the boy's mother, one hand on her son as if she could pull him away from the soldier. "He's not a thief!"

"Ha!" Gisborne's focus was so wholly on the child that he must not have recognized Rob's voice. I gripped my dagger tighter just in case Gisborne suddenly realized. "He'd say anything to save his hand!"

Rob inclined his head, perhaps letting Gisborne think he agreed.

"I didn't lie! Or steal!" cried Elton. "It was given to me."

My heart dropped. I knew where Elton's gold had come from.

Me. Us. They mustn't have melted it down like we told them to.

I wished I hadn't come searching for the crying child. I was about to witness the consequences of not heeding Gisborne's warnings.

Yet, Rob wasn't ready to give up. "It's a little harsh to take his hand, don't you think? He's only a boy. And he says he didn't do it." He aimed his question at the other soldier. Probably safer than looking at Gisborne, even with his hood up.

Gisborne whirled on him. "Do you really think I'm that stupid? The child has in his possession gold with Lord Herman's crest stamped into it. Lord Herman was robbed right here in the forest earlier this week." Gisborne glared at Rob as if to say, you make the connection.

I wondered if Rob realized this was the gold his friends had stolen. Probably.

Rob laughed. It sounded harsh and not like Rob at all. "You think a scrawny boy could force Lord Herman to hand over all his gold? Surely you underestimate the power of a man protecting his fortune."

"The boy has the gold in his possession. That's all I need to know." Gisborne turned away. Conversation over. "Hold the boy's arm against the log," he demanded of the other soldier while he readied his sword.

Elton's mother screamed. She was long since past the point of making any sense. Tears streamed down her face and my heart broke for her.

I flexed my grip on my dagger, focusing on the point between Gisborne's shoulder blades. I would run out and stab Gisborne before I let him take the boy's hand.

Rob clearly had a similar idea. With a ringing that split the early morning birdsong, he drew his sword and in one motion, brought it down on the arm of the soldier holding the boy. The soldier screamed and dropped to the leaf-covered ground, blood spurting from his wound.

"Run." Rob spoke calmly to the boy before turning to block the blow already coming from Gisborne.

As he turned, his hood fell back. For a split second, I thought Gisborne's surprise at seeing his brother might have been enough to give Rob the advantage, but Gisborne didn't waver. If anything, his blows came harder. Faster. "Well, well," he said, breathing heavily. "If it isn't my big brother. I've been looking everywhere for you."

Rob was a good swordsman, well above average. Gisborne was his match or better in every way. Probably because he'd benefited from training Rob hadn't had after he was cast out into the forest to die. But anger and hatred were powerful motivators driving Rob's every move. Each blow by one was blocked by the other.

They circled each other, using the moment to catch their breath. "You're going to die today." Gisborne sneered.

"One of us will, but it won't be me." Rob bounced on his toes, circling Gisborne.

I checked the image from my dreams. Could *this* be the place I kept seeing? The time of day was right, possibly a fraction earlier than I'd imagined but close enough. But the rest, no. Not possible. The place in my dreams was open, on a slight hill, not on a flat trail surrounded by trees. And he never died by a sword. It was always an arrow in his back.

It didn't make me feel any better. I'd begun to wonder if the location didn't matter. Based on what I was currently seeing, that was potentially true.

Gisborne swung at Rob, the clash of their blades making my ears ring.

My mind raced and I wished I'd never heard that boy crying. I wished I'd never brought Rob this close to Gisborne.

Rob stumbled, the trail a mess of holes and rutted ground beneath his feet. He regained his footing immediately, but Gisborne pounced, hitting Rob with three fast swings and knocking the sword from his hand. It fell on the dirt with a soft thud.

This was bad. I flexed my hand on my dagger. I needed to do something; I just wasn't sure how much damage I could do with such a small weapon.

OUTPLAYED

Rob scrambled for his sword, but Gisborne was quicker, kicking it along the trail and raising his sword.

I pushed through the bracken and yelled at the top of my voice. "Stop." He would not kill Rob. I refused to let him. I'd seen it too many times these past months to sit back and watch it happen when I could do something about it.

Maud's face still affected Gisborne. He turned to me and his expression softened for just a moment. Then he caught himself. His shoulders stiffened and he jeered. "I won't fall for that again." He turned his back and brought his sword down hard and fast. Rob scrambled away, backwards on hands and feet, but not fast enough. Gisborne's sword sliced into his thigh.

Never until the day I die, will I forget the scream that ripped from Rob's lips. It almost split me in two. And it lit an anger inside me like I'd never felt before. An anger that made my hands shake and my breath tremble from my lips. Anger that refused to allow Gisborne the final say, no matter what. Anger that turned from molten lava into something cold and hard.

Gisborne raised his sword again.

"Gisborne." This time, I spoke softly the way Tabitha had suggested, trying to sound as much like Maud as possible. I had few options to get him away from Rob, especially without my bow, but I would use those I had to the very best of my ability. Rob was always calm when he dealt with Gisborne. I was going to be the same. "Gisborne, it's me. Maud."

Mid-swing, Gisborne stopped. "No. Maud would never live out here in the forest. She'd never go with him." He spat the final word and raised his sword again. But I knew I had him. Otherwise, he wouldn't have stopped.

"It really is me. How can I prove it to you?"

Gisborne stalled. He wanted me to be her, his voice saying one thing, his actions another. "You can't. I know it wasn't you at the tournament. Eliza explained."

"Did she also explain that after I caught the two of you together, after I scratched her face, she followed me into the forest then had her witch of a sister send me away? Did she tell you she banished me to another place where I barely survived?"

Gisborne turned, his eyes wary. She had told him that. Whether he believed or not was a different story, but his eyebrows lifted to hear the same from me.

"I've been trying to get back here ever since." I held up my left hand, thanking my good luck and the stars that Maud had given me her engagement ring. And that Tabitha made me wear it. "I wouldn't have this if I wasn't your fiancé, would I?"

He blinked and stepped toward me. "The ring? You still have it?" He shook his head. "She didn't have it. The other...you."

I nodded, taking a careful step toward him. My heart hammered and my breath came in short, sharp bursts. I pulled my hand back under my cloak so Gisborne couldn't see it shaking. Rob's life relied on me getting this right.

Rob groaned quietly on the ground, but I couldn't look at him, not if I wanted Gisborne to believe me. And I needed him to believe. "That wasn't me. You know that. But I'm back now. Of course, I have your ring. I've worn it every day for the past two years. It means everything to me." My other hand gripped the little knife beneath my cloak, waiting for the right moment. "Will you please take me home?"

Gisborne's eyes jumped between my face and the place where his ring hid beneath my cloak. He held out his hand.

I smiled, wide and long, needing him to think I was looking at the best sight I'd ever seen. When he nodded and smiled back, I knew I had him. Keeping my eyes locked with his, I whipped out my knife and aimed for the soft skin beneath his ribs. At the last second, he saw it and twisted away. Not fast enough, though. I drove the knife into his upper arm, twisting it as it went in. "That's for hurting Rob."

"You little bitch!" he screamed, staggering as he glanced down at the knife sticking from his body. But it didn't slow him down as much as I'd hoped. Or at all, actually. He drew back his sword and swung at me, grunting with the force. I dodged, and only the tip scratched my arm.

Hatred lit his eyes. I'd fooled him again and this time, he wasn't going to let me away with it. He advanced on me.

"Run, Maryanne." Rob's voice was rough, weak. I needed him to hold on. I'd get us out of this. Exactly how, was yet to be decided.

"It's okay. I've got this." I threw him a quick smile. Or at least something I hoped looked like a smile, because this wasn't looking good. That quick glance at Rob had shown me blood running from the cut on his leg and soaking into the ground beneath him. I no longer had a weapon, and in another moment, Gisborne would be close enough to slash me with his sword.

But with that glance, I also saw Rob's sword lying where Gisborne had kicked it into the middle of the trail behind me. I dived for it, gripping the handle so tight my hands ached, and whirled around on Gisborne, the sword out in front of me. I put everything into that blow, hoping to connect. Gisborne saw it coming and danced out of the way with a smirk.

"Now I'm certain you're not Maud. She would never pick up a sword, let alone attempt to use one." Gisborne shook his head in disgust.

"Gisborne!" Rob's voice was stronger than I expected, stronger than I'd thought possible from that glimpse at him a moment ago.

Gisborne's eyes flicked to Rob, looking away from me for the briefest of moments. It was all I needed. I raised Rob's sword and brought it down toward Gisborne. I aimed for the place his neck and shoulder met, but Rob's sword was heavy, and my aim was bad. It bit into Gisborne's arm, just above the place I'd shoved my dagger into him.

He screamed, dropping to his knees and clutching his bleeding arm, shouting expletives at me.

I didn't care. This was the opportunity we needed. I turned to Rob, expecting to see him on his feet based on the strength of his voice a moment ago. But no. He was lying on the ground where he'd fallen, eyes closed and breathing fast. It had cost him a lot to draw Gisborne's attention from me. I wasn't going to waste whatever time it had brought us.

I dropped the sword and rushed to Rob, crouching beside him. "Rob. We have to go. Can you walk?" I glanced over my shoulder. The soldier Rob had injured was lying quietly on the ground, either dead or passed out from pain. Gisborne was clutching his wound with one hand while trying to use the other hand to get at something on his belt, probably first aid supplies. His injured arm wasn't working properly, and he let out a growl, released his grip on the bleeding wound and used the other hand to pull out some bandages. We didn't have much time. "Rob?"

Rob nodded. "I'm fine." His face was pale, but at least the blood wasn't spurting from his wound. Gisborne had missed Rob's artery. I took his good arm and put it over my shoulder, helping him off the ground.

"Get back here!" Gisborne screamed, wrapping the bandage around his arm.

I pulled Rob along the trail. Gisborne might not be able to use both arms, but he could run, and that was something we couldn't do. Rob could barely walk. He dragged his injured leg behind him, grunting with each step.

I glanced behind us again. Gisborne was attempting to tie off the bandage using one hand. "Come on." I urged Rob forward with my arm around his waist, while I searched the ground for a rock. I'd use anything to keep us both alive.

The trail turned, and Gisborne disappeared from view. I cast my hearing wide, listening for his footsteps as I tried not to think about how bad Rob's wound might be. And what we'd need to do to keep him alive.

Instead of Gisborne's feet, horse's hooves pounded on the trail behind us. "Here." I dragged Rob into the bracken, pushing him to the ground. I picked up a stick and stood sentry, hidden behind a tree. I wasn't dying here today. Not without a fight, at least.

The horse slowed and came to a stop beside us. "Rob? Maryanne?" Tuck called into the undergrowth.

"Tuck?" I let out a huge breath. I'd expected the rider to be a soldier.

"Come out," he called. "It's only me. I took Gisborne's horse. It was tied up farther along the trail."

"Rob's hurt." I stepped out from behind the tree so Tuck could see me.

His lips shifted into a thin line. "I know. I heard him scream."

"And Gisborne's not badly injured. He'll be here in a moment, I imagine." My grip was still tight around the stick.

"He's a little more injured than he was a moment ago." Tuck climbed off the horse, his bow in one hand. "I hit him with an arrow on the way past. Just above the shoulder blade."

Now he mentioned it, Gisborne's yells had changed. They were still angry and expletive-ridden, but pain-slurred as well.

"Bad shot, Tuck," murmured Rob, pulling himself to sitting. "Should have aimed for his heart."

"I did," said Tuck. "But the noises you made earlier had me half scared out of my wits."

"Didn't make any noises," mumbled Rob, as we helped him to his feet. His breath came in shallow, fast gasps, and his skin was paler than I'd ever seen it.

"We need to stop the bleeding," I said, hoping I'd hidden any fear from my voice. Rob's pale color could be from blood loss or shock. Either way, we needed to attend to his injuries.

Tuck made an affirmative sound in his throat. "We have to get away from here first, so Gisborne's men can't find us. Help me get him on the horse. I'll take him to the apple grove near Mansfield. You go back to the cave, find John and Miller and meet us there."

"I don't know where the grove is." Panic rose inside of me at the thought of them leaving me alone in the forest with Gisborne nearby. Panic that made me want to curl into a ball and close my eyes.

"John and Miller know. Just find them." Tuck eyed the horse, probably considering the best way to heft Rob on its back.

"I can't," I whispered. What if they'd heard Rob's cry and gone searching for him, the way Tuck had? What if they'd followed Tuck to find the horse? What if they weren't at Black Hole anymore? I couldn't hide in the forest alone, not with Gisborne angry and searching. Not when they were riding off to safety without me.

Tuck ducked out from under Rob's arm, looking at me. "I'll help him on from this side. You go around the other side of the horse in case he overbalances."

I stood still. They were leaving me alone, with Gisborne nearby.

"Maryanne." Rob adjusted his weight to his good leg and turned to look at me. "You can do this. If you don't, John and Miller won't know what happened to me. Or where we've gone." His voice was slurring, and he wobbled on his feet.

I shook my head. He had far too much faith in me. I could hide. But I couldn't run through the forest to find the others.

He ducked into my vision, something that must have been close to impossible with his injury.

"Weren't you the one just telling me to face my fears?"

I had told him to do that, and look where it had gotten us. "You shouldn't have listened."

"I should have, because it needed to be said. And, so does this." His words slurred again, and he wobbled so much I threw my other hand out to steady him. "You are more than capable of finding our friends and bringing them to Tuck and me. You're not going to cower here on the side of the trail waiting for Gisborne to find you. All right?"

I nodded. What choice did I have?

"Good." He blinked three times, like he was clearing his vision. "Now, get me on that horse before I pass out."

Rob wasn't joking about passing out. Whatever strength he'd found to talk to me and then get onto the horse, left him the moment he was seated. He wobbled so much, Tuck had to grab hold of him as he climbed on behind.

"You need to stop the bleeding." I looked up at Tuck. The leg of Rob's pants was wet with his blood.

"I know." Tuck's reply was terse; he was as worried as I was. And that worried me all the more.

"You need to make a tourniquet." He stared blankly at me. "A bandage that you tie tightly up higher than the bleeding."

"Yes," said Tuck, like he knew already.

"And you need to clean it. The wound. Maybe with whiskey?" My mind was racing. "And use clean linen for bandages. Everything needs to be clean." My words were getting faster and faster as I realized I wouldn't be in control of Rob's recovery. Infection was a killer in the twelfth century. I didn't want him to die.

Tuck's reply was soft. Softer than I'd ever heard him speak. "It's all right. I know what to do. I've done it before."

I glanced again at the blood on Rob's leg, too scared to ask how often he'd dealt with wounds this bad.

John and Miller were waiting at Black Hole. I'd been terrified for no reason. They'd packed up everyone's gear and were ready to leave the moment I arrived. As we walked, I relayed the morning's events. They listened in silence as if they already knew what I would tell them. They probably did. Tuck had sent me back to them alone, with a message to meet them at the apple grove. Combined with Rob's scream when Gisborne's sword hit him, it didn't take much to guess what had happened.

When I finished speaking, Miller nodded at my arm and said, "You're bleeding."

"It's just a graze." Gisborne's sword had cut a slit in my tunic, right through to my skin. My blood had soaked through the surrounding tunic making it wet and cold. Something I hadn't noticed until Miller reminded me of the cut.

"You should bandage it. We've got a long walk ahead." The bruises on Miller's face were already turning from purple to yellow. It was good to hear him focusing on something else, even if he shouldn't be worried for me.

I nodded, taking the cloth he held out and winding it around my arm before following him along the trail toward the apple grove. I'd clean it properly once we were somewhere Gisborne couldn't find us.

Once, a long time ago, someone had built a home in the apple grove. No one lived here now, but a tiny hut stood in the center of the grove. After the caves we'd been sleeping in since I returned, this was practically luxury.

The apple grove was Miller's favorite place in the whole forest, and he'd talked about it non-stop while we walked. It probably helped put Rob further back in his mind, and it eased some of my worry to hear light in Miller's voice after days of lifelessness.

Gisborne's horse, munching grass at the edge of the grove eased my worry further. They were here. Gisborne hadn't captured them.

Tuck strode outside when he heard our voices. The neck of his robe was dark with sweat and his forehead creased into a frown. "I need firewood." The lack of pleasantries, or even a greeting, made me stride toward the little hut to check on Rob.

John and Miller dropped their packs and retreated into the forest without another word.

"How is he?" I asked to Tuck's back. He'd turned back to the hut the moment John and Miller left.

"See for yourself."

Rob sat with his legs out in front of him, his back resting against a wall that was cracked and badly in need of repair work. Beside him was a stone-lined fireplace that was cold and empty. There was no chimney, just a small hole in the roof—I really hoped there was no rain on the way.

Around Rob's leg was a tourniquet, as well as another blood-smeared bandage covering the wound. A pile of linen, also covered in blood, lay beside him. The corners of his lips were pinched with pain, and he focused on an invisible spot beside his feet we entered.

I turned to Tuck. "I thought you knew how to fix him."

"I do," snarled Tuck.

"Well...?" Because he wasn't fixed. Rob was no different to how he'd been a couple of hours ago when I last saw him.

"We haven't been here long. We couldn't ride fast because Rob was having trouble staying on the horse."

That would explain the empty fireplace and Rob's bleeding wound.

Tuck ran his hands down his face, his voice softer when he spoke again. "I need to cauterize it, but every time I go in search of firewood, he tries to follow. Makes the wound start bleeding again."

"Got to look out for you in case Gisborne followed." Rob's words slurred together, worse than he'd slurred earlier.

I glanced at Tuck. There was no way Rob could look out for anyone in his present state. I was surprised he could walk. He must be delirious with pain.

Tuck shook his head, dropping his voice. "If I don't do this soon, things are going to get bad. I'm pretty sure it's just the pain bothering him at the moment, but the longer I leave it, the greater risk of infection."

Tuck didn't have to tell me. I understood all too well. I started for the door. "I'll go help them with the firewood."

He stopped me with a hand on my arm. "If Rob wouldn't let me go on my own, he's not going to let you."

I glanced at Rob. In his pain-riddled state, he mustn't have realized Miller and John were here and already searching for firewood.

The hut was well set up with six crudely formed hammocks strung side-by-side between poles, and pots and pans on a shelf above the fire. I picked up one of the pots. "I'll go and get some water to boil." At least that would make me feel like I was helping. And the river was close enough to see from the hut, just a short walk through the apple grove.

Tuck nodded in agreement.

By the time I got back, John and Miller had returned, dumped their arms full of wood and left again. Tuck was coaxing a flame from the tinder, a large flat-bladed knife lying beside the fire.

Rob's eyes were closed, his hands balled into fists.

"How do we do this?" I whispered to Tuck.

Tuck glanced over his shoulder at Rob. "It's going to hurt like hell, so I might need you to hold him down. If the others aren't back, that is."

Once the fire was roaring, and the water in the pot had boiled, I cleaned Rob's wound. It was a straight cut, and so far, showed no sign of infection. No matter how gentle I was, his body stiffened with pain whenever I touched him. I'd never been so glad to see Miller and John arrive back—we would all help Rob through the next part.

Tuck pulled the knife from the fire. In silence the rest of us took hold of Rob—Miller gripping his ankle, John his hips and me his chest. Without a word of warning, Tuck pressed the knife to the wound. Rob bucked and screamed, and although the sound tore at my heart, it was short. I glanced at Tuck. He nodded.

It was done.

I sighed, feeling like I could breathe for the first time in hours. I bandaged the wound, and John and Tuck moved Rob onto the hammock closest to the fire.

John, with a few quiet words to Tuck, walked out the door with his pack on his back. He didn't say where he was going, and no one seemed to have the energy to ask.

I sat on the dirt floor next to Tuck in front of the fire, watching Rob doze. "He'll be okay now?"

"Hopefully." Tuck shrugged. "Won't know until morning."

I kept my eyes on Rob, waiting to see his chest rise and fall, the stress of the day catching up with me. A tear escaped down my cheek. He couldn't die. There were things I needed to tell him.

"He's alive, Maryanne. There's no infection. That's all we can hope for at the moment," Tuck said, gently. Probably the kindest tone he'd ever used with me.

Rob was no longer pale, and the bleeding had stopped. Still, I wasn't taking any chances. "I'll watch him for a bit if you want some fresh air."

Our peace of mind didn't last long. Minutes after we'd all settled into our hammocks for the night, Rob cried out. I slid out of my hammock, the ground freezing against my bare feet, and ran the few steps to Rob, my way lit by the glowing coals of the fire. Tuck was faster, beating me there.

He swore under his breath.

I took Rob's hand, then touched my fingers to Rob's forehead.

Fever.

Tuck unwrapped the bandages around his wound. Even in the dim light, it was red and angry. He swore again.

"Miller," Tuck called. "We need to get..." Tuck stopped himself and I knew what he'd been about to say.

A healer.

We needed a healer because Rob's wound was infected.

I shook my head. We weren't sending Miller. Not after what happened last time. Tuck caught my eye, then spoke almost to himself. "I'll go."

I released Rob's hand and nodded toward the fire. "Miller. Bring me that pot of water." I pulled my first aid kit from my pack and wet one of the bandages in it, pressing it to Rob's head.

He growled and pushed it away, curling into a ball without opening his eyes. "Cold. Too cold."

Tuck pulled on his boots, watching Rob with a set jaw.

I didn't want to risk Tuck's life by sending him out into the forest alone in search of a healer. And I didn't want Rob to die. "Wait," I called. "I can help him."

Tuck's eyebrows lifted. "Cool cloths won't fix that infection. A healer's the only one who could. And even then..." He shook his head. A healer might not save Rob, either.

I riffled through my first aid kit. "No, but these will."

Carrie had insisted I bring antibiotics in my first aid kit. We didn't know any doctors personally and telling a medical professional I was about to travel eight hundred years back in time would probably have gotten me a different type of medication. Instead, she made an appointment with our family doctor, made him believe she had a urine infection—I had no idea how she pulled it off—and he gave her a course of antibiotics. Which she gave to me.

One course. Five tablets.

Make sure you don't die, she'd said as she handed them to me. I hoped she'd agree that keeping Rob alive was just as important.

I held up the tablets, and Tuck scoffed.

"I don't know what they are, but I know they can't help my friend."

"Please, Tuck." I tipped a tablet from the container into my palm. "Just give me this chance." I met his eyes. "You know I'm going to do everything I can to save him. This is what we use for infection in my time."

Tuck blew out a breath and walked over to the fire, throwing a log on and raking up the coals. "If he dies..."

"He won't." I'd never hoped more that I was right.

Sixteen

I WOKE, three nights later, down at the river. My feet were soaking in the icy water and my dripping clothes stuck to my body. I didn't remember coming down here. Must have sleepwalked. And taken a sleep swim. I'd been dreaming of Rob dying with an arrow in his back over and again, I remembered that much. At least swimming made the dream disappear.

Shivering, I trudged back to the hut, kicking my saturated boots off at the door. I glanced at Rob, sleeping in his hammock by the fire, his face peaceful and relaxed. His fever had broken, and his wound was no longer red and puffy. He was through the worst thanks to Carrie, though he'd done nothing but sleep these past few days.

I threw another log on the fire and watched the flames dance and catch on the dry bark, the warmth soothing on my cold skin. Shaking off my wet clothes, I lay them in front of the fire to dry. I wrapped my cloak around my shoulders—the cold fabric making my teeth chatter—and moved closer to the flames to warm up and lie down.

I hadn't even closed my eyes before the dreams returned. This time Rob's death was interspersed with the villagers from Oxham, the letter G carved into their faces, showing off their injuries. Eye sockets without eyes, mouths without tongues, hands without fingers. And always Gisborne's laughter.

"Maryanne. Maryanne. Maryanne!" The villagers knew my name, called it over and over. They wanted my attention; I wanted to look away. The dream wouldn't allow it. I was stuck here. Trapped, looking at their injuries or watching Rob die.

I fought against it, finally dragging my eyes open to find Rob awake and sitting on the ground beside me, his injured leg sticking out in front of him. His hand was on my forehead and he stared at me with frown lines between his eyes. "Maryanne? Are you okay?"

I nodded and pushed myself up to sit. "I'm fine. How are you?" It was good to see him awake.

The frown didn't move as he watched me before finally nodding. "I'm feeling okay. Sore, but okay. Unlike you, I think."

Miller sprinted into the hut, a pot in his hand. "I got the water you asked for. Does she need cold cloths, like you did, Rob?"

"I'm fine, Miller." I rubbed my eyes. I wouldn't admit it, but I still felt like I was inside my dreams. "I didn't mean to wake you."

Rob touched his palm to my forehead again. "You're not fine. You have a fever."

A laugh bubbled up from my chest. That was absurd. "There's nothing wrong with me." Apart from the dreams.

Rob raised an eyebrow. "Really? So how do you explain your pants and tunic?" He nodded to them, lying in front of the fire.

I folded my cloak tighter around my body. Now he mentioned it, I did recall swimming in the river then removing my clothes. Which meant I was close to naked beneath the cloak. "I was hot. I went for a swim." I felt a little warm now, especially when reminded of my nakedness.

Rob beckoned Miller closer. "You're not fine, Maryanne. But you will be soon. Put your clothes on so you can take off your cloak. We need to cool you down."

I shook my head. It was sore and heavy. I needed a drink, but apart from that, I was okay. "How's your leg?"

Rob looked pointedly at my clothes then gingerly turned away. His message was clear. He'd talk once I was dressed.

I pulled on my clothes – now mostly dry. My arm was tender where Gisborne's sword had nicked me. I'd cleaned it each day since we arrived at the apple grove, as well as smearing it with anti-bacterial cream from my first aid kit. It was nothing to worry about. A scratch compared to the wound he'd given Rob. "Dressed," I said.

"Good. Miller, wet some linen and wrap her in it. It should cool her down."

"No, Miller, don't." I didn't need their fussing. Apart from a slight headache and a sore arm, and feeling sluggish when I moved, there was nothing wrong with me. If they'd let me lie down and sleep like I wanted to, my headache would be gone by morning.

"Your...arm." Miller pointed. "It's bleeding."

I looked down. The sleeve on my tunic was wet and red. I must have removed the bandage when

I went swimming. As if reminded the wound existed, my arm began to throb.

Rob shuffled closer. "Jesus, Maryanne. What happened?" He took my arm.

I pulled away. "I'm fine."

"I don't think you are. Did Gisborne do this?" He rolled up my sleeve, easing it gently over the wound. Then he let out a quiet curse. "Okay. Change of plan. Miller, wake Tuck. Tell him he needs to go get the healer from Mansfield and bring him here. And bring me the whiskey bottle." He cursed again.

I glanced at my arm. It was throbbing badly now.

Gisborne's sword had slashed from one side all the way to the other. The cut wasn't deep. But it was puffy, and the edges were red and angry. I knew what that meant, and it terrified me. Especially because there were no more antibiotics in my first aid kit. "It's infected." I shook my head. How had this happened? I'd been careful with it, cleaned it each day.

Rob's face was grim as he took the whiskey bottle from Miller. "This might hurt." He took hold of my upper arm and poured the alcohol over it.

I bit back the scream that wanted to tear from my body. "Ouch," I whispered. Understatement.

"Sorry. I need to do that again." Rob glanced at Miller. "Miller, can you bring me the pills Maryanne gave me. There's still a couple left, and she needs them more than me."

I shook my head. "You have to finish them. Or your infection will come back. Anyway, there's not enough left to fix me."

After that, things grew hazy. I was cold again, but Rob insisted on draping me with freezing, wet linen. I protested, but he did it anyway. I remember curling up into a ball and shaking so hard the world distorted and I had to close my eyes. All that did was give the dreams an opening to return, and I watched Rob die, again and again.

If the dreams allowed it and I opened my eyes, Rob was always right there beside me, his face pale and lips pressed into a thin line as he held my hand, his injured leg propped out in front of him. He kept telling me the healer would be here soon, and I would be fine.

It was a lie. There was nothing a healer could do to fix my infected arm, or stop the infection spreading. "I don't want to die," I rasped.

"Good," said Rob, dribbling some water into my mouth. "Because I'm not planning on letting you. There's a carriage coming through the forest in a day or two, carrying more gold than we've ever seen. I'm going to need your help to stop it."

That carriage would have to come and go. Neither Rob nor I would be in any state to be there. Maybe I wouldn't ever stop a carriage again.

I must have slept a little because it was suddenly the middle of the day and the healer was here. He looked at my arm and frowned.

Rob climbed unsteadily to his feet and took the healer aside. I didn't hear what they said, but Rob reached into the neck of his tunic and pulled out the chain where his mother's wedding ring hung. He'd shown it to me once, when he spoke of his mother, but mostly he kept it hidden beneath his clothing.

When the healer nodded, Rob pulled the chain from around his neck and pressed it into his hand, shaking it vigorously.

No! He'd kept that ring safe for all the years he'd lived in the forest and he had so few reminders of his mother. He couldn't give it away.

I couldn't make any noise though. Or if I did, no one listened, and soon they moved me off the floor into one of the hammocks and the healer hovered over me, while Rob, Tuck and Miller crowded behind him.

"Are you sure about this?" asked Miller, disgust filling his voice.

The healer made a sound in his throat while looking inside his bag.

"But…" Both hesitation *and* disgust from Miller, now. Whatever was happening couldn't be good.

I started to sit up, but a firm hand—not sure who's—held me down. I tried to ask what was happening, but my mouth was so dry, and my tongue so huge, I couldn't form the words.

The healer took my arm. "This might hurt a little," he mumbled.

Burning pain shot through my arm as he pushed his fingers into my wound. It felt like he was digging in right down to the bone. I pulled at my arm trying to get away, but someone held it tight and placed a cold cloth on my forehead.

"That's the worst bit." The healer's voice floated down to me. "Just had to open the wound a little." His hand moved over my arm, gentle this time.

Footsteps pounded, sprinting from the hut and I opened my eyes—didn't recall closing them—just as Tuck disappeared outside. The sound of retching drifted into us.

"Tuck never did have a strong stomach," Rob said, lightly. But his cheeks were pale and his lips pinched, and he kept looking from my arm to the door where Tuck had disappeared.

I moved my head, the motion catching Rob's attention. He met my eyes. "Hi," he whispered. "The healer is just…healing you."

"With maggots! He's putting them inside your wound!" added Miller, disgust and awe mixing in his voice.

Yuck. I shook my head. I didn't want maggots in the same room as me, let alone inside my body. I pulled my arm away, but someone held it tight. "Just relax and lie still."

Rob spoke softly, his voice close to my ear. "It's all right, Maryanne. You're going to be fine."

I slept after that. Properly, without dreams. When I woke, it was dark. Tuck and Miller were sleeping, but Rob was sitting beside my hammock, the way I'd sat beside his. He held my hand in his, twisting Maud's ring around my finger. "Where did you get this?" he whispered.

"Maud," I croaked. "She's living with my family." I wanted to tell him how she'd pretended to be me, but Josh knew she was a fake, but my mouth was too dry.

Or maybe I did tell him, because the next time I opened my eyes, Rob swiped away a tear and whispered, "Josh loves you as much as you love him." He squeezed my hand. "Don't die, Maryanne," he whispered. "You can't die. It's not supposed to go this way."

How's it supposed to go? I tried to ask, but my mouth had gone dry again. My tongue felt huge, and the words wouldn't form.

"There are things I need to tell you. Things I shouldn't have kept from you. I thought you were her, and I've been so stupid. But I know now." He swiped a hand across his cheek. "Live, Maryanne. Give me the chance to explain. Please."

He sat in silence for a long time, just watching me. I might have slept again, but I woke to hear him talking. "I missed you so much while you were gone. I miss you since you came back, too. I want..." He shook his head and his voice turned hard. "I'll kill him. If you die, I'll march right into Nottingham and kill my bastard brother. I don't care what they'd do to me for it. It won't matter, if you're dead."

Seventeen

My eyes fluttered open to Miller stoking the fire. My throat was drier than the desert sands and I was ravenous. I sat up, swinging my legs over the side of the hammock, the foggy haze gone from my mind along with the fever and infection. "I'm so thirsty." My voice was a rasp in my throat.

Miller turned, a grin splitting his face. "The maggots worked." He shook his head, like he couldn't quite believe it. "The healer put them in your arm, and they ate all the dead flesh including the infection."

I screwed up my nose. That was something I really didn't need to hear. "Thanks for the visual." I held back a shiver. It was far too easy to imagine those tiny little grains of rice crawling around inside my arm and eating the dead tissue. It made me feel ill. "Are you sure he removed them all?" Because, it might be my imagination, but it felt like there was still something crawling around in the wound.

"Certain," smiled Miller. "He checked before he left."

I shivered again at the thought, then looked around the empty hut. "Where is everyone?"

"John's hunting." Miller put up a hand as if he knew what I was going to say. "Before you get too incited, he's using a slingshot, not his bow."

I couldn't help but smile. "I'll always be *excited* to hear you mix up words and tell me John is feeling better." Maybe Miller had done some healing of his own while he was waiting for me to recuperate. "Where's Tuck? And Rob?"

Miller scratched the back of his neck. "Tuck's…out. And Rob's…"

The door to the hut opened, and Rob stood on the threshold, the late afternoon sun at his back. "Thought I heard voices." His eyes fell on me. "You're all right." He let out a breath so deep, his shoulders shook.

I nodded. I felt so much better. "So are you."

He continued to look at me as if he'd never seen me before. Or perhaps like he'd never expected to see me again. "The infection's gone and my leg is healing well."

"Thank you," I whispered. "For using your mother's ring to pay for the healer. I'll repay you. I promise." I was so happy to see him standing up. I'd been terrified for him, and even once his fever broke, I'd still worried he might not recover.

He shook his head. "No need. You saved me with the pills. I'd say we're even."

I nodded as we continued to take each other in.

He took a hesitant step forward. "We need to talk, Maryanne. There's some things you need to know."

Miller got to his feet, as if he was going to leave to give us privacy, but Rob shook his head and motioned for him to sit. "Not now, Miller. I have to relieve Tuck."

"But, I thought since Maryanne is better, you'd wait another day…"

Rob shook his head. "You know I'd stay if I could."

"You're leaving?" Going to whatever it was that was dividing his loyalties. "Are you sure you're well enough?"

He gave a slow nod. "Tuck's been there for the past few days. John was there before him. It's time." His lips flickered like he was trying to smile, but his eyes were sad. "Sorry."

OUTPLAYED

There were two ways to deal with this. Act like a baby and sulk or be the friend I wanted to be for him. "Don't be." I gave him a proper smile. "You've done more than enough since I got sick. And Miller and I should get dinner started, anyway." Once I got out of this hammock. "Be careful."

He pulled his quiver over his shoulder and picked up his bow. "See you in a few days. Then, we'll talk. Okay?"

I nodded.

"Bye, Miller."

Miller, his face completely healed now, didn't even acknowledge Rob's goodbye, instead busying himself with making the fire burn hotter, smoke wafting through the hut. Rob cast a final glance in my direction, then walked out the door, shutting it quietly behind him.

Miller kneeled in front of the fire, a log in his hand. His shoulders were tight with tension.

"Are you all right?" I thought Miller was angry, though I couldn't see his face. Whether it was because of Rob leaving, or something else, I wasn't sure.

He stood and threw the log at the door so hard, the top hinge shattered, and the door fell sideways, held in place by just the bottom hinge.

Definitely angry. "Miller?"

"I'm fine." He crossed his arms over his chest.

I stood and made my unsteady way over to him. "Why don't you sit down for a bit? Relax. I'll look after the fire." I watched him from the corner of my eye, as I bent and placed a piece of wood on the fire. His cheeks were a mottled pink and his body hummed with tension. *Fine* was not the word I would use to describe him at this second.

He watched me for a moment then sighed and went to his pack. Pulling out the book I'd given him, he lay down on his hammock.

I let out a breath. He could get lost in that book for hours, by which time he'd have let go of his anger at Rob.

"It's shit, you know." Miller stood, glaring at me with the book in one hand.

"What is?" As if I couldn't guess.

"Rob."

It was. Miller had been through a horrible ordeal at Gisborne's hand, and Rob had always made him feel safe. It stood to reason he'd be upset and scared to see Rob striding off without a backward glance. I had no words of comfort for him. All I had were the words Rob had given me. "He's trying to protect the people he loves. You know that."

Miller shook his head. "He says that, but it's not true. If he cared, he'd be here with us, not..."

He threw his arms in the air, as if that explained where Rob had gone.

"I think leaving is a very hard decision for Rob. I think he really wants to be here but feels obligated to be elsewhere." I was surprised to find, I believed what I said. Rob kept spending time with us in between going wherever it was he went. He wouldn't come to us if he didn't want to.

"Well, then, he should grow a pair!" Pink flooded Miller's cheeks again. "No one is in charge of him. He can do what he wants. If he wants to be here, he should say so, and then do it!" His voice grew louder and more agitated, and the hand that held his book shook with fury.

We were deep in the forest, and far from any of the main trails, but it was never wise to risk anything by raising a voice. "Miller." I put my hand out walking carefully toward him, hoping to calm him the way I'd calm a scared animal. "It's okay. The rest of us are here for you." That was really what this was about. He felt abandoned. I couldn't even blame him for thinking that way; I felt pretty abandoned every time Rob left, too.

He batted my hand away and raised his voice anyway. "I don't need you! I don't even want you! Or anyone. I can look after myself perfectly well. Rob got along fine when he was my age. I can do the same." Glaring at me, he tossed his book at the fire.

"Miller, no!" I scrambled after it. He might be angry now, but he'd be devastated to lose it once he calmed down.

The book landed at the edge of the embers, the top right corner catching alight immediately. I scooped it out with my fingers and picked up my boot—sitting in front of the fire—to put the flames out. When I looked up again, Miller had pushed through the broken door and was gone.

The top corner of the first half of the book was burnt. There were singe marks all over the front cover and it was blackened with soot. Plus, I'd burned my hand as I plucked it from the embers.

My burn was easy enough to fix. The same remedy as if I were at home—cold water, from the pot beside the fire. The burnt book was an entirely different matter.

"What happened?" John asked, his eyes on the sagging door as he sidled inside. "And, hello, milady. It's good to see you feeling better."

I gave him a weak smile from my seat on the floor and pulled my hand from the pot of water. "Miller's a little upset."

"He burned you?"

I shook my head and held up his book. "I said the wrong thing, annoyed him and he tossed it into the fire. I burned myself getting it out."

John let out a low whistle. "That boy's going to be pretty annoyed at himself when he calms down."

I thought so, too. "I'm going to try to clean it up. Once my hand stops hurting."

John frowned at the book. "Good luck to you. I'll leave you to it." John held up a rabbit, showing me his catch before going outside to skin it.

I got a cloth, dunked it in water and wiped the front cover. The soot wiped away easily leaving dirty smudges, which lessened the more I wiped. The pages were much harder to repair. Impossible, actually. But I'd pulled it from the fire quickly and it was only the margins that were singed. He could still look at the pictures.

Tuck pushed the hut door open as I began working on the back cover.

"Rob said you were better," he said, by way of a greeting. "Where's Miller?" He threw his pack on the ground as John followed him inside, the skinned rabbit in his hand.

I glanced at John, letting him answer. "Don't know."

Tuck glared from John to me through narrowed eyes. It was clear he was in a wonderful mood. "How can you possibly not know?"

"Do we know where you are every second of the day?" I snapped. It had been days since I'd eaten, and I had no energy—felt like lying down again. I wouldn't until I'd fixed Miller's book, but right now, I had about as much tolerance for one of Tuck's moods as he had for me.

John stepped between us. "He's upset. He's taken a few moments for himself." It was much longer than a few moments, but if John didn't think Tuck needed to know that, then neither did I.

"I would be too if you'd thrown my treasured possession into the fire." Tuck's words were mumbled as he bent over and fiddled with his pack, but still loud enough that I couldn't miss them.

"Because that's clearly what I've done," I said, sarcastically. I turned pleading eyes on John, hoping for some help. I didn't want to fight with Tuck.

John gave me a half-smile and handed me some dried meat from his pack. "Eat that. You look like you're about to fall over." He looked at Tuck. "Maryanne didn't do this. Miller did."

Tuck looked between us again, understanding dawning on his face. He held his hand out and I passed the book to him. "Did this happen after Rob left, by any chance?"

I nodded.

John looked at Tuck over my head. "I told you we needed to keep an eye on him. This thing with Rob is hard on him."

"It's hard on everyone. But yes, it would appear you were right." Tuck sighed and sat down in front of the fire, pulling his robe down over his knees.

"Do we need to go and look for him?" I wouldn't have wanted to be out in the forest alone at night at his age. It was nearly dark and searching for him would be almost impossible. Still, we were all recalling what happened the last time we'd left him alone at night.

Tuck shook his head. "He'll be fine. Don't imagine he's gone far."

I took the book back from Tuck and continued working on it. Hopefully I'd have it in a much better state by the time Miller returned. But if John and Tuck were expecting a reaction like this from him, it begged a question. "Why do you let Rob do this? You all know how much Miller looks up to him, so why let Rob think it's okay to live somewhere else?"

John's gaze was thoughtful. "You think we can stop him once he has his mind set?"

"Of course you can! Or you could at least try." They were his best friends. He'd listen to them. Especially if they explained how Miller was feeling.

John shook his head with a laugh. "In all the years I've known Rob, there's only ever been one person who could change his mind once it was set. And it's not me."

I looked at Tuck. He put his hands in the air. "Nor me."

"Then, who?" They both stared my way. "Me?" I shook my head. "No. Rob and I aren't close." Anymore, at least. "He certainly doesn't listen to me."

John sat down in front of the fire and leaned back on his hands. "Should we talk about the way you first managed to get him to rob carriages?"

He hadn't wanted to, true. But he was going to be a legend, so it was hardly any work to change his mind.

"Or how he marched down to fight his brother for you."

"I never asked him to do that. I was fine on my own." I would never expect Rob, or anyone, to rescue me the way John was suggesting.

"You were. But he came to help you anyway. Even though it meant showing his face to the one person he'd hidden from for years. What about how he wasn't keen on helping that child in the forest two weeks ago? Like I said, you are the only one who can ever change Rob's mind about anything. The question is, why haven't you tried?"

OUTPLAYED

My mind froze. "You can't think I'm to blame for Rob not being here?"

John placed a comforting hand on my knee. "No. This situation is all Rob's doing. I'm just asking why you, as the only one of us who can ever make him do something he thought he didn't want to, haven't asked him to come back?"

Well, that was obvious. "Because the moment he stopped trusting me, his personal life became none of my business."

"Stopped trusting you?" John's eyebrows lifted. He seemed genuinely surprised.

"He's never told me where he goes, or who he's protecting, yet he's told all of you." That hurt more than I wanted to admit.

John ran a hand through his already messy hair. "And there's no reason you can think of that might have given him pause?"

I shook my head.

"There's no reason for him to think—because you once told him there was no way you could return to him—that you might be someone else?" He stared at my hands.

I shook my head again, but his stare lingered, becoming more pointed. I looked down. He couldn't be serious. "The ring? He thinks I'm Maud? He thinks Gisborne sent me here?"

"Thought. You cleared that misunderstanding up by stabbing Gisborne with your dagger to save his life." John gave a sheepish shrug. "And we all might have thought you were Maud at one point or another."

"But..." How was this possible? I'd lived with them for weeks. They'd never called me Maud. But they had questioned me. *Are you trying to make us ignore the pain you're bringing our way?* John asked me that on my first night back with them. Tuck had questioned me that night, too. At the time, I thought they were worried about me leaving again. Instead, they thought I was a spy for Gisborne. Even Eliza had seen the ring on my finger in her chamber at Woodhurst Manor and decided I was Maud. "But when Rob first saw me, when he came to Kings Cave with the rabbits in his hand that first night, it was like it used to be between us. He didn't think I was her then."

John lifted a shoulder. "None of us did. Until you removed your gloves and we saw Gisborne's ring."

Yes, everything had changed once I sat down beside the fire that first night. There had been that weird vibe that I couldn't put my finger on, which had slowly disappeared as they started to trust me again. Now I knew why.

Part of me wanted to be outraged; surely they knew me better. But another part knew how similar we looked. "I met Maud, when I was back in my time. That's where she is." I twisted her ring around my finger. "She wants Gisborne to have this back. Tabitha thought I should wear it. For safety, so Gisborne would think I was Maud." Which was how I'd grabbed his attention out on the trail the other day. I softened my voice. "You should have asked me about it."

John's voice was just as quiet. "You didn't exactly make it easy on us, Maryanne. You turned up out of nowhere wearing her ring, and the first thing you did was stop off in Eliza Thatcher's chamber."

"I had a gift for her! From her sister." I sighed. I could see how it looked. "But you all believe me now? You all know I'm Maryanne, right?"

"I know it. Started to suspect when you stepped out onto the trail to stop that carriage on the way to Oxham. Learned the hard way not long after." John was almost whispering. "Not trusting you was the stupidest thing I've ever done. Someone almost died because of it."

I frowned. "Who?"

He shook his head, lips clamped shut and eyes on the ground. It wasn't often John refused to talk. Which probably meant I shouldn't push him. For now.

We sat in silence a moment before he spoke again. "Just know, I'm certain of who you are now. Which means I know you can talk Rob into anything. But Maryanne, if you want him to trust you, maybe you first need to trust him with whatever it is that wakes you up screaming in the night. I know it's something to do with Rob."

I shook my head. That was something I could never tell. And worse, I couldn't even explain why.

John shrugged, that little movement telling me that what I wanted, what we all wanted, was in my hands. If only it were as easy as he thought it was.

Miller pushed the door open and strolled back into the hut—Tuck had fixed the door hinge. He sat down to warm his hands on the fire as though nothing out of the ordinary had happened. When he saw the book on my lap, his eyes widened. "You saved it?"

"It's a little damaged. I'm sorry I didn't get to it sooner."

Miller took it from me, his hands gentle. He hugged it to his chest. "No. I'm sorry for yelling at you. And I'm sorry your hand got burned saving my stuff." He rested the book on his lap, flicking through the pages by the light of the fire.

John gave me a nudge, his eyes going pointedly to Miller. "Talk to Rob. If not for yourself, then for someone else who needs him."

EIGHTEEN

"ARE you waiting for that fish to jump into your lap?" Rob said from behind, stepping onto the huge rocks beside the river.

I had a fishing pole in the water, hoping to catch something for dinner while the boys went out to rob a carriage, and Rob had caught me dozing in the sunshine. Now he mentioned it, the line was jumping with a fish on the end.

In one fluid movement, he pulled the fish from the water and killed it on a rock.

"I was waiting for a big, strong man to come back and help me out." Or daydreaming about one. I batted my eyelashes, hoping to hide that I'd been thinking about him. And about what John said two nights ago. I'd never actually asked Rob to come back. Not in so many words. And he'd never told me he thought I was Maud. A decent conversation was long past due.

Rob met my eyes with a grin. "I don't think you've ever waited for a *big, strong man* to do anything for you in your entire life."

"Not true. I let you lead me away from the fighting on the day we met." I wrapped my arms around my knees, watching as he pulled out his knife and began gutting the fish.

He threw the fish gut into the river and met my eyes. "Careful, Maryanne. You've called me big and strong twice in five minutes. I might start to think you mean it."

I shook my head, ignoring the way his eyes on me made my heart beat out of my chest. No change there. "If you ever do, just remember how you came to save me once and ended up almost getting both of us hanged."

He put a hand to his chest. "Ow. Harsh."

"It was a little, wasn't it?" I smiled. "I'm sorry."

"Unfortunately for me, it's entirely true and any criticism of that day will be taken under consideration."

I leaned back on my hands, watching him wash the fish in the river. He'd rolled up his sleeves and the muscles in his forearms danced with each movement. "Believe it or not, I have very little criticism about that day. No one's ever ridden to my rescue before."

He bit back a grin. "And no one's ever come to mine. I guess that makes us even."

"Glad to hear it. Since we are even, and now you know I'm not Maud, perhaps you should come back and live with us." Good one. Just throw it out there with no warning or lead-up.

He washed his hands in the river and sat down crossed-legged on the rock beside me. "Have you got a minute? We really need to talk."

I swallowed down my nerves. He sounded so serious. "Let me guess, you still think I'm Maud?" It was a joke, because John said Rob had worked out I wasn't her.

But Rob didn't smile. He licked his lips.

He hadn't answered. Why hadn't he answered? "Do you think I'm Maud bloody Fitzwalter?"

"No."

But the pause had been too long. That there was a pause at all spoke volumes. "Jesus Christ. You do." I stood up and turned away from him. John knew me for Maryanne, and he didn't know me half as well as Rob did. How was it Rob couldn't see me for who I was?

"I did. Don't anymore. Let me explain." He scrambled to his feet, took hold of my wrist and turned me back to face him.

I shook my head, feeling like I'd taken a punch to the gut. "Don't bother." I thought we had a connection. I thought he'd know me, no matter what. I thought we were past this.

His grip on my wrist tightened incrementally. "What would you think, knowing the girl you'd fallen for could never come back to you, but then she suddenly did? What would you think when that same girl went to Eliza Thatcher within hours of returning? What would you think if that girl was now suddenly wearing a ring she'd never worn before, a ring given to another girl on her engagement to my brother?"

A huge misunderstanding, all because of a ring. A ring that saved Rob's life. Had I not been wearing it, Gisborne would never have believed I was Maud.

"I did think you were her." His voice was quiet, eyes focused on the rock beneath our feet. "My head, hell, my eyes told me you couldn't be Maryanne. Maryanne hated Eliza and she'd never worn that ring before. And Maryanne said if she went home, she could never come back."

How was it possible for Rob to mistake me for Maud again?

OUTPLAYED

Because based on all the reasons he'd just given, I wouldn't have trusted me either. No wonder the two of us had found conversation difficult. "Maud Fitzwalter is...living with my family, in my time. She gave me her ring to return to Gisborne. Tabitha suggested I wear it for safety." She was right. It had kept me safe by getting Gisborne's attention long enough to stab him. "I wish you'd just asked me, but I understand why you didn't."

"I wish I'd asked you, too. But as time went on, I didn't need to. I knew it was you when I saw you waiting for Miller at Kings Cave, and when you were cleaning his face up after he escaped from Gisborne. And when I saw you march after that child because you thought he was in trouble. And when you stabbed Gisborne in the arm with your knife. I know who you are, Maryanne, because of what you do, not because of what you look like. The others know, too. I'm just sorry it took us so long to work it out."

"As long as you know now, then I guess we're all good."

He swallowed deeply. "When you were sick, I made myself some promises that I've been ignoring since. The reason I came here today wasn't to rob a carriage." He jingled the pouch of gold on his belt. "Although that is a positive side-effect. It was because I needed to talk to you. Really talk."

"Okay," I said slowly. My heart thudded in my chest and his tone made the nerves jump in my stomach.

"I kept this secret from you because I thought you were working with Gisborne. The only reason we didn't kill you to ensure our secret remained safe, was because I was holding out a small hope you really were Maryanne, impossibly returned from the future."

"It's something big, then." I couldn't even begin to guess. All I knew was I was likely lucky to be alive.

Rob nodded. "I also did this for his protection. I thought the best way forward was to keep everyone separate. I don't think it's working, but I have no clue what will."

"Trust me. It's not working." Miller could attest to that. We all could.

He drew in a deep breath and let the words tumble out. "I have another brother. I've been living with him. His name is Alan. And he's...different. Gisborne knows of him."

There were so many things in those sentences that needed clarification. Another brother was not what I expected, but it made my next question easy. "Can I meet him?" To keep Rob safe from Gisborne's arrow, I needed to keep him close—I couldn't help him when I didn't know where he was. That started with getting to know his brother. Plus, if he was important to Rob, he was important to me.

His eyebrows shot up and he gave a confused half-smile. "Meet him?"

"Well, if he's coming to live with us, he should really meet me first. You know, to make sure he's happy to have me around. I'm assuming he's met the others before?" He knew John and Tuck, for sure. They'd looked after him while I was sick and Rob was sitting with me.

Rob shook his head. "I didn't say he was coming to the forest to live. I just wanted to stop lying to you. Make you understand where I go, and why."

I turned toward him. This was the best opportunity—maybe my only opportunity—to get Rob to come back and live with us without telling him of the danger he was in if he didn't. I had to make him see it was in everyone's best interest. "I do understand, Rob. He's your brother. He's important to you and you're worried Gisborne will use that against you. Miller is your brother, too, even if not by blood. Doesn't he also deserve to have you around?" Didn't all of us?

Rob hesitated.

"Do you want to come back and live with us, Rob?"

"With every bone in my body. I'm just...unsure whether my own desire might be clouding my judgment. What if I bring him here and he can't adjust? What if he's not comfortable living like we do? What if I bring him here and something happens to him?"

Those were all good points, and I might have agreed with them all were I not so worried for Rob's life. "What if you leave him wherever you currently have him hidden and something happens while you're stopping carriages, or hunting, or running back and forth between us and him?" A fish jumped in the pool in front of us. I watched the water rings expand and disappear. There was another what if. What if whatever made Alan different—that was the word Rob used—made him unsuitable for living in the forest? I didn't know how to voice that question though, not without saying the wrong thing. "Take me to meet him. Then we'll decide together what to do next."

Alan and Rob's current home was the village of Bidworth, with a monk who'd been Alan's caregiver since he was eight.

I recognized Alan the moment I saw him. He was playing some sort of throwing game with the kids in the village. With his back to me, he could have been Rob. Same height. Same blond hair.

Exact same cloak, right down to the fur on the inside of the hood. "You two even dress the same." I laughed.

"Got the cloaks made a couple of years back, once we'd found—or thought we'd found—a safe place for Alan to stay. Wanted to remind him how much he meant to me." He waved to his brother. "Alan!"

Alan turned, a huge smile bursting across his face. From the front, the likeness wasn't as pronounced. Alan had the flattened face and upward slanting eyes that would one day be known as Down Syndrome. He loped across to us, enveloping Rob in a bear hug. "Rob! You're back!"

Rob squeezed Alan tight. "Sure am." When he extracted himself from his brother's grasp, he said, "Alan, this is my friend, Maryanne."

Alan's smile was wide. "Is she your *girl*friend, Rob? She's pretty."

"Nice to meet you, Alan. I can tell you and Rob are brothers—you both try to flatter me." I grinned and leaned toward Alan, speaking in a loud whisper. "You're much better at it than him, though."

"Hey!" Rob shook his head, laughing.

If it was possible, Alan's smile grew even wider. He turned to Rob. "I like her. You should try harder to flatter her if you want her to fall in love with you."

I couldn't hold back the laugh that bubbled from my chest.

Rob's cheeks turned red. "She's much too clever to fall in love with someone like me, brother."

If only that were true.

Alan's eyes moved back to his game. "I was about to win. Can I go and play some more?"

Rob nodded and Alan ran back to his friends.

"Is he Gisborne's brother, too?" I hoped it wasn't an insensitive question. Rob hadn't given me any specifics and his family wasn't the easiest to understand.

"Half-brother. Same as me. He's Mother's son with her first husband. Father was her second husband." And Gisborne's father her third. "He lived with us until just after she died. Looking back, I can see now that Father...I mean, Jerimiah—he was never my father. Jerimiah saw Alan as another threat to Gisborne's inheritance. As a child, I stupidly believed everything Jerimiah said." Rob retied the leather that kept his hair from his face. "After Ma died, Jerimiah said he couldn't look after Alan and that Alan would be happier in a monastery where the monks would give him all the attention he needed." He blew out a deep breath. "I'll never stop feeling bad about that."

OUTPLAYED

"It's not your fault, Rob. You were a child, too." Gisborne's father had a lot to answer for. Pity he'd died before anyone had the chance to make him pay.

"I assumed his new life was best for him. I believed Jerimiah when he said so." He gave a deep sigh. "It was Tuck who found him. In the monastery in Mansfield. He'd lived his whole life in this tiny room, all but forgotten. It was awful."

It sounded hideous, though I didn't expect anything done by Gisborne's father to be pleasant. "So, you got him out of there?"

"There was one monk, Francis, who treated Alan better than the rest. Brought him extra food, toys, treats. He knew who I was, how I was living. He thought Alan would struggle to adjust to our living arrangement, so he offered to leave the monastery and look after Alan elsewhere for me. They lived at Oxham for the last year. Before that, they were in other villages, like Bligh, Overton and Hamilton. We moved them if we felt it wasn't safe. Tuck and I took them game every week, and at Oxham, Alan was working in the fields."

I watched him playing with the village kids, throwing rocks at a target, the closest one the winner. Which, judging by Alan's excited shouts, was often him. There was no discrimination. The other kids didn't seem to care he was much older than them. They did seem to love that he did everything he could to try to beat them all.

I didn't know much about Down Syndrome. Nothing actually. There'd been a girl with it at my school, just a year older than me. Chloe was her name. I could still remember the entire school cheering her on as she swam the length of the pool at swimming sports and how she'd thrown her hands in the air in excitement when she was told she'd made it through to Zones. Last I'd seen her, she was working at a local café. Even biked to and from her job herself. If she could do all that, maybe Alan could come and live with us. Surely, we could teach him about the forest. "What about Francis? Would his caregiver want to come into the forest to live?"

Rob looked at me sideways. "Should we decide that living in the forest is in everyone's best interest, then I would imagine he'll come. He's been part of Alan's life for so many years. I can't imagine him abandoning Alan now."

Two more mouths to feed. Two more people to keep quiet when soldiers were nearby. Totally worth it to see Miller happy again. "Then bring them into the forest. He wants to be where you are, I could see it in his eyes when he hugged you. Miller wants to be where you are. I might even want to be where you are." There was no might about that statement. "It's the best option all around."

Rob backed away heading toward the forest, our visit with Alan over. He pointed a finger at me. "There's something in that sentence that requires further clarification. Later. But, as for what to do with Alan, I'll think about it."

"What's going on?" I asked, as I returned from washing at the river a week later. A boy stood in front of the hut talking to Miller, who adamantly shook his head. Tuck and John watched out the corner of their eyes as they readied themselves for the day ahead.

"Kid's looking for Robin Hood." John tucked a slingshot into the back of his pants. It was his go-to hunting weapon these days. Said he wasn't so good with the bow anymore because of his fingers. I hadn't seen him try and wondered if he just didn't want to fail. I knew exactly how it felt to think that way. The next time we had the chance, I'd have to do something about it.

The boy turned at the sound of my voice. His mouth opened and shut, and he pointed to me. "It's you."

"It's you," I smiled to the boy who would currently be minus a hand had it not been for Rob. "Elton, right?"

The boy nodded. "Is he here? Robin Hood?"

Miller blew out a disgusted breath and folded his arms. "He's not here. He's never bloody here."

I glanced at John and Tuck, both of whom returned my worried stare. A moment ago, Miller was denying all knowledge of Rob—it was the safest option when we didn't know who sent the boy. Once he realized the boy wasn't a threat, he'd given up protecting Rob. Probably because Rob hadn't been near us for an entire week. Miller was taking it hard.

No one knew why he hadn't come around. Either I'd pushed too far when I insisted Alan come and live with us, or Rob was using the time without us to see if he could be without us always. Neither option made me feel good. And Miller was worse than ever, see-sawing between yelling and screaming at the top of his voice, and sitting quietly staring at his book for hours. Without turning a page.

"Ma wants you—and Robin Hood, or whoever it was that rescued me..." He glanced around the clearing at the other boys. "All of you actually, to come and celebrate St Valentine's Day with us in Huxley. To say thank you for what you did for me."

Wow, how had time gone so fast? Valentine's Day was also my birthday, and I hadn't even realized it was so close. "I'm not sure that would be safe for your village. If we could manage to find Robin Hood and bring him with us, he is a wanted man. If he were found with you, the entire village would pay the price. It's what happened in Oxham." The very mention of Oxham sent a shiver up my spine. My dreams continued to show up every night even though Rob had gotten away from that place with his life.

"Ma said you'd say that. She said to tell you the village knows the risk. But we also believe the chance of soldiers finding you there at night is slim. And we owe you." Elton sat himself down on the dirt near our extinguished campfire. "They also told me I wasn't to leave until you all agreed."

"You drive a hard bargain, but we can't put you at risk." I glanced around the apple grove, hoping for some back up, but no one met my eyes. "Right, Tuck?"

Tuck and John looked at each other, some silent conversation happening before John said, "It wouldn't really be a risk. Not if it's at night."

I narrowed my eyes. "But you said the soldiers come into the forest at night sometimes now."

"Aye." He nodded. "They do, sometimes. But not usually in as far as Huxley. Isn't that right, boy?" He looked at the child for confirmation.

Elton nodded.

"And it's St Valentine's Day," said Miller wistfully.

"And it would be rude to decline." Tuck spoke as if he didn't have a clue what it was like to be rude.

"Let me get this straight, you all want to go? You all think it would be safe to go?" I couldn't keep the surprise from my voice.

They all nodded.

"Why?"

Elton scrambled to his feet. "Because St Valentine's Day in Huxley is famous throughout the forest. I'll tell Ma to expect you."

"I don't think that's—"

"See you next week!" he yelled, already on his way.

Miller nudged John as Elton left. "Looks like you'll get a party on your birthday this year."

"Valentine's Day is your birthday?" It was no wonder I got along so well with him.

John nodded.

"Mine, too."

"Birthday twins." John grinned.

"It's settled then," said Miller, his smile larger than it'd been for a long time. "We're going to the party."

Nineteen

"Maryanne? What are you doing?" Rob's shadow darkened the door to his hut and his voice was hesitant. I turned to find him leaning on the doorframe.

I'd come to Bidworth alone this morning, leaving the apple grove before the others awoke. Before they could stop me. I couldn't find Rob or Alan when I arrived, so I went to their hut and began to pile their belongings into a pack from one of the shelves. "Packing. What does it look like?" I batted my eyelashes, feigning innocence.

"Hmmm. I can see that. Might I ask why?" He folded his arms across his chest.

His hair was loose, falling around his face. I liked it when he wore it this way. "Because you have to pack if you're going to leave, of course." I was on a mission today. I'd already stopped in at Clipstone this morning to ask John's sister for help with John's birthday present. Now I was at Bidworth to achieve the second item on my to do list.

"Oh, yes?" His lips twitched like he was trying not to smile. "And where might I be going?"

I turned back to my packing. I was almost done, but I took my time folding the final blanket. "Not just you. Alan, too. You're coming back to live in the forest with us." I'd made some decisions overnight. I hoped bringing the two of them back to the forest to live would stop the dreams, because what I'd done so far had failed. Even if it didn't, I hoped it would make Miller happy again. But the bottom line was Rob had more chance of surviving Gisborne's sword if he had his three best friends nearby and looking out for him.

He sighed, and the lightness left his voice. "Maryanne." His tone told me we'd already had this conversation, and nothing had changed.

"It's okay." I'd thought it all out, considered what his arguments might be and had answers for every one of them. "We can teach Alan how to use a bow. Or a sword. Or if he doesn't like the idea of using either of those, a knife. Then he'll be able to fight back if he needs to. I think maybe a set routine might be good for him, so we can teach him things like getting wood for the fire, and he'll know that's the first thing we do when we make camp."

Rob shook his head. "Maryanne. It's not that easy."

"It is!" If he wanted it to be. "You're the one who's making it difficult!"

He walked over to me, all of two steps. "What's really going on? Because I know you understand the risks."

He really needed to ask? "Miller is a mess without you! And John misses his best friend. And Tuck—"

Rob took my shoulders and turned me to face him, then he ducked into my line of vision. "Yes, but what is it really?"

I don't want you to die. Right from the moment Maud first explained what would happen if I told anyone about the dreams, I'd understood what I was signing up for. I'd hoped to stop Rob dying and live happily ever after, but I'd known what my options were if the dreams kept coming. The sole purpose I was here was to cement the legend as Dad knew it into history. Seeing how much Elton wanted to meet Robin Hood had reminded me of that. There would be no legend if Rob was dead, and that left me with just one option.

Save Rob's life by telling him about my dreams.

I'd die. But he'd live. All I could hope was that I had a little more time before that happened. "Did you ever wonder how I knew you needed to leave Oxham?"

Rob looked at me sideways. "You didn't tell me to leave Oxham."

"Well, no, not in person, but..." Miller and John had done it for me.

"But what?"

I half-laughed. "It was me who made Miller and John talk to you." Surely they mentioned this when they told him to leave.

He shook his head. "It wasn't because of them that I left Oxham, Maryanne. It was stupid luck that Alan, Francis and I weren't there when the soldiers came. Alan had been asking to camp out in the forest for a night. That happened to be the night we chose. We left right after Miller and John left."

"But...the hut was almost empty." There were next to no possessions in there, the day Oxham was attacked.

He gave a sheepish shrug. "What can I say? I don't own much, and the things I do own—like the plates and mugs Alan and I use for eating, and our blankets—I took for comfort while we camped out."

Huh. "So, Miller and John said *what* exactly to you that day?"

He turned his lips down. "Not a lot. They handed out gold. We had a quick chat. I asked after you. What do you think they told me?"

"That you were in danger. That you needed to leave." My voice sounded small as the pieces fell into place. *This* was the advice John hadn't followed, the advice that had almost caused someone—Rob—to die. The reason he began to suspect I was Maryanne and not Maud. He hadn't told Rob that he needed to leave Oxham because he thought I was her. Probably thought I'd hatched some plan with Gisborne to draw Rob out, so Gisborne could hunt him down.

"And you knew this how?"

I felt sick. That day had been so very close to total disaster.

"How did you know?" An edge crept into his voice.

I drew in a deep breath and signed my own death warrant. Not that I was going to make it easy on whoever— or whatever—came to kill me for sharing this secret. I planned to fight tooth and nail to stay here with Rob and his friends. "You're not safe."

A ghost of a smile crossed Rob's face. "Understatement of the year."

"I've been having these...dreams." I shrugged one shoulder. "About you."

He started to grin.

I shook my head and held up one hand. "Don't." The sort of dreams he was imagining would have been far more welcome than the ones I saw night after night.

His expression turned immediately serious. He'd probably heard something in my tone.

I forced my voice to remain steady. "I dream of you dying at Gisborne's hand with an arrow through your back. Before Oxham, I told Tuck, Miller and John of the place I kept seeing, where I thought you were most in danger, and they all said it was Oxham. I made them go and get you out of there. At least, I thought that's what they were doing." I shook my head. John's decision could have cost Rob his life. The thought stole my breath. "The dreams stopped for a night or two after you left there, and I thought everything was fixed."

He frowned. "But then they came back?"

I nodded. "I wasn't supposed to tell you, but I think you'll be safe now. I've done what I needed to make sure of that." I wouldn't tell him of the consequences I was yet to face. I wouldn't make him feel guilty for the choices I made. "And if not, you'll be in the forest where Gisborne has to get past four of us before he can kill you."

OUTPLAYED

His eyes moved from me to look through the door, toward the forest. "It just seems dangerous. Like I'd be putting more people in danger for no reason."

Rob didn't fool me. He might be saying what he thought he should, but I could see how the forest called to him. He wanted to come back as much as we all wanted him back. "Good. It's settled." I picked up the blanket and folded it again, my heart beating loudly. I didn't want to die, but I didn't want him to, either.

"But I didn't say—"

"You were going to."

He pressed his lips together, trying not to smile. "I feel like we've had a version of this conversation before."

We had. Only last time, it was him making decisions for me. "Is there anything else you want to take?"

He shook his head. "Just Alan."

We headed out the door. Alan was playing with the kids again, throwing rocks at a target in a very loud, very competitive game just outside the door. So loud, it blocked out the thumping of horses' hooves until they were closer than they should have been.

Rob and I heard them at the same moment. "Run! Soldiers!" He yelled to whoever would listen. He sprinted to Alan, pulling on his arm. I started for the forest. It wasn't far. Rob's house was one of the closest to the trees.

I glanced over my shoulder to find Rob and Alan stopped in the middle of the rutted trail outside the hut. Rob moved his hands wildly while Alan shook his head and folded his arms across his chest.

I ran back to them. "What's the matter?'

"Francis," said Alan. "We have to find Francis." Alan's caregiver.

I glanced at Rob. All around us, people were running. Francis had surely run, too. "He's probably in the forest already. Or almost there, at least."

Alan shook his head, blond hair swinging across his face. "He's not. He's taking a nap." He pointed along the hut-lined street to the one his friend was sleeping in.

My heart began to thump. We had to leave. As it was, we'd be lucky to make the forest before the soldiers arrived. "I'll get him."

Rob shook his head. "Maryanne…"

There was no time for arguments. "You get Alan to safety, then come back for me if you need to." I shrugged, hoping to sound less worried than I actually was. Rob and Alan had to get to the safety of the forest. "Hopefully you won't have to come back."

OUTPLAYED

Without waiting for his answer, I ran toward Francis' hut, pulling my bow from my back just as the first soldier emerged from the forest.

His sword was already drawn, and he brought it down on a woman who changed direction the moment he appeared. She was almost to the forest—where she could have found somewhere safe to hide—when his sword cut into her and she dropped like a stone.

"Francis!" I dodged around people running in every direction, raising my voice above their screams.

He poked his head out of his hut. I recognized him immediately. Like Tuck, he wore monk's robes. That was where the likeness ended. Francis was short and skinny, his greying hair thin on his head. "I'm a friend of Rob's. He has Alan. We need to get to the forest and hide. Now."

The old man's eyes rounded as he watched something behind my back.

I took his arm, pulling gently. There was no time for anything except running. "We have to go."

My touch started him moving. He nodded. "Yes. Yes. We must go."

He was faster than I expected, though not as fast as I would have liked. I held his arm as he half-ran, half-stumbled over the rough ground of the partially sown field, the footsteps and panting of running villagers loud in my ears. The forest that had seemed so close before now seemed so very far away. There were soldiers everywhere. Metal clashed with metal as some of the villagers chose to stand and fight. Screams hung in the air, sometimes cut short, sometimes so long they made the hair on my arms stand on end.

I couldn't see Rob or Alan, but I was okay with that. They should have reached the forest by now. So long as they hadn't met a soldier on the way.

I urged Francis forward. He shook himself free of my grasp. "You go ahead, dear. I'm too slow."

There was no way that was happening. If Francis was important to Alan, he was important to me. "You're not. We're almost there." I took his arm again, wishing we really were almost there.

He stalled again; his eyes stuck on something ahead.

I followed his gaze to find a soldier bearing down on us. Letting go of him, I whipped an arrow from my quiver, lined up the soldier and shot.

My arrow wedged in the opposite shoulder from his sword arm. It did as much damage as missing would have, and he kept riding toward us.

I nocked a second arrow and let it go. Then I grabbed Francis' arm. "Run!"

OUTPLAYED

This arrow hit the soldier in the chest. He toppled forward, falling beside us as his horse galloped past. We were safe, for now. But we were still at least a hundred steps from safety. Once we reached the forest, if we stayed off the trails, the soldiers would have to dismount to follow. The foliage off the trails was too thick to properly swing their swords, and they didn't carry bows. There was no way they'd follow us in there, not unless they wanted to die. "Almost there."

My gut was hollow. This was exactly what Maud promised. Tell anyone about the dreams; die a violent death. I hadn't expected the consequence to come so fast. Although, if I had any say, it wasn't happening at all. I wasn't dying here today.

Another soldier galloped toward us, sword shining in the sunlight. His burgundy cloak streamed out behind him, floating up and down in the same rhythm as his horse. People in front of us changed direction, trying to get out of his way.

I let go of Francis and pulled out another arrow, firing on the soldier.

I missed, the arrow sailing over his shoulder to land somewhere in the ruined field behind him.

The soldier charged; his eyes focused on us and sword raised.

I pulled at Francis, but he was too slow. The soldier too close.

His sword came down as if in slow motion. It sliced into the place between Francis' shoulder and neck as if it were slicing into butter. The impact shook Francis' body. I felt it through his hand in the moment before he crumpled onto the ground with a stifled scream in his throat.

"No!" I pulled out another arrow, shooting at the soldier's back as his horse carried him past in search of his next victim. I felt nothing but satisfaction to see him fall to the ground, my arrow protruding from his body.

Blood spurted from the wound high on Francis' shoulder as if a faucet had opened. I was no doctor, but with that much blood coming so fast, it looked like he'd hit an artery. I took Francis under the arms, gripping onto his blood-slicked tunic, and dragged him toward the forest.

The pounding of hooves sounded everywhere around me. So did the screams of the injured or dying. There was noise everywhere, except from Francis. He was silent. And heavy. He was going to die, but at least he'd die with people he knew around him.

The shadow of a horse fell across my feet. I hadn't heard it arrive. I thought I'd been keeping watch.

OUTPLAYED

Wishing the horse was riderless, I straightened, just as the cool tip of a sword touched my neck.

"There you are." Gisborne smirked down at me from atop a white horse.

Twenty

Gisborne was straight-backed upon his horse, the sword in his hand dripping with blood. I had no idea how he'd found me amid the panic surrounding us. "Sorry, my lord." I smiled tightly. "We'll have to catch up some other time. I was just leaving." I tugged on Francis' arms. He felt heavier and more blood-covered than moments ago.

Gisborne slid from his horse in one movement, his hand clamping around my bicep. "I don't believe you're going anywhere. My lady." His final words were spoken through clenched teeth and with flared nostrils.

I pulled at my arm, but his grip was strong. "Let go of me."

"Not today. Not unless you're willing to swap your freedom for that of my brother?"

I clamped my lips shut. That wasn't happening. With any luck, Rob had gotten Alan far enough away that they couldn't see me. He'd be down here in a second if he was watching, and that was the worst thing he could do.

"Thought so. Never mind. I'm certain you'll be changing your mind soon enough."

"That's one thing you really shouldn't be certain about, my lord." He'd have no more luck finding Rob's location from me than he'd had with John or Miller. A sense of mild panic ran through me with that thought. Mild because I still backed myself to reach the edge of the forest. Panic because if Gisborne did manage to kidnap me, I wasn't sure I would be able to deal with whatever he chose to do to me. I certainly wouldn't handle it as bravely as John or Miller.

Not that it mattered. I wasn't going anywhere with him. I yanked my arm from his grasp, then pulled at Francis, changing our course to go around Gisborne.

Gisborne's hand clamped around my arm again. "I believe you misunderstand me, Lady Maud. Or whoever you are today. You have only one place to be this afternoon. And that is with me." Spinning me around so I lost my grip on

Francis, he placed his hands on my waist and hoisted me onto his horse—he was stronger than I'd imagined. A second later, before I even had the chance to think about wriggling out of his grasp and sliding back to the ground, he was sitting behind me, breathing in my ear.

He made a clicking sound, and his horse began to move. An arrow whistled past us, with it, Rob's voice. "Let her go, Gisborne!"

I'd known he'd try to stop Gisborne. Hadn't wanted him to put himself in the danger it would bring but I knew he'd do it anyway. Still, I wished he'd stayed hidden.

Gisborne turned his horse to face Rob.

"Take me!" yelled Rob, over the racket of Gisborne's men wreaking havoc among the villagers.

"Don't be stupid, Rob. He's not going to hurt me." There'd been plenty of chances in the past, but Gisborne never took advantage of them. I believed he still loved Maud and wouldn't hurt her. Which meant he couldn't hurt me either, because he didn't know for certain which one of us I was.

"Your lady is incorrect, brother. I do intend to hurt her. Probably in much the same way I hurt your other friends. How hurt she gets, depends on how long you take to find her. But because I'm nothing if not fair, I'll give you a fighting chance and tell you where we're headed."

Rob dropped his bow on the ground and stepped toward us with his hands raised beside his ears. "Let her go. Take me instead. I'm the one you want." His voice shook and I wasn't sure if it was from fear or anger.

Gisborne shrugged. I felt his shoulders move. "Perhaps. But I'll have you on my terms, and I'll have you once I'm sure hurting your friends will no longer hurt you. Consider it payback for all the punishment I received growing up."

"Any punishment was your own doing, not mine." Rob's eyes moved from Gisborne to me, and back again.

Gisborne shook his head. "Not when it was Mother. You were always in her ear."

Rob shook his head. "That's ridiculous."

"Is it? Why did she let you sneak into her bed when you were scared on stormy nights, but force me to clean silverware with the servants when I tried to do the same thing? Why did she allow you to play outside later than your curfew, but send me to bed without supper for missing mine? Why didn't she make you clean your own dirty clothes or stand over you while you mended a hole in the knee of your pants." He spat the words at Rob, his anger still raw.

Rob gave his head a slow shake. "Are they the worst examples you can come up with? Those are the reasons you've spent months hunting me and my friends down? You're pathetic, brother. Did anyone ever tell you that? Mother loved you. You think she wronged you? Try being the child Father didn't want in the house, then you'll know what it feels like to be unloved." His hands were still up near his ears.

"You were her favorite. In her eyes, I never existed." His face hardened. "I hope it hurts knowing how helpless you are to stop this. That's how I felt when Mother picked on me." He made that clicking sound again with his tongue, and the horse started to move, turning away from Rob. "I'm taking Maud to a place we used to know well." There was a smirk in his voice as he called over his shoulder.

"No! Stop, Gisborne!"

Gisborne laughed, his breath warm against my neck.

I shivered.

I tried to twist around, to look at Rob, but Gisborne caught my shoulder and pushed me back. In that brief second, I saw Rob scoop up his bow. A moment later, an arrow whistled past us. Gisborne laughed again. "Bad shot, brother," he called over his shoulder. Then he jumped and cursed in my ear.

I turned again and glimpsed the end of an arrow lodged in his shoulder blade. "Are you hurt, my lord? Maybe we should stop and fix your wound." I tried to keep the smugness from my voice. That shot would be enough to force Gisborne to stop for help, allowing me to escape. The arrow sticking out of him would jar every time his horse took a step, something I imagined to be painful. It had been a couple of weeks since my last run in with him, but he was possibly still weak from the wounds he received that day. There was no way he could keep riding. I looked to the nearby forest, searching for the best place to run the moment he slowed, somewhere a horse couldn't follow.

"Not a chance." Gisborne gritted his teeth and wound one arm tightly around my waist. He kicked his horse in the sides and we sped up, galloping away from the village, away from Rob.

I struggled against him. I'd take my chances with a broken bone from a fall from this horse rather than meekly go where Gisborne wanted to take me. But his grip was firm, and I could do nothing but watch the scenery go by.

We stayed on the main trail for a long time before turning onto an overgrown trail wide enough for just one horse. It felt like we'd ridden for hours, but we couldn't have, or the sun would be lower in the sky. It just felt that way because every step took me farther from Rob and closer to an uncertain future.

We stopped at the edge of a large clearing that appeared often used by Gisborne's soldiers. There were a handful here already, waiting for us. They saw Gisborne, and the arrow in his shoulder, and jumped to action. "Are you all right, my lord?" one asked, taking the horse's reins.

"Fine," snapped Gisborne, sliding to the ground with a hiss. "Get down." He glared at me until I climbed off his horse, then he nodded to one of the soldiers. "Watch the girl. If she escapes, it'll be your neck. I'll be back for her shortly." He cast his eyes around the clearing, and startled soldiers jumped back into whatever tasks they had been doing before we appeared. "Where's Antonio?"

"Here, my lord." Tall and thin, Antonio pushed his way through the bushes and into the clearing.

"Get this damned arrow out of me as fast as you can. I have things to do."

Antonio nodded, disappearing back the way he'd come with Gisborne following in his wake.

I lunged for Gisborne's horse—I could escape on it. I was about to swing myself up onto the animal's back when the soldier dug his fingers into my shoulders and dragged me down, dropping me on the ground.

"Get up," he grunted. When I didn't move, he wound his hand in my ponytail and pulled me to the nearest tree, dropping a length of rope on the ground.

"You're tying me up?" He didn't speak and probably didn't need to. The answer was clear.

I wasn't sticking around for him to bind me to a tree. He had to loosen his grip on my hair if he wanted to wrap that rope around me. The moment he did, I ran.

I'd only taken three steps before he tackled me and knocked me to the ground. My chin smacked on the dirt and I bit my tongue. Blood fill my mouth. I spat it out and kicked him, but he was too strong, and my kicks glanced off his legs. He dragged me to my feet with a pinching grip on my wrist and pulled me back to the tree. "I'm not dying because of you," he muttered.

He tied the rope around my wrists while I kicked and bucked. I fought even knowing he was stronger, knowing that no matter how much I wanted to, I couldn't get away. Once he was done, he sat a few steps from me, never taking his eyes off me.

"Just let me go. Gisborne won't really kill you because of it." I was still panting from the effort of trying to escape and didn't believe my own words. All I could hope was that the soldier was new and didn't know Gisborne well. "Just tell him it was an accident."

The soldier gave a disgusted shake of his head. Not new, then.

"If he kills me, it'll be all your fault, you know. For holding me here like this." That probably wouldn't help either. I'd seen what Gisborne's soldiers did to the villages they visited. I doubted any of them had a conscience.

"No," the soldier said quietly. "It'll be your own fault for antagonizing him and then not running fast enough to get away today."

I shook my head. What he said was true. I had continuously provoked Gisborne since the first time I met him. It was little wonder he wanted some payback.

We fell into silence and I took another look around the huge clearing, memorizing it in case I had the chance to escape. Shelters were erected side-by-side around the edge opposite me. They were A-frames made of large sticks which were then covered by smaller sticks, leaves, and anything else that might keep the weather out. There was a large fire in the center and the smell of cooking meat wafted from it. Horses were tied up somewhere out of sight—I could hear them snuffling—and there was running water somewhere nearby.

Footsteps made me turn as Gisborne marched toward us. He crouched in front of me, talking to the soldier without looking at him. "You may go, soldier. I have this now."

The soldier shot to his feet and scurried away, as if pleased his post was over.

Gisborne worked at the end of the rope, untying the knot that kept me strapped to the tree. Slowly, he unwrapped the ties from around my body, took my hands and helped me to my feet. "I'm not stupid enough to imagine my brother is sitting on his hands awaiting your return."

I didn't imagine he was either, though that was likely the safer option.

"But just in case, where are you all based at the moment?" He moved stiffly, his shoulder obviously sore, the bandaging invisible beneath his cloak.

I laughed. "I'm sure you're also not stupid enough to think I'm going to tell you that." Miller and John had survived Gisborne while keeping Rob safe, I could, too.

His eyes wandered over my face from my eyes, to my mouth, then back to my nose, my hair. I knew what he was searching for. He wanted to know if I was her. Maud. I'd been sleeping with my hair plaited hoping the waviness would give the impression of curls and I hoped he couldn't tell the difference between the two of us.

He made a sound in his throat that gave no indication what conclusion he'd come to. "I think you misunderstand me. Not giving me that information would be stupid. Handing it over would prove you to be of above average intellect." He gave me a beaming smile.

The man was an idiot. If he thought he'd just paid me a compliment, he needed to brush up on his courting skills. "And what, exactly, do you plan to do with that information, once I give it to you?" The longer we talked, the more time I had to come up with a plan to get out of here.

He linked his hands behind his back, hissing as his wound bit. "That's of little consequence to you, my lady."

"See, that's where you're wrong. If you're going to kill my friends, why would I share that information?"

Gisborne watched me again, his tongue flicking out to lick his lips. "Very well. I have no intention of hurting your friends. I'd just like to know where their current abode is. Maybe stop by for a visit next time I'm in the area."

Yeah, right. "Sorry, my lord, but I can't recall the name of the place we're staying."

"Perhaps, then, you could describe it. So I'll know it if I'm passing."

He either thought I was stupid, or terrified of what he would do to me. I was a little of the second, but not enough to give him what he wanted. "So, you'll keep them all safe? If I tell you?"

He leaned forward, nodding. "Of course."

I stared at him, hoping he'd think I was deciding. "We live in the most beautiful part of the whole forest. The trees are huge and very old."

He nodded again, his eyes bright. "What town is nearest?"

I looked over his shoulder into the distance, as if I was thinking. "I'm not sure. Edwinstowe. No, Mansfield. No, I think Rainworth."

"None of those towns are close to each other. Which one is it?" There was agitation in his voice, though a smile remained on his face.

"I'm sorry. We've moved a lot lately, and I get so confused." I was just a girl, after all. At least, that's how I hoped he saw it. "There's this one massive tree, so big two people can't get their arms around it."

"The Big Tree?" He looked at me sideways.

"No. Not the Big Tree. I know that place well enough to have told you if we were staying there."

He barely heard my answer before asking his next question. "Is this place near a trail?"

"Yes. But not too close to the main trail. There's a smaller one that leads there. There's a hill on the far side."

His eyes lit. He hadn't seen it for the lie it was. "I think I might know the place. Anything else?"

"There's a valley on the other side."

Gisborne's nod was fast, excited.

Time to put a stop to that. "And it's filled with rainbows. And unicorns. And candy." Take that Gisborne. As if I'd ever tell you anything about any of the places we stayed.

His fist to my gut folded me in two, driving all the air from my lungs. I dropped like a stone to the ground. I hadn't seen it coming. I knew Gisborne would try to strike me. It was just the kind of man he was. But I thought I'd have time to react or at least brace myself for it.

He stood over me with his hands on his hips, waiting until I'd taken those first couple of breaths. "Let's try that again. Where are they staying?"

I pulled myself up to my knees and wheezed, "High in the forest. In a huge tree house." Gisborne was getting nothing from me.

The toe of his boot connected with my thigh with such force it knocked me onto my side. I held back the cry that pushed up in my throat. I imagined I'd be screaming in pain soon enough, might as well hold it back while I could, and hope it pissed Gisborne off.

Taking a fistful of my hair, Gisborne dragged me to my feet. "Where. Are. They?"

If he didn't get it by now, he never would. "Nottingham Castle."

This time, his open hand slammed into my cheek, the impact so hard it made my ear ring. I stumbled backward, catching the smirk on his lips before I looked away. I didn't need to see how much he enjoyed my pain. Blood trickled down my chin, my lip already swollen and bleeding. I wiped it away.

"Last chance. Where is my brother?"

I lifted my head and threw every bit of hatred for all the things he'd done into my stare. "Woodhurst Manor." I must have bit my tongue the last time he hit me, because the words were heavy in my mouth. I knew I should stop. Maybe beg for his forgiveness, tell him some minute detail. The smallest thing would keep him happy. I also knew it wouldn't matter what I said. We'd end up in the same place anyway. I'd likely chosen the faster route. Plus seeing him so riled up gave me a small sense of satisfaction.

Another open-handed blow slammed into my face. The other side this time. I staggered back, the world shrinking to that one point that screamed in pain. Rob would tell me riling Gisborne was stupid. I guessed I'd learned from the best. I'd seen Rob do it more than once and I finally understood it. Even now, as he drew his hand back and hit me again, I couldn't be sorry.

My breath came in uneven pants and the cry I'd kept inside earlier ripped from my lips when he hit me the next time. Each of his blows hurt. That last one felt like he'd put every ounce of strength he contained into it. I leaned on a tree behind me and pulled deep breaths into my lungs, trying not to let him see that my legs were about to give way. I'd expected more questions, but there were none. Just another blow that rocked my head back and slammed it into the rough bark of the tree. Then another, to my stomach. My legs finally collapsed, and I was on the musty-smelling forest floor.

I clenched my hands, wishing I had the energy and strength to hit Gisborne back. He couldn't treat me this way. I was a person, too. He didn't get to put his fists on me just because he felt like it. He didn't get to hit me until I was too hurt to move just because everyone was too terrified to stop him.

Except, of course, he did.

I wasn't physically strong enough to block his blows. Now he'd hurt me, I could barely move. I certainly couldn't run, and fighting back without a weapon was impossible.

Gisborne raised his hand again and I screamed at him to stop. Wished I hadn't. I hated the idea of begging this man for anything.

Whether he heard me or not, the blows didn't end. There wasn't a place on my body that he left unscathed.

I must have passed out after that because the next time I opened my eyes, Gisborne was gone, and the sound of birdsong rang loud in my ears. Someone had moved me. The trees seemed closer than they had before, and whatever I was lying on was rough and uncomfortable.

I struggled to sit, and the world swayed. Every muscle, every tendon, every bone in my body screamed with pain. My face was so tight, I felt like I'd never be able to talk again. The inside of my mouth was raw and bloody from where I'd bitten my tongue.

"Be still." Eliza Thatcher gazed at me in the disappearing evening light. Between us was a set of wooden bars. A cage. I was inside a cage. And it was no wonder the world felt like it was moving. My cage—made of heavy branches crossed over each other and lashed together with rope—was hoisted high in the air, dangling via ropes from a branch about five meters off the ground. There were massive gaps between each of the sticks I sat on, and though I couldn't fall through, I wasn't convinced the binding would hold. "Please. Get me out of here." I was at the edge of the clearing, dangling to one side of the shelters I'd noticed earlier. The fire was hidden behind one, but not the light it threw off. That brightened the undersides of the trees and I wondered if I'd been wrong about the time of day. Perhaps it was later than I'd realized.

Eliza shook her head and brought one finger to her lips. "Don't make any noise. If they find me up here, we're both in trouble." She held a damp cloth between the bars.

I stared at it, draped over her hand.

"For your face. Or your ribs. Whatever hurts most. Is anything broken?" Eliza sat with her legs dangling over the edge of a platform that reminded me of the floor of a tree house. A rope ladder was swinging in the slight breeze below her. At the other end of her platform, made out of lengths of flat wood rather than round sticks like my cage, was an actual tree house. Walls, a roof, a door and a gap for a window.

Moving slowly because everything hurt, and because it was best to use caution around Eliza, I took the cloth from her and pressed it to my left eye, which was almost swollen shut. The cold was soothing. I shook my head to answer her question. I might be stiff and sore, but nothing seemed broken.

"I put some cream on your wounds and tried to stop the swelling with cold cloths." She nodded at my knees.

I followed her gaze to find a second cloth lying discarded beside me. My movement made the cage sway and creak.

"Keep still." Eliza reached out, took hold of one of the bars and pulled the cage to a stop.

"Please can you let me out?" I begged.

Eliza shook her head. "I can't. If Gisborne finds me up here now, I'll get the same treatment you've just had. And then there'll be no one to look after either of us."

"Where is he?" I croaked, feeling sick at the thought of him.

Eliza nodded in the direction of the fire. "Drinking. Eating. Celebrating."

"Celebrating?" As far as I knew Gisborne had nothing out of the ordinary to celebrate. "Because of what he did to me?"

Eliza nodded. Her dress was plainer than I'd seen her wear in the past, dark green and lacking the usual jewels and embellishments. Strands of hair had escaped the clasp at her neck, but she still looked as stunning as always. Even the scar on her cheek didn't detract.

"Why are you helping me?" I'd thought the two of us were as much enemies as Gisborne and me.

She looked out to where the fire glowed. The murmur of voices drifted up to us along with the occasional burst of raucous laughter. "Because you brought me a gift from my sister when you could easily have thrown it in the fire."

Yes, well, it wasn't like I'd gone out of my way.

"Oh, I know you didn't come to Woodhurst that night just for me. But I also know you could have walked straight past my chamber without giving me that...painting of Tabitha, and I'd never have known you had it. This is my way of making us even. And saying thank you." She held her hand through the bars again and I passed her the cloth. She dunked it in a small jar of water before handing it back. "You shouldn't have provoked him the way you did, you know." Her voice was quiet. An observation, not a reprimand. "Gisborne never responds well to provocation."

Tell me something I didn't know. I tried to shrug, but it hurt to lift my shoulder. "The outcome would likely have been the same whether I spoke up or remained silent." We both knew I would hold the information Gisborne wanted for as long as I could.

Her silence told me she agreed.

The wind moved through the trees, pushing the cage from side to side. Eliza took hold of it again, steadying it.

"What is this place?" I asked.

"This is where the Woodhurst boys spent many happy summer days."

I wasn't that gullible. "I doubt it. Not together, anyway." Rob and Gisborne had always hated each other.

She turned her lips down. "Sure, they didn't get along as they got older. But before that, and before Uncle Jerimiah began teaching Gisborne to be just like him, they were true brothers. They played here in summer, like their fathers did before them." She smiled softly. "Tabitha and I played here sometimes, too. Always loved this tree house." A burst of laughter came from around the fire. "Not anymore, though. Gisborne's made sure of that."

I watched the orange light dancing on the nearby trees. "Why would he bring me here rather than to Woodhurst?" I assumed we were near his home if Rob had played here as a child. It seemed strange that he wouldn't just continue on if we were that close.

"Because he has an image to uphold. Wouldn't do his reputation any good if someone saw him beating the life out of Lady Maud Fitzwalter before her father or the Sheriff had gotten hold of her. Especially given how you behaved at the Sheriff's tournament."

Eliza got to her feet. "I have to go. It's best you don't tell anyone I was here. The cream should help those bruises and cuts feel better by tomorrow." She dunked my cloths in the jar of water and handed them back one last time before tipping the water over the side of the platform and tucking the jar inside her dress. Then she shimmied down the ladder and disappeared into the darkness.

I woke to find my cage swinging wildly as Gisborne's men lowered it to the ground. They cut the ties and threw the door open. Gisborne stood in front of me, arms folded. My heart rate tripled when I saw him. I was stuck in this cage, couldn't get away. He was about to hurt me all over again; I could tell by the disgusted smirk on his face.

"Good morning, Lady Maud."

I wondered if Gisborne would ever see me as anyone but her.

"Would you like to elaborate on any of the things we discussed last night?" He gave little reaction as he looked at me. My face was surely as battered as Miller's had been, but the sight bothered Gisborne not at all. His slight smirk said he liked what he saw and was waiting to see me cower, waiting for me to beg for mercy.

"You want details about the valley we're staying in?" I stood at the back of the cage, gripping the wooden bars behind my back.

He raised his eyebrows, the only sign of encouragement he seemed willing to give. He might think he was hiding it, but his eyes widened in eagerness to hear my answer. He expected I would give him what he asked for.

Well, screw him. That wasn't happening. "It's filled with fluffy white clouds the unicorns sleep on." With a growl he dragged me from the cage by my tunic. I dodged the kick he aimed at my stomach. Didn't make it any less painful when his foot bit into my leg. That was the only blow I managed to dodge. The rest landed exactly where Gisborne aimed them; legs, face, gut and arms.

My eyes snapped open to see the sun blazing through the canopy of trees, high in the sky. I was back in the cage high above the ground. A jug of water and a chunk of bread sat on Eliza's platform, but there was no one around, even down in camp. I dragged the food and water into my cage, but my face was so swollen I could barely open my mouth. I had to dip the bread in the water just to eat it.

I needed to get out of here. I was fairly certain Rob would come and I wanted to be gone before he got here. If I didn't escape, Gisborne would kill me. I'd told Rob about my dreams. A violent death was my punishment.

The cage door was tied shut. I shuffled over to it, trying to keep the cage from moving, and started working on the ties. My fingers weren't injured, but the ties were tight, and my arms were bruised and stiff, and I had to stop to rest every few minutes. I tried kicking the door out, but that didn't work either.

Just before dawn, I managed to unravel the final tie. I allowed myself a moment to smile. I was free, and I was getting out of here.

I crawled through the door and onto the platform, then hurried down the rope ladder, my arms screaming in agony. The clearing was silent. Too much longer getting those ties undone and I'd have been too late. Everyone would be starting their day. But for now, while the forest was lit only by the last shafts of moonlight, I was free.

I crept around the base of the tree. A trail led away from the clearing here, I'd seen it from above. I didn't care where it went, all I needed was to go. And I was. I was on the trail. I was escaping.

Behind me, a stick cracked. My heart rate increased. So did my speed.

But I wasn't fast enough.

"Lady Maud." Gisborne's voice boomed through the quiet morning forest at my back.

Twenty-One

I RAN, but Gisborne was faster, his strides crushing leaves and twigs as he covered the distance between us in just a few steps. He caught the end of my hair and pulled me to a stop.

"Let me go!" I couldn't take another beating. "Stop!" He pulled me back toward his camp. He moved fast, and I had to run beside him to keep my hair from ripping from my head. The second he stopped, I would kick him. Between the legs if I could. Aimed right, it would give me a few moments to get away.

I tripped on a tree root—morning was coming fast, but not fast enough to light the trail. I landed on my knees, strands of hair ripping from my scalp before Gisborne released his grip. "Get up." His voice was icy and laced with fury.

I considered disobeying his order, then saw the tip of his boot and remembered what he'd do if I refused. I got to my feet, keeping my eyes down. As I straightened, I drove the heel of my boot into Gisborne's foot.

He growled then swore, reaching out for me, but I was already gone.

I sprinted down the trail for the second time this morning, pumping my arms and legs as fast as I could. And for the second time, he caught me in seconds. He tackled me around the legs, and I dropped to the ground.

I kicked but he held me tight, cursing.

I wasn't going back with him. I would not let him beat me again.

My hand closed around a rock lying on the trail. His grip on my legs loosened. Without giving him a chance to take hold of my arm and drag me to my feet, I twisted and smashed the rock into the side of his face.

He was stunned for about a second—a second I should have used to get the hell out of there—before he pulled me to standing. His face was harder than I'd ever seen it, his eyes void of emotion. He was going to hit me again. And this time, he wouldn't stop. He drew his hand back to hit me and I saw my chance. I slammed the rock into the side of his face, bracing for his fist, but it never came.

The moment I hit him, something shifted in the air. The movement was the same as I'd felt at the tournament; the magic realigning itself.

Gisborne screamed in pain and staggered back, releasing his grip on me. He sagged against the tree behind him, standing awkwardly and holding his jaw with one hand. "How lovely of you to join us." Gisborne's words were slurred, and blood ran down one side of his face. He kept blinking as if he was trying to clear his vision.

It took a moment to register why Gisborne was no longer coming at me.

Apart from the fact that my blow with the rock had him wobbling on his feet, the hand he'd raised to strike me was nailed to the tree behind him. An arrow had pierced his wrist, traveling so fast it lodged into the tree with Gisborne still attached. I had serious doubts that he could have hit me after what I'd done to him; his head swayed as he focused on something over my shoulder. He didn't seem to have registered the arrow through his wrist.

I followed his gaze and Rob stepped out onto the trail beside me. His face hardened as he looked me over, his eyes stalling on my bruised face, before moving to stare at Gisborne. "Seems I'm a little late. Maryanne appears to have taken care of you all on her own."

At the sound of his brother's voice, some of Gisborne's focus returned. He pulled at the arrow, snapping it in half and, with gritted teeth, pulled his wrist off the shaft. "Screw you, Woodhurst. Guards!"

In a movement almost too fast to see, Rob pulled an arrow from his quiver, nocked it and fired, pinning Gisborne to the tree again through the fleshy part of his shoulder.

Gisborne screamed, then held his head. It gave me a small sense of satisfaction to see how much my blow hurt him.

"There's no point yelling. Your guards are currently incapacitated." Rob fired another arrow, this one pinning Gisborne to the tree by his other arm.

Gisborne screamed again. "Guards!"

"They can't help you, Gisborne. My men are…taking care of them." Rob's jaw was tight, the only indication that he might be close to losing it. He waited until his brother stopped yelling. "Do you know what happens when you terrorize people who are weaker than yourself? When you hurt people who have no opportunity to fight back?"

Gisborne's mouth twisted with contempt and he lifted his chin. Even nailed to a tree, his men captured, Gisborne was still looking down at the world. "My men get to loot their village and keep any valuables."

Rob took a predatory step forward, running the tips of his fingers lightly up and down the shaft of his bow. Gisborne's eyes followed. "I can see how you might think that. The trouble is, when you act like a bastard over and over, the world has a way of turning on you. Eventually, everything you've done will come back and bite you on the backside." He reached over his shoulder and drew an arrow from the quiver. As he nocked it, he stepped backward until he was beside me, putting enough distance between him and Gisborne to ensure that arrow had enough speed to hurt Gisborne.

Gisborne's lips turned down as he looked at Rob with disgust. "Go on. Kill me. It's what you've wanted for the last six years."

"Oh, I intend to." Rob pulled the bowstring back to his cheek. And held it there.

Shoot it. This was the chance Rob had waited for. The chance to rid the world of his brother.

Gisborne laughed; a cruel, hard sound. He shook his head. "You always were too soft. That's why you could never have been the lord of the manor."

Rob's hand flexed around his bow. "No. I could never be lord of the manor because you traded away my life, looking for your father's approval."

Gisborne moved his shoulder like he was shrugging, then hissed in pain. "I knew he wanted you gone, and I saw an opportunity to make it happen. Unlike you, I didn't hesitate." His eyes snagged on the arrow pointed at his chest.

"Shooting me didn't get you what you wanted. Did it? Father might have loved you more than me, but that man barely knew how to love. And he didn't love you any better once he thought I was dead." Rob's voice was even as he looked down on Gisborne, his nostrils flaring. The hand holding his bow was deadly still, but I was certain it was an act. He had to be filled with fury at Gisborne, but he was hiding it well.

Gisborne smirked and shook his head. "Why did I need love? Without you in my way, I had land and titles I'd never have received. People began to treat me with respect. Killing you was the best thing I ever did. I only wish I'd done a better job." He'd certainly been trying to make that happen recently.

"Why? Worried the Sheriff might return all your land and titles to the rightful owner now he knows I'm not dead?" Rob shot the words back like a bullet.

I glanced at Rob. I didn't think him getting his home back was an option. Not since I killed that deer and Rob took the blame.

Gisborne shifted uncomfortably; his tone no longer quite so certain. "I believe the Sheriff sees this issue in the same light as me." He might, but there was obviously some other reason that kept him hunting Rob since the day he discovered him alive last summer.

"And King Richard? Should he return home suddenly and take over from the Sheriff, would he see the issue in the same light?" Rob let his question hang in the air.

Gisborne stared directly at him, but his lips remained firmly shut.

Rob was right. It was the King's reaction that concerned Gisborne. That was why he wanted his brother dead. "Would he agree the land and titles of Woodhurst should go to the person who attempted to murder the rightful Earl of Woodhurst?"

Gisborne swallowed. "Of course. Especially since the so-called rightful Earl of Woodhurst is a thief who kills the King's own game." The smug confidence was gone from Gisborne's voice. It was the first time I'd ever heard him uncertain.

"Or perhaps he'll see that I had no choice but to live in the forest, and live any way possible."

Gisborne glared. "Do it. Kill me. That's what all this is about."

Rob stared at him.

He wasn't going to.

After everything. After all the times Gisborne had tried to kill Rob, all the times he'd hurt one of us to get to Rob, after everything, Rob wasn't going to take this opportunity.

A laugh bubbled from Gisborne's chest. He knew it, too. "This is the reason, brother. This is why you could never have been the Earl of Woodhurst. You can't make the tough decisions. You're too soft."

Rob's arrow whistled as it flew through the air and buried in the flesh of Gisborne's thigh.

Gisborne screamed and struggled against the bindings Rob had made from his arrows.

Rob caught my eye and nodded along the trail. "Let's go. We'll leave him for the animals."

Gisborne cursed us at the top of his voice.

Rob ignored him and took my hand and walked me up the trail, away from Gisborne's screams.

Neither of us spoke as Rob guided me along the trail with his hand in mine. Once we made a turn that put us out of Gisborne's view, he stopped and looked at me. The pain in his eyes shattered my heart. "Maryanne." His voice wobbled but he held out an arm and I sank into his chest. "Are you all right?"

Bruised, not broken. "Better for seeing you." Now we were safe, the pain of my injuries came rushing back. My face was tight and swollen, and my head ached, my ribs ached. My entire body ached. "He would have killed me if you hadn't turned up." I'd seen the look in Gisborne's eyes before I hit him with the rock. He wouldn't have stopped this time. Tears pricked at my eyes. I refused to give in to them. I refused to let Gisborne have that sort of power over me.

Rob shook his head. "You didn't need me. That last blow with the rock disoriented him enough that you could have escaped. I just made sure he could never chase you." He pulled back and his jaw tightened as he swept his eyes over my battered face. "You should have told him where to find me. I assume keeping quiet was the reason he gave you all those bruises?"

"I was never going to tell him." That had never been an option. He knew that.

"I wish you had," he whispered, running his fingers with extreme gentleness down the side of my face. "I hate seeing you hurt. When I look at you, I can imagine the kick that caused that bruise on your cheek, or the slap that made that cut below your eye, the punch that produced that mark on your neck. It makes me so furious." His jaw tightened. "I wanted to keep you safe from him."

It was never going to be that easy. "It's okay. We don't have to worry about him anymore." Not when we had blood loss, the elements and wild animals all working toward the outcome we wanted for Gisborne. "You could have killed him."

He let out a deep sigh and nodded.

"Why didn't you?"

"Couldn't do it. I wanted to, but..." He shook his head and I wasn't sure if he was upset or disgusted with himself. "He looks so much like Mother, has her eyes. He reminded me of her."

"But last time, you did it."

"Last time, at the Big Tree, you weren't safe. I stuck my sword in him so I could get to you. This time you were perfectly safe, so there was no need. And I found I lacked the will to do it." He put his hand on my back, guiding me along the trail. "He will die, Maryanne. There's no way he can free himself. It's just not going to be me that lands the final blow."

He fell into silence and I couldn't gauge his mood. "Do you wish you had killed him?"

"No." He sighed. "The place he took you, we used to call it Little Manor. I remember helping him up that rope ladder when he was barely old enough to walk. We battled so many imaginary enemies in that place. Together. This part of the forest is the one place I have some good memories of my family. Of him. I could never kill him here." He met my eyes and I wondered if Gisborne had somehow known that would be the case.

"Well, I might have some good news."

Rob smiled. "Yes?"

"I haven't had any dreams since I told you about them. Which is what I expected. The price for telling you about them was supposed to be my death."

His eyes widened. "What? Why would you do that?"

"To keep you safe." I shook my head. "I was supposed to die here, with Gisborne. When I hit him with the rock, the magic moved. Something feels different. I think it's over. I've done enough to stop either of us dying." The heavy weight I'd carried on my shoulders for weeks lifted.

The dreams were gone.

We were safe.

We reached the clearing that had been my prison for two days to find Miller, Tuck and John there, each guarding three tied up and gagged soldiers. No wonder the camp was so silent as I escaped.

"Where's Eliza?" I asked, looking from soldier to soldier again just to make sure I hadn't missed her.

Tuck shook his head. "Not here."

"She is." I ran to the closest shelter, threw aside the tarpaulin door and looked inside. Just sleeping mattresses spread across the floor. No people. Same in the next shelter.

Rob stopped me on my way to the third, his hands on my shoulders. "She isn't here, Maryanne."

I pulled out of his grip. "She is. Was." I turned to the boys. "Are you certain?"

Four heads nodded.

"Then she's..." I didn't finish, already knowing where she was. I turned and sprinted up the trail we'd just come down, Rob's footsteps close behind.

My body ached each time my foot pounded into the dirt. I ignored it, desperate to get to Gisborne before Eliza. He was supposed to die. Slowly. He was no longer screaming, and that filled me with fear.

I rounded the corner that should have brought me face-to-face with Gisborne and stopped dead. "He's gone."

Rob came to a puffing halt half a step behind me.

The broken ends of four arrows lay on the trail. The rest of their bloody shafts were still embedded in the tree. "She saved him." My voice wobbled. We'd been so close. We should have killed him.

"We didn't even know she was here." Rob shook his head. His face was bleak, hands buried in his hair.

"We can search for them. They can't have gone far."

Rob nodded, but neither of us expected to find them. Rob might have known this part of the forest well as a child, but Gisborne knew it well now.

Twenty-Two

"Put the wood down there in a pile," I used my head to nod, my arms too full of my own wood to point. We hadn't found Gisborne. By mutual unspoken agreement, we were all ignoring the fact that he was still alive when he should have been dead. We'd missed our chance to kill him, but apart from that, life was no different to what it had been. Except in one major way. Rob and Alan were living with us in the forest.

"Here?" asked Alan.

Everyone was pleased to have them with us. There was more spring in their step, more laughter in their talk. The boys started hunting again, all of them going out together. Which left me with time to get to know Alan.

I nodded, dropping my pile, then bending to stack it nicely. Alan did the same.

Getting firewood was the first thing Miller had taught Alan when he came to live with us. He seemed to enjoy the responsibility, and he loved to learn. I'd discovered we needed to show him correctly the first time or he would recall the wrong way of doing something easier than any way I tried to correct him. He was constantly surprising me. Rob had given him a lesson with a bow, which Alan had loved, but he was far more interested in how John cooked a meal for all of us. Last night, he'd helped with the cooking, too.

"Do you like my brother?" Alan asked, as he set the fire.

"Of course. He's a wonderful person." That was as vague an answer as I'd ever given. Rob and I needed to spend some time together, something we'd been slowly working up to in the days since I returned from Gisborne.

"Yes, but do you *like* him? Are you his girlfriend?"

I shook my head. "I'm not his girlfriend."

"Huh," he said quietly. "You should be. He was worried for you when Gisborne took you, and I've never seen him that worried about anyone. And you're nice. Not mean to me, like some people."

My head shot up. "Who's mean to you, Alan?"

He shrugged. "People, sometimes. They call me stupid. I don't like it when they call me stupid."

"You shouldn't," I said, carefully. "Because you're not." He wasn't. He just learned in a different way from the rest of us.

He picked a stick out of my hand and put it back on the pile, deeming it too large to use to start the fire. "Sometimes when I can't do things, like run fast or kick a ball hard, I think they might be right."

Something tightened in my chest. "You're not stupid. Who says these things? Does Rob know?" I wanted to hurt the person who'd said it. I couldn't imagine what Rob might do if he knew.

Alan grinned. "He clipped a kid around the ear once when he heard him say it. Kid was 'bout the same size as him, but he never called me stupid again." His speech grew slurred as he got excited. It made me smile and reminded me in a way of Miller. Rob's brothers, blood or not, were more similar than any of them realized.

"Well, if anyone does, you tell me. Okay? Because no one should say things like that."

Alan nodded. "Are they really going to keep teaching me how to shoot a bow, so I'll be the same as Rob?" He held his breath as he waited for my answer. We'd talked about it again this morning. John needed more practice, which gave Alan the perfect opportunity to learn. If he wanted to.

"That depends," I said. "Do you want to keep learning?" I hoped he did but had no idea if he'd be able to master it. He deserved the chance to learn the way both his younger brothers had.

He nodded so hard his hair escaped the tie and fell across his face.

"Good." I stood up and brushed off my hands. Alan did the same. "Do you know what?"

He shook his head.

"You're nice, too."

Alan beamed and pulled something out of his pocket. He held it out to me. "I found this for you."

It was an early spring wildflower, slightly crushed, but the sentiment remained. "Thank you, Alan. It's beautiful." I threaded it through my hair. "Did you know we're going to a party tomorrow night?" It seemed like so long ago since the invitation had come, but it had only been a week.

"A party? Here?" He looked around the tiny campsite. We'd moved back to Kings Cave, and it certainly wasn't big enough for a party.

OUTPLAYED

I shook my head. "No. We've been invited to a party for St Valentine's Day at the village of Huxley." I didn't know what to expect from a Valentine's Day party, apart from dancing—according to John, there would be plenty of dancing.

Rob and John crested the hill beside the cave and Alan got to his feet, eyes on his brother. "Huxley. That's where the waterfall slide is, right? The one you told me about last summer?"

"You've got a good memory," smiled Rob, looking between the two of us.

"That's because it sounded fun. Can we go there? After the party? Or before?"

"It's winter." Rob said it as if that explained everything.

"Almost spring," argued Alan. "Have you been, Maryanne?"

I shook my head. "I've never been nor ever heard about this waterfall slide."

"It was just a place we found last summer—"

"And it was so much fun!" Miller said, coming up the hill, a pheasant in his hand.

"So, you'll take me?" Alan asked.

"I don't know." Rob hesitated.

"Maybe we could go. Just to look at it, the day after the party." What harm was there? If Alan wanted to see it and we were so close.

"Yes! Let's!" said Alan.

Rob sighed. "All right. I'll take you both. After the party."

The boys were more excited than I realized. They spent the day getting ready; bathing in the river, washing their clothes, and slicking back their hair. John even made some rabbit stew to give our hosts. I had a surprise to share tonight, plus I could get dressed up, so I was looking forward to the party as much as anyone. Before I left home, I'd packed the dress the Sheriff had given me the first time I came to the twelfth century. I'd carted it around each time we moved camp. And finally tonight, I had a reason to wear it.

When we were almost at Huxley, I stopped, feigning a problem with my boot. I sat on a log at the edge of the trail and unlaced it, pulling the boot off and emptying out a non-existent stone. As I retied my laces, Rob drew his sword, slowly and quietly. I put a hand on his arm and stepped in front of him.

"Maryanne," he whispered. "Get out of the way. There's someone out there."

I shook my head and held up my hand as the others drew their swords. "It's okay."

The trees beside us rustled and out stepped Josephine and her little boy, Luke. I smiled at John. "Happy birthday."

John dropped his staff on the ground. "Jo. What the...?" He wrapped his arms around his sister, lifting her off the ground, closing his eyes tight as they hugged. "You shouldn't be out here alone," he said, pulling away.

"We were careful. Anyway, isn't a big sister allowed to wish her brother a happy birthday?" Jo's smile was huge. She had the same brown hair as John. Normally, strands fell loose from her hair clips, but tonight, like the rest of us, she'd spent time on her appearance, and her hair was pulled neatly to the back of her neck. Her dress was simple, navy blue in color, and her cheeks were pink with excitement.

"You look beautiful." John beamed and I wondered how long it had been since he'd heard her call him her brother. At least four years, I guessed. "You did this?" He looked at me.

"You said you missed her. That you wanted to spend some time with her and Luke. Tonight seemed like a good opportunity. She's coming to Huxley with us. The three of you have all evening to get to know each other again."

He strode over and wrapped his arms around me. "This is about the best present anyone's ever given me. How can I ever thank you?" he whispered.

"By getting to know your nephew. Then telling me about him at every chance you get." Because that was the real kicker about being far from the people you loved, not having anyone to share your memories with.

"Deal," he said. He put one arm around Jo, picked up Luke and started up the trail toward Huxley, a spring in his step.

Rob sidled up beside me. "You know you've screwed things up for the rest of us, right?" His eyes danced when he looked my way.

"Really? And how's that?"

"We're never going to be able to give him a birthday present better than this one, no matter how many years we try."

I laughed. "Just don't go getting any ideas. There's no way I'm inviting your younger brother to spend your birthday with us. Unless you have any other brothers tucked away that I don't know about?" It was possible. He'd kept Alan secret for a long time.

He shook his head. "No. Just the two."

"Thank goodness. I don't think I could cope with any more."

He laughed softly, watching John and Josephine ahead of us on the trail.

He seemed quiet and I wondered if he was worried for their safety. "John and Jo don't have to come to Huxley tonight. I just thought it would be safer if we're all together. I also wanted her to be with us when we arrived. Better that the people of Huxley don't know she's come from another village. Don't want anyone to tell Gisborne."

"You've thought it all out, haven't you?"

"I tried." I just wanted John to have a good birthday. And to spend it with the family he seemed to miss so much.

"I don't even know how you managed this." He shook his head like it was beyond his comprehension.

"Woke up one morning last week feeling like I needed to change the world. Or at least, change my part of the world. Went to Clipstone, talked to Jo. Then found you and asked you to come home." Then told him about the dreams and spent two nights at Gisborne's camp for my troubles.

He laughed. "I don't recall much *asking* happening that day."

I pushed past him, glancing over my shoulder. "That's because you listen better when I tell you what to do than when I ask nicely." I continued up the trail with a smile on my lips.

His reply drifted quietly to me. "I know. And that's exactly why I like you so much."

It was just on dark when we arrived in Huxley and the party was already beginning. Music filled the air as we walked down the rutted street that ran the length of the village toward the glowing field where a bonfire roared. Flaming torches marked the pathway down to the field.

Elton and his mother, Hannah, met us beside the first torch, smiles on their faces today rather than terror. Hannah hugged Rob, then me, and thanked us again and again for saving her son's hand.

She pointed us toward tables piled with food; pheasant and duck, carrots, parsnips, potatoes, bread and some green thing I couldn't identify. And pork roasting on a spit. I'd never tasted anything so good. "I thought the villages were struggling," I whispered to Rob between mouthfuls.

"They are." He licked his fingers. "They've likely been hoarding food for months for this feast. And fattening up the pig." He glanced at the area beside the fire where dancing had just begun. "Want to dance?"

There were a range of instruments playing by the fire. When we arrived, three girls had danced a jig to a set of bagpipes. But they'd disappeared and someone else was now playing a violin so fast and with so much joy I could barely see his fingers on the strings. "The fiddler's very good," Rob added, as if that would help make up my mind.

I shook my head. I wasn't dancing. Couldn't would be the more accurate term. Not the way they were dancing beside the bonfire, anyway. They had partners and set steps they all did at the same time. I was pretty sure the step-tap I used at school dances back home wasn't going to cut it.

Rob narrowed his eyes. "Scared, are we?"

I shook my head. He'd talked me into something using this tactic before. It wasn't happening today. "Totally. And it's not something I'm going to get over in a hurry."

He leaned forward and spoke into my ear. "I could help you."

A shiver went up my spine as his breath touched my skin. I hoped we'd have some time together tonight. To talk. To get to know each other again. It wasn't going to happen on the dance floor, though. "Tempting. But no." The dancing was way too complicated for my two left feet. "You go, though. There's a young lady over there who looks like she'd love to dance with you."

Rob's eyes followed the direction of my nod. The girl smiled at him. "I'd rather dance with you." His fingers tapped against his thighs in time to the beat.

I gave him a shove. "Go. Show me how it's done."

Rob might have been about to refuse, but the girl walked over and took his hand.

He was a good dancer, moving around his partner on light feet, and with a huge smile on his face. I didn't know why I was surprised. He was good at everything.

"He was brought up learning the more formal versions of these dances." Tuck stopped beside me, speaking as though he could read my mind.

"What about you?" I asked. "Do you know these dances?"

He nodded. "It's been a very long time since I've been near a dance floor, though, and I don't see it happening tonight." No sooner had he said it than a girl a little older than me ran up to Tuck, took his hand and pulled him into the dance. He was good, too. But not as good as Rob.

I didn't want to watch only Rob—there were plenty of others dancing who were almost as good—but my eyes kept finding him as if he was the only other person here. I enjoyed seeing him happy and relaxed. There hadn't been a lot of time for either emotion in the months I'd known him.

He moved from partner to partner, twisting and turning amongst the villagers as if he were one of them.

Rob beckoned to me. I shook my head. Not happening.

"Go. Dance!" Miller took a swig from the tankard in his hand. It was the first time I'd seen him since we arrived. He danced on the spot, the same moves Rob and Tuck were doing with their partners.

I narrowed my eyes. "What are you drinking? Is there whiskey in that mug? You're too young." Tuck had been firm about his thoughts on hard liquor. It wasn't something he allowed any of us to partake in, even though he always had a flask of whiskey in his pack. For emergencies and medicinal purposes, apparently.

Miller shook his head, hard and fast, a definite indication he had whiskey in there. I took the mug and tipped it on the ground.

"Maryanne!"

"Would you rather I do that now, or leave it for Tuck to catch you sculling whiskey?" Plus, I had a nagging fear left over from weeks of running from Gisborne that we might need to get out of this place fast, should soldiers come. We didn't need to be dealing with drunkenness or hangovers if that happened.

He sighed and folded his arms across his chest. "You should dance with him. You two haven't spent much colony time together lately."

I tried not to laugh. It felt like forever since I'd heard Miller misuse a word, but I'd take it any day. Colony time or quality time were all the same to me, so long as I saw Miller recovering from what Gisborne did to him. I shook my head. "Don't know how."

Miller lifted his eyebrows, looking very much like Rob. "You know he'll show you."

I did know that, and I was suddenly nervous. There had always been a reason for Rob and me to skip over whatever the thing was between us; I was going to return home; we had to look out for Gisborne; he was keeping Alan safe. Tonight, we had no reason and I was terrified.

"Maryanne!" Alan ran up to me. He'd been dancing with one of the local girls and his hair was plastered to his head. He'd taken off his cloak and opened the top two buttons of his tunic to cool down. "Let's dance!"

He took my hand and pulled me around the fire toward the music without allowing me the opportunity to refuse. He pushed into the dance circle, making sure I was on the outside with the rest of the girls and women. I couldn't walk away, not when he looked so excited. Instead, I shook my head. "I don't know how."

"I do." He took my hand and moved us forward. Then backward. Then he spun me around. All in time with everyone else.

"You're a good dancer," I laughed, as I missed standing on his foot by millimeters.

"Not as good as Rob." He glanced across the circle at his brother, who was smiling over some girl's head at the two of us.

"Better," I grinned. "He couldn't teach me to dance."

He hugged me then threw himself into the moves. Soon, I was too busy trying to keep up to feel self-conscious.

I was out of breath and covered in sweat, and my cheeks hurt from smiling when the fiddler finally took a break. I'd danced with almost every man here for a beat or two, and I felt happier than I had in a long time.

The fire had died down to embers and in the sudden quietness, the fiddler directed everyone to sit around it. It was time for The Match. With a title like that, I imagined some sort of sports tournament, and was contemplating how that might happen in the dark when Hannah moved through the ring of people to stand next to the fire, a hat in her hand.

Rob squeezed in to sit beside me. "I believe the excuse was, *I can't dance.*"

I looked at my hands resting against my crossed knees and hid my smile. That might have been the reason I gave him when I said no to dancing.

"Yet it didn't seem like that at all a few moments ago when the fiddler was playing."

I laughed. Every man I'd danced with had had his foot trod on at least twice. "I wouldn't call it dancing. And we can't all be as accomplished at everything as you."

"Says the woman who's bested my greatest enemy three times now, while I can barely land a blow on him."

Not entirely true. "That, Robin of Woodhurst, has not a thing to do with skill, and everything to do with hatred." It was a horrible thing to admit, but it was true. My absolute loathing of Gisborne and the way he'd treated Rob drove my actions almost every time I was near the man. It had certainly been hatred that made me stab my knife into his arm. And hatred mixed with fear that made me smash a rock into his face three different times.

"If it only came down to hate, my brother would be dead a hundred times over by now." Probably more. Rob and I were far from the only ones who disliked him.

"Could it be the greatest archer the forest has ever seen is admitting defeat?" Tonight was for

OUTPLAYED

fun, not for dwelling on what might have been. And he'd given me the opening.

A slow grin crossed his face and the pit of my stomach filled with butterflies. "I told you already, Lady Maryanne. If you want that title, you'll have to fight me for it."

Hannah called out two names, and all around us, people cheered.

"Really? And how exactly should I take you up on that offer. You know, should I ever want to make you admit you're the second-best archer in Sherwood Forest?" I smiled to myself. Tonight was exactly what Rob and I needed to get back to normal.

His grin grew wider and if possible, even more wicked. "Oh, I can think of plenty of ways. None of which can be discussed with so many people around."

God help me, but my cheeks heated. With any luck, he couldn't see by the light of the fire. "I'll remind you to explain, then. Next time we're alone."

He laughed into his chest and waited while Hannah called a new set of names before leaning in and whispering, "You won't dance with me, but you spend the entire night dancing with my brother? How is that fair?"

Not entirely true. Rob and I had danced together twice, but each time I was twirled off to a new partner before I was ready to leave. "Not jealous, are you?"

Rob grinned. "Why would I be jealous?" His eyes sparkled. "My brother's a great dancer. He's fun to be around, and he didn't even have to ask you to dance with him." Unlike me, were his unspoken words.

"He's good-looking, too." I could play his game. And I could do it without blushing. "You forgot to add that to the list."

"That goes without saying. He *is* my brother, after all."

I choked back a laugh as Hannah called out two more names to more loud cheers.

When the cheering stopped, Rob put a hand on his chest and let the amusement drain completely from his face. "I am totally, utterly and entirely jealous of anyone who gets to spend time with you, my lady."

My lady. He hadn't called me that in the longest time. I liked the way it sounded when he said it. It sent shivers through my body. "Even your brother?"

He gave a single nod. "Especially my brother."

"Rob...I hope you don't think..." My heart fell to my feet. I was just trying to be a good friend to Alan. Nothing more.

He held up his hand for me to stop. "You're so relaxed with him. Your friendship is new, but it looks...easy."

OUTPLAYED

"It is easy." Alan was fun, and I enjoyed hanging out with him.

"Unlike...us, for instance."

The crowd cheered again.

I knew exactly what Rob was getting at. "You don't think this is easy?" Because tonight had been better than it had been in a long time.

He shrugged. "Sometimes. Until we argue. Or when I sit up night after night watching you thrashing in your sleep wondering if the fever will steal you away. Or until I see my brother dragging you onto a horse or beating the life out of you. None of that was easy." He swallowed. "You should have told Gisborne we were staying at Kings Cave." He ran his eyes over my face, still bruised, but healing fast. "You knew he'd hurt you if you kept quiet."

"I knew he'd hurt *you* if I didn't."

Rob rested his hand on mine. "Like I said, *we* are not easy."

"And you wish we were." I wasn't sure how that made me feel. Disappointed, I guessed. Life wasn't easy with Rob. It was like living on a roller coaster, but I wouldn't wish it away, no matter what.

He squeezed my hand. "Never in a million years would I wish that. I know for certain I'm alive when I'm around you, and there's nothing better than feeling alive. I just...miss talking. The way we used to."

He wasn't the only one.

Hannah called another pair of names and we watched while two people made their way to the front, kissed on the cheek then sat down. "What is actually going on here?" It seemed to be some sort of ritual, but I'd been too busy talking with Rob to take any notice.

"It's The Match. Guess I'm going to have to get used to that jealous feeling, when they call your name."

I shook my head. "I don't know what the match is." Other than a rugby game.

He turned his head, checking to see if I was kidding. "It's St Valentine's Day. You don't do this?"

"I'm not sure what *this* is." Valentine's Day wasn't a huge thing in my country. Unless you were a couple. Then you got suckered into buying flowers on the most expensive day of the year.

"One of the village elders calls out pairs of names. The person you're paired with is your Valentine, and you can either kiss them, or give them a gift. Then, if you want to hang out for the rest of the night, you can. Or you can go your separate ways. No pressure."

Oh. That was kind of romantic. "So, anyone who's married automatically has their partner's name called?"

Rob shook his head then grinned as my eyes widened. "St Valentine's Day is the one day anyone can be single again. If they want to."

Not quite so romantic as I'd first thought, then. "Don't people care?" Especially if they're married.

He shrugged, watching as an old lady kissed a guy about Rob's age on the cheek. He grinned and kissed her back. On the lips. "Some do, I guess. Some have an agreement to do what they like on St Valentine's Day. Mostly, it's only a kiss on the cheek."

"Unless they decide to hang out after."

He pressed his lips together. "Unless, that."

Hannah called Tuck's name and he pressed a kiss to the cheek of the pretty young girl who'd asked him to dance. He smiled as she spoke to him, then returned to sit next to her in the circle, to a huge chorus of claps and cheers.

Miller's partner was a girl close in age to him, and his cheeks and the back of his neck turned a mottled red as he kissed her. And John's was a young woman with lush black hair, who John didn't seem to mind kissing at all.

Rob leaned in to speak in my ear. "I would."

I narrowed my eyes and turned to him wondering where this was going. "You would what?"

"Care."

"About what?" But I didn't need to ask. I knew what he was referring to. It was just that my heart was racing so fast, I wasn't sure I could speak more than two words. I hadn't known until then, not for sure, how Rob felt about me.

"If you kissed someone else." His breath tickled my ear and I didn't know how I was going to draw the next breath into my lungs.

"I wasn't aware we had a reason to have an *arrangement* discussion." I tried to sound flippant, but it came out breathless.

Hannah called my name and I rose, but Rob took my arm and pulled me back down. "There will always be a need for an *arrangement* discussion between us on St Valentine's Day."

He let my arm go and I got to my feet. Leaning down, I said, "Right back at you."

Twenty-Three

I MADE my way to Hannah, my heart racing. Mostly because of my conversation with Rob, but also because I was about to share a kiss with a complete stranger, and I wasn't sure I wanted to. My twenty-first century-self kicked into gear. What if they hadn't washed? What if they had some sort of disease? What if they wanted to hang out tonight and I didn't?

My hands were shaking, and I wasn't sure if it was nerves or left-over adrenalin from talking to Rob. I stopped in front of Hannah and John called out, "Happy Birthday, Maryanne. Hope you like your present as much as I liked mine."

I nodded, not sure I needed everyone to know it was my birthday. And then heard the name Hannah called next.

Rob.

He grinned as he walked up to me. "Never have I been so glad of anyone's birthday and their present from someone else in my whole life."

We stared at each other, both waiting for the other to make the first move. Finally, I shook my head. "I'm not kissing you. I have a gift." I did. By accident, but a gift that would work perfectly just the same.

His lips flickered. "I also have a gift. But I don't intend to give it to you here." He took my hand with a grin, and pulled me away from the bonfire, out into the darkness of the open field. As the crowd grew loud and raucous at our hasty retreat, he slid his arm around my waist and urged me toward the forest, both of us laughing as we ran from the bonfire.

We stopped, still giggling, when we were too far from the bonfire to hear anything but the occasional cheers, at a spot right at the edge of the forest. He indicated I should sit on a log poking out the edge of the bracken, and he took a seat next to me. I tried to ignore my rapid heartbeat, and instead focused on finding the present I'd carried around since I'd returned to his time. I finally found it at the bottom of my bag.

"Happy Valentine's Day," I said, holding it out to him.

Rob took the paper-wrapped present and turned it over in his hands. I was suddenly nervous. At home, this had seemed like the perfect gift for Rob, but now I wasn't sure if he'd even like it, let alone remember why I chose it.

He brought the package up to his nose, still unopened, and inhaled deeply. "I love it," he said.

"You haven't opened it yet."

"Don't need to. Recognize the smell. My most favorite smell in the world." He unfolded the paper to reveal two bars of handmade vanilla and raspberry soap. Not very manly, but it had seemed right when I brought them. "Reminds me of one of my favorite days in the world."

"You remember?" He'd seen me in my underwear that day. Of course he remembered.

"Never smelled anything as good as the soap you used that day. And you got me two pieces?" He brought a piece to his nose and took another deep inhale. "I don't think my gifts are going to compare."

He rested the soap on his lap and pulled a package from his pocket. "Happy birthday, Maryanne."

I unwrapped the paper to find a jewel encrusted hairclip inside. "It's beautiful. Where did you get it?" Because it looked expensive and would be better used to help a village in need.

He took it from my hand and indicated I should turn around. Then he ran his fingers through my hair, pulling it back and sliding the clip in place. "I don't have many things that were Mother's. Just this and a couple of other small pieces. She'd have been pleased for you to have it. Even if it's not very practical." He stood and pulled me to my feet.

"Thank you." I touched the clip in my hair, humbled by his choice of gift and by the fact it had once belonged to his mother. It was the most beautiful thing I'd ever owned, and combined with the dress I was wearing, I felt like a princess. Looking up at a prince.

"I have something else for you." He pulled me toward him so close I had to tip my head back to see him. His fingers were linked in mine and his eyes fell on my lips. My heart rate ramped up another notch and I blew out a long, nervous breath.

He watched me carefully, could probably feel my hand shaking in his fingers. Finally, he narrowed his eyes. "So long as you can bear to come close to me before I use my new soap to bathe?"

I'd once said he had no idea what to do with a piece of soap.

"That depends. Are you going to tell me how all the jewels in the world couldn't match my beauty?" It was a line he used often to get women to part with their rings, necklaces and hairclips when he stopped their carriages. A line which made every one of them blush and giggle, no matter their age. A line he'd never said to me.

He drew his head back to look at me properly, then shook his head, his face losing its lightness. He brought one hand up and brushed it across my cheek. I shivered.

"You are more beautiful than all the jewels in the world, Maryanne Warren. More attractive than anyone I've ever known and every time I look at you, I can't catch my breath. But your beauty is by far the least desirable thing about you. You're smart, and brave and caring, too. And I love all those things more."

My breath caught. Rob always knew how to say the exact thing that would stop me in my tracks.

His grin returned. I guess he'd seen my blush in the moonlight. Or he just knew me well enough to know that when I looked at my feet, I was hiding my cheeks. "Now, will you let me kiss you?"

"That depends." I needed a moment to re-balance myself.

His smile grew wider. "Does it now? On what?"

"There's this guy, he's a bit of an idiot at times. He told me that we needed to come to some sort of arrangement before I could kiss anyone tonight. I'm just not sure we came to that arrangement."

"Oh, you did." His eyes were flitting between my mouth and my eyes.

"Really? And what was it?" Actually, I was over this conversation. If he just wanted to cut to the chase and kiss me, I'd be good with that. Didn't need an answer.

Rob leaned in a little more and I thought he was going to do exactly that, but he stopped short of my lips. "It was that you could kiss him, and only him, tonight, tomorrow night and any night of your choosing."

I swallowed. "What if I choose never to kiss him?"

Rob's head shake was so minute, it almost wasn't there. "Oh, you won't."

His confidence made my knees weak. He put his arm around my waist, holding me up and drawing me closer, then filled the rest of the distance between us, leaning in until our lips met. My breath caught immediately, and I wrapped my arms around his neck. I'd wanted this since the day I returned, had day-dreamed about it from my own time. And even when I'd been pushing all those thoughts away because I thought he had someone else, they were still there. And the kiss I'd dreamed of had never been half as good as this.

He tilted my head back, and I dragged my fingers through his hair, arching into him. This was all the things we hadn't said since that first kiss, all the things we had yet to say. He ran his hands up my back, grasping the hair at the base of my neck. Tingles erupted along my spine, fanning out across the rest of my body.

Despite what he'd said, he'd used some sort of fragrant soap today; he smelled like lemon, and smoke from the bonfire. He smelled like Rob.

When I didn't think I could draw another breath due to my racing heart, he pulled away. He gave me a shy smile, his breath coming in quick bursts. "I've wanted to do that for forever."

"I hope it was worth the wait." I wasn't stupid enough to think I was the only girl he'd ever kissed. I saw how the women in the carriages looked at him. I was at the low end of experience and I didn't want him to be disappointed.

"Are you kidding me? I'd wait that long again knowing kissing you would feel that way."

"Me too," I whispered.

He wrapped his fingers through mine. "We should get back. I poured whiskey out of Miller's mug earlier. Better go check he hasn't found any more."

Twenty-Four

SOMETHING woke me the next morning while it was still dark. I wasn't sure what. I just knew it wasn't a bad dream. I hadn't had a nightmare in days. I lay still and listened, waiting to see if there was another sound that would tell me why I'd woken, but there was no noise apart from the sounds of sleep.

We'd slept at the village last night. By the time Rob and I found Miller, he was already passed out in some unsuspecting family's home—must have found more whiskey after he'd seen Rob and me. It was too difficult to carry him back to Kings Cave, and Tuck, John and Alan wanted to stay. So, we did, sleeping on the floor of an empty home,

John slipping in after he walked Josephine and Luke back to Clipstone. We would leave here at dawn so as not to cause any problems for the villagers should soldiers arrive.

I listened to the steady breathing of my friends. They might all be asleep, but I was now wide awake and desperate to relieve myself.

Pulling on my boots and wrapping my cloak around my shoulders, I crept outside. The village was deserted, muffled snores coming from every hut. It was cold out, and after I used the communal outhouse, I headed for the remains of the bonfire, the last coals still glowing in the darkness and hopefully giving off a little heat.

Last night had been amazing and I was happier than I could remember being in a long time. Certainly, since Josh's accident. Probably since before that. I had good friends who listened to me, a place in their group, somewhere to live. And Rob. Thinking about the way he kissed me last night still sent tingles up my spine, even now, all these hours later.

It was that I focused on as I settled beside the embers of the bonfire, drawing my cloak tightly around me.

Everything had worked out. Rob was living in the forest again, and my dreams were gone. Yet, I still didn't feel safe. We hadn't heard a thing from

OUTPLAYED

Gisborne since Eliza helped him escape. He was too quiet, and I couldn't help but wonder what was coming next.

Light slowly chased away the night. In the village behind me, the sounds of people rising wafted out on the wind, and the birds began to chirp.

Down at the bottom of the field, at the place it almost disappeared into forest, a man walked away from the village. Not just any man. Rob. Even this far away and in the low light I could tell by his cloak and the color of his hair. I stood up, ready to wave the moment he turned this way. He could come and sit with me beside the bonfire embers while we waited for everyone to wake. He turned slightly and time slowed.

The field in front of me was suddenly the field I'd seen in a hundred dreams. A thousand.

Nausea welled inside me.

This was the place.

I'd seen it so many times in my head. How was it I'd been here since last night and only just realized?

Because we'd arrived in the dark to lanterns and a bonfire. Only now the light was coming could I see it plainly.

"Rob!" I screamed his name, picked up the hem of my cloak and sprinted down the slope toward him. "Rob! Run!" The dreams might have stopped but there was no way I was sitting here waiting, watching and doing nothing, even if there was no danger coming.

My thoughts flew in every direction as I sprinted, panicking and yelling his name. The only way for him to be safe was if he didn't stay here. He had to move. Go back to the village.

"Rob!" My scream hurt right down into my chest, but still he didn't look up. Or even turn. Why didn't he hear me?

I ran. Faster than I'd thought possible in boots and a heavy cloak. If I could get there first, make him move into the forest, we might be all right. Because it never happened in the forest. It always happened out here. Right at the edge of this field, with the birds singing and a river bubbling somewhere nearby.

The uneven ground stole my footing. I stumbled, landed on my knees in the damp and frosty grass. Wetness soaked through my dress. I jumped up, Rob's name on my lips. Just like in my dream, I felt entirely helpless.

The *thwang* of the bowstring sounded as I screamed his name. An arrow flew from somewhere over my right shoulder. A moment later, it buried in Rob's back. He made a surprised grunt and fell forward, just as I'd seen him do a million times before.

"Rob!" My legs moved but I felt like I wasn't getting anywhere.

Horses hooves pounded into the earth behind me. I braced for the same treatment as Rob, for an arrow to pierce my body. But they passed me by. Ten. Fifteen horses. And bringing up the rear, the magnificent beast that belonged to Sir Guy of Gisborne.

They formed a semi-circle between Rob and me. Gisborne slid down from his horse, less graceful than I'd ever seen him.

"Gisborne!" I screamed, racing toward them. How was he well enough to ride?

Gisborne turned slowly then indicated to two of his soldiers on horseback. They nocked their arrows and pointed them at me. "I would stop, Lady Maud, if I were you." His movements were stiff, his elbows tucked in beside his ribs. He was still hurting from Rob's arrows.

One of the soldiers let his arrow fly. It landed a centimeter in front of my left boot. I stopped short. "Leave him alone!"

Gisborne glanced over his shoulder at me. "Sorry, but no." He reached down and twisted the arrow in Rob's back, pulling until it came free. Rob's body convulsed and he contorted in pain. I screamed, too, and ran.

An arrow landed between my feet.

"Consider that your final warning, my lady." Gisborne barely glanced my way. He ordered one of his men to pick Rob up and lay him, face down, across a horse, strapping him there with a long piece of rope.

"You can't take him away!" My voice was shrill in the morning air, the only tool I had to keep Rob safe. He couldn't take Rob from us. From the world. From me. I felt like I'd only just got him back.

"How is it you intend to stop me?"

I shook my head, wishing I'd killed him with that rock. Or Rob had killed him with his arrows. This morning I had no weapon, nothing to fight with. Hadn't taken a single thing when I left the others sleeping. How had I been so stupid? I'd been so wrapped up in memories of Rob's kiss that I hadn't even bothered to consider the danger. I couldn't move toward him, not without receiving an arrow through my leg. Or heart. I couldn't do a goddamned thing. Just like in my dream.

Gisborne smirked. "Smart girl." He climbed onto his horse. "I have some fun times planned for the two of us. Unless he dies. Then he'll receive a shallow grave and a party." He glanced over my shoulder, up the hill to the village. "Word has it, your father is due to return home. Because I have no way of knowing if that is true, I'm not going to take you as well. This time. But don't worry, my lady. I'll be back. And we'll have all sorts of fun once I return." He made a clicking sound and kicked his horse's sides.

And they were gone. Back into the forest where they'd come from mere moments ago.

Behind me, footsteps pounded down the hill. Voices yelling. At me. At Rob. At Gisborne. Tuck's the loudest of them all. I heard them. Didn't turn. Was watching the place Gisborne's soldiers entered the forest. The place they'd taken an injured and probably dying Rob.

I was sick. Sick of being the victim. Sick of feeling like I was shattering into a million pieces. Sick of it always happening because of an arrow. Gisborne didn't get to threaten me, to take away people I loved, to hurt them, without ever having any recourse on him.

I no longer cared about rules, or laws, or following procedures. I didn't care that Rob saw his mother in that man. Because next time I had the chance to kill him, he was dead.

All I wanted was to find my way back to the place I'd been last night. The place where I'd been happier than I'd ever known.

If Rob died today, I had nothing to lose. If he didn't, I'd do everything I could to get him back.

Either way, Gisborne should be terrified.

He wasn't coming for me.

I was coming for him.

Get the Sherwood Outlaws Prequel Novella for Free

Thanks for reading Outplayed.

I really enjoy getting to know my readers, it's one of the best things about being a writer. I send a newsletter to my readers group once a month, and that group is the first to find out about new releases and special offers.

If you sign up to my readers group, I'll send you a copy of Outcast for free. Outcast is a novella narrated by Rob, set before he met Maryanne. And my readers group is the only place it's available.

Just use the link below, then complete your email address. I'm looking forward to meeting you.

www.hayleyosborn.com/outcast

Enjoy This Book?

You can make a difference.

Honest reviews are an important part of a book's success as they help new readers discover new stories to enjoy. They are the most powerful thing for getting attention for my books.

If you enjoyed this book, I'd be forever grateful if you could take five minutes to leave a review on the book's Amazon page—it can be as short as you like.

Thank you!

Also by Hayley Osborn

Outlawed
Outlasted

Go to www.hayleyosborn.com to find out more.

Acknowledgments

Outplayed was the hardest book in this series to write. Don't ask me why—I couldn't tell you. I just know it took a lot more effort than the other books to get it to the place it's at now.

So, I need to thank a few people.

Melissa, thank you for editing this book. It would have been something completely different—and terrible—without you.

Kat, thanks for reading this and suggesting changes. I will always be grateful for all the time you give me when you could be writing your own books.

Mum, Dad and Kelly, thanks for being the supportive cheerleaders of my work that you always are.

Hayden, Jacob, Ashleigh and Zach—there's just one more book in this series. Once that's released, I promise to put aside the laptop for a while.

To everyone who read this book—thank you. It means so much to have amazing fans like you.

About the Author

Hayley Osborn lives in Christchurch, New Zealand, with her husband and three children, cat and dog.

Online, you can find her at:
www.hayleyosborn.com.

To connect with her on social media, you can find her on Facebook at HayleyOsbornAuthor, or on Twitter at @Hayley__Osborn. Or if you prefer to make contact via email, you can contact her at hayley@hayleyosborn.com.

Ingram Content Group UK Ltd.
Milton Keynes UK
UKHW011807230323
419066UK00002B/181